D1306416

Raven's Peak

Book I, World on Fire

by

Lincoln Cole

Table of Contents

This one is for my grandma.

If I got rid of my demons, I'd lose my angels.
—Tennessee Williams

Prologue – The Reverend

"Reverend, you have a visitor."

He couldn't remember when he fell in love with the pain. When agony first turned to pleasure, and then to joy. Of course, it hadn't always been like this. He remembered screaming all those years ago when first they put him in this cell; those memories were vague, though, like reflections in a dusty mirror.

"Open D4."

A buzz as the door slid open, inconsequential. The aching *need* was what drove him in this moment, and nothing else mattered. It was a primal desire: a longing for the tingly rush of adrenaline each time the lash licked his flesh. The blood dripping down his parched skin fulfilled him like biting into a juicy strawberry on a warm summer's day.

"Some woman. Says she needs to speak with you immediately. She says her name is Frieda."

A pause, the lash hovering in the air like a poised snake. The Reverend remembered that name, found it dancing in the recesses of his mind. He tried to pull himself back from the ritual, back to reality, but it was an uphill slog through knee-deep mud to reclaim those memories.

It was always difficult to focus when he was in the midst of his cleansing. All he managed to cling to was the name. *Frieda.* It was the name of an angel, he knew. . . or perhaps a devil.

One and the same when all was said and done.

She belonged to a past life, only the whispers of which he could recall. The ritual reclaimed him, embraced him with its fiery need. His memories were nothing compared to the whip in his hand, its nine tails gracing his flesh.

The lash struck down on his left shoulder blade, scattering droplets of blood against the wall behind him. Those droplets would stain the granite for months, he knew, before finally fading away. He clenched his teeth in a feral grin as the whip landed with a sickening, wet slapping sound.

"Jesus," a new voice whispered from the doorway. "Does he always do that?"

"Every morning."

"You'll cuff him?"

9

"Why? Are you scared?"

The Reverend raised the lash into the air, poised for another strike.

"Just...man, you said he was crazy...but this..."

The lash came down, lapping at his back and the tender muscles hidden there. He let out a groan of mixed agony and pleasure.

These men were meaningless, their voices only echoes amid the rest, an endless drone. He wanted them to leave him alone with his ritual. They weren't worth his time.

"I think we can spare the handcuffs this time; the last guy who tried spent a month in the hospital."

"Regulation says we have to."

"Then you do it."

The guards fell silent. The cat-o'-nine-tails, his friend, his love, became the only sound in the roughhewn cell, echoing off the granite walls. He took a rasping breath, blew it out, and cracked the lash again. More blood. More agony. More pleasure.

"I don't think we need to cuff him," the second guard decided.

"Good idea. Besides, the Reverend isn't going to cause us any trouble. He only hurts himself. Right, Reverend?"

The air tasted of copper, sickly sweet. He wished he could see his back and the scars, but there were no mirrors in his cell. They removed the only one he had when he broke shards off to slice into his arms and legs. They were afraid he would kill himself.

How ironic was that?

"Right, Reverend?"

Mirrors were dangerous things, he remembered from that past life. They called the other side, the darker side. An imperfect reflection stared back, threatening to steal pieces of the soul away forever.

"Reverend? Can you hear me?"

The guard reached out to tap the Reverend on the shoulder. Just a tap, no danger at all, but his hand never even came close. Honed reflexes reacted before anyone could possibly understand what was happening.

Suddenly the Reverend was standing. He hovered above the guard who was down on his knees. The man let out a sharp cry, his left shoulder twisted up at an uncomfortable angle by the Reverend's iron grip.

The lash hung in the air, ready to strike at its new prey.

The Reverend looked curiously at the man, seeing him for the first time. He recognized him as one of the first guardsmen he'd ever spoken with when placed in this cell. A nice European chap with a wife and two young children. A little overweight and balding, but well-intentioned.

Most of him didn't want to hurt this man, but there was a part—a hungry, needful part—that did. That part wanted to hurt this man in ways neither of them could even imagine. One twist would snap his arm. Two would shatter the bone; the sound as it snapped would be . . .

A symphony rivaling Tchaikovsky.

The second guard—the younger one that smelled of fear—stumbled back, struggling to draw his gun.

"No! No, don't!"

That from the first, on his knees as if praying. The Reverend wondered if he prayed at night with his family before heading to bed. Doubtless, he prayed that he would make it home safely from work and that one of the inmates wouldn't rip his throat out or gouge out his eyes. Right now, he was waving his free hand at his partner to get his attention, to stop him.

The younger guard finally worked the gun free and pointed it at the Reverend. His hands were shaking as he said, "Let him go!"

"Don't shoot, Ed!"

"Let him *go*!"

The older guard, pleading this time: "Don't piss him off!"

The look that crossed his young partner's face in that moment was precious: primal fear. It was an expression the Reverend had seen many times in his life, and he understood the thoughts going through the man's mind: he couldn't imagine *how* he might die in this cell, but he *believed* he could. That belief stemmed from something deeper than what his eyes could see. A terror so profound it beggared reality.

An immutable silence hung in the air. Both guards twitched and shifted, one in pain and the other in terror. The Reverend was immovable, a statue in his sanctuary, eyes boring into the man's soul.

"Don't shoot," the guard on his knees murmured. "You'll miss, and we'll be dead."

"I have a clear shot. I *can't* miss."

This time, the response was weaker. "We'll still be dead."

A hesitation. The guard lowered his gun in confused fear, pointing it at the floor. The Reverend curled his lips and released, freeing the kneeling guard.

The man rubbed his shoulder and climbed shakily to his feet. He backed away from the Reverend and stood beside the other, red-faced and panting.

"I heard you," the Reverend said. The words were hard to come by; he'd rarely spoken these last five years.

"I'm sorry, Reverend," the guard replied meekly. "My mistake."

"Bring me to Frieda," he whispered.

"You don't—" the younger guard began. A sharp look from his companion silenced him.

"Right away, sir."

"Steve, we should cuff…"

Steve ignored him, turning and stepping outside the cell. The Reverend looked longingly at the lash in his hand before dropping it onto his hard bed. His cultivated pain had faded to a dull ache. He would need to begin anew when he returned, restart the cleansing.

There was always more to cleanse.

They traveled through the black-site prison deep below the earth's surface, past neglected cells and through rough cut stone. A few of the rusty cages held prisoners, but most stood empty and silent. These prisoners were relics of a forgotten time, most of whom couldn't even remember the misdeed that had brought them here.

The Reverend remembered his misdeeds. Every day he thought of the pain and terror he had inflicted, and every day he prayed it would wash away.

They were deep within the earth, but not enough to benefit from the world's core heat. It was kept unnaturally cold as well to keep the prisoners docile. That meant there were only a few lights and frigid temperatures. Last winter he thought he might lose a finger to frostbite. He'd cherished the idea, but it wasn't to be. He had looked forward to cutting it off.

There were only a handful of guards in this section of the prison, maybe one every twenty meters. The actual security system relied on a single exit shaft as the only means of escape. Sure, he could fight his way free, but locking the elevator meant he would never reach the surface.

And pumping out the oxygen meant the situation would be contained.

The Council didn't want to bring civilians in on the secretive depths of their hellhole prison. The fewer guards they needed to hire, the fewer people knew of their existence, and any guards who were brought in were fed half-truths and lies about their true purpose. How many such men and women, he'd always wondered, knew who he was or why he was here?

Probably none. That was for the best. If they knew, they never would have been able to do their jobs.

As they walked, the Reverend felt the ritual wash away and he became himself once more. Just a man getting on in years: broken, pathetic, and alone as he paid for his mistakes.

Finally, they arrived at the entrance of the prison: an enclosed set of rooms cut into the stone walls backing up to a shaft. A solitary elevator bridged the prison to the world above, guarded by six men, but that wasn't where they took him.

They guided him to one of the side rooms, opening the door but waiting outside. Inside were a plain brown table and one-way mirror, similar to a police station, but nothing else.

A woman sat at the table facing away from the door. She had brown hair and a white business suit with matching heels. Very pristine; Frieda was always so well-dressed.

"Here we are," the guard said. The Reverend didn't acknowledge the man, but he did walk into the chamber. He strode past the table and sat in the chair facing Frieda.

He studied her: she had deep blue eyes and a mole on her left cheek. She looked older, and he couldn't remember the last time she'd come to visit him.

Probably not since the day she helped lock him in that cell.

"Close the door," Frieda said to the guards while still facing the Reverend.

"But ma'am, we are supposed to—"

"Close the door," she reiterated. Her tone was exactly the same, but an undercurrent was there. Hers was a powerful presence, the type normal people obeyed instinctually. She was always in charge, no matter the situation.

"We will be right out here," Steve replied finally, pulling the heavy metal door closed.

Silence enveloped the room, a humming emptiness.

He stared at her, and she stared at him. Seconds slipped past.

He wondered how she saw him. What must he look like today? His hair and beard must be shaggy and unkempt with strands of gray mixed into the black. He imagined his face, but with eyes that were sunken, skin that was pale and leathery. Doubtless, he looked thinner, almost emaciated.

He was also covered in blood, the smell of which would be overpowering. It disgusted him; he hated how his daily ritual left him, battering his body to maintain control, yet he answered its call without question.

"Do you remember what you told me the first time we met?" the Reverend asked finally, facing Frieda again.

"We need your help," Frieda said, ignoring his question. "You've been here for a long time, and things have been getting worse."

"You quoted Nietzsche, that first meeting. I thought it was pessimistic and rhetorical," he continued.

"Crime is getting worse. The world is getting darker and…"

"I thought you were talking about something that might happen to someone else but never to me. I had no idea just how spot on you were: that you were prophesizing my future," he spoke. "Do you remember your exact words?"

"We need your help," Frieda finished. Then she added softer: "*I* need your help."

He didn't respond. Instead, he said: "Do you remember?"

She sighed. "I do."

"Repeat it for me."

She frowned. "When we first met, I said to you: 'Whoever fights monsters should see to it that in the process he does not become a monster.'"

He nodded. "You were right. Now I am a monster."

"You *aren't* a monster," she whispered.

"No," he said. "I am *your* monster."

"Reverend…"

Rage exploded through his body, and he felt every muscle tense. "That is *not* my name!" he roared, slamming his fist on the table. It made a loud crashing sound, shredding the silence, and the wood nearly folded beneath the impact.

Frieda slid her chair back in an instant, falling into a fighting stance. One hand gripped the cross hanging around her neck, and the other slid into her vest pocket. She wore an expression he could barely recognize, something he'd never seen on her face before.

Fear.

She was afraid of him. The realization stung, and more than a little bit.

The Reverend didn't move from his seat, but he could still feel heat coursing through his veins. He forced his pulse to slow, his emotions to subside. He loved the feeling of rage but was terrified of what would happen if he gave into it; if he embraced it.

He glanced at the hand in her pocket and realized what weapon she had chosen to defend herself. A pang shot through his chest.

"Would it work?" he asked.

She didn't answer, but a minute trace of shame crossed her face. He stood slowly and walked around the table, reaching a hand toward her. To her credit, she barely flinched as he touched her. He gently pulled her fist out of the pocket and opened it. In her grip was a small vial filled with water.

"*Will* it work?" he asked.

"Arthur…" she breathed.

The name brought a flood of memories, furrowing his brow. A little girl playing in a field, picking blueberries and laughing. A wife with auburn hair who watched him with love and longing as he played with their daughter. He quashed them; he feared the pain the memories would bring.

That was a pain he did not cherish.

"I need to know," he whispered.

He slid the vial from her hand and popped the top off. She watched in resignation as he held up his right arm and poured a few droplets onto his exposed skin. It tingled where it touched, little more than a tickle, and he felt his skin turn hot.

But it didn't burn.

He let out the shuddering breath he hadn't realized he was holding.

"Thank God," Frieda whispered.

"I'm not sure She deserves it," Arthur replied.

"We need your help," Frieda said again. When he looked at her face once more, he saw moisture in her eyes. He couldn't tell if it was from relief that the blessed water didn't work, or sadness that it almost had.

"How can I possibly help?" he asked, gesturing at his body helplessly with his arms. "You see what I am. What I've become."

"I know what you were."

14

"What I am no longer," he corrected. "I was ignorant and foolish. I can never be that man again."

"Three girls are missing," she said.

"Three girls are always missing," he said, "and countless more."

"But not like these," she said. "These are ours."

He was quiet for a moment. "Rescues?"

She nodded. "Two showed potential. All three were being fostered by the Greathouse family."

He remembered Charles Greathouse, an old and idealistic man who just wanted to help. "Of course, you went to Charles," Arthur said. "He took care of your little witches until they were ready to become soldiers."

"He volunteered."

"And now he's dead," Arthur said. Frieda didn't correct him. "Who took the girls?"

"We don't know. But there's more. It killed three of ours."

"Hunters?"

"Yes."

"Who?"

"Michael and Rachael Felton."

"And the third?"

"Abigail."

He cursed. "You know she wasn't ready. Not for this."

"You've been here for five years," Frieda said. "She grew up."

"She's still a child."

"She wasn't anymore."

"She's my child."

Frieda hesitated, frowning. He knew as well as she did what had happened to put him in this prison and what part Abigail had played in it. If Abigail hadn't stopped him…

"We didn't expect . . ." Frieda said finally, sliding away from the minefield in the conversation.

"You never do."

"I'm sorry," Frieda said. "I know you were close."

The Reverend—Arthur—had trained Abigail. Raised her from a child after rescuing her from a cult many years earlier. It was after his own child had been murdered, and he had needed a reason to go on with his life. His faith was wavering, and she had become his salvation. They were more than close. They were family.

And now she was dead.

"What took them? Was it the Ninth Circle?"

"I don't think so," she said. "Our informants haven't heard anything."

"A demon?"

15

"Probably several."

"Where did it take them?" he asked.

"We don't know."

"What is it going to do with them?"

This time, she didn't answer. She didn't need to.

"So you want me to clean up your mess?"

"It killed three of our best," Frieda said. "I don't...I don't know what else to do."

"What does the Council want you to do?"

"Wait and see."

"And you disagree?"

"I'm afraid that it'll be too late by the time the Council decides to act."

"You have others you could send."

"Not that can handle something like this," she said.

"You mean none that you could send without the Council finding out and reprimanding you?"

"You were always the best, Arthur."

"Now I am in prison."

"You are here voluntarily," she said. "I've taken care of everything. There is a car waiting topside and a jet idling. So, will you help?"

He was silent for a moment, thinking. "I'm not that man anymore."

"I trust you."

"You shouldn't."

"I do."

"What happens if I say 'no'?"

"I don't know," Frieda said, shaking her head. "You are my last hope."

"What happens," he began, a lump in his throat, "when I don't come back? What happens when I become the new threat and you have no one else to send?"

Frieda wouldn't even look him in the eyes.

"When that day comes," she said softly, staring at the table, "I'll have an answer to a question I've wondered about for a long time."

"What question is that?"

She looked up at him. "What is my faith worth?"

✳✳✳

The Reverend—Arthur, he reminded himself; his name was Arthur—sat on the red-velvet chair inside the private jet, high in the clouds and traveling at several hundred kilometers per hour. He felt out of place, sickened by the luxury and ostentation of this trip. He'd spent the last five years living in his roughhewn cell, and it had become his home.

He missed it, the cell with its lumpy mattress and low ceiling. It had become

16

his sanctuary, a place to hide away from the world. Things had gotten to be too much for him to handle, and the utter simplicity of the cage took away his choices. It took away his free will and his ability to make mistakes.

Out here in the real world, mistakes were all he had left.

He looked out the window at the clouds and saw his face reflected there, but this time, it was more like the face he remembered. He'd shaved off the beard and cut his hair, and now he was wearing comfortable and light clothing. It would be cold in the mountains where he was heading, but he didn't fear the cold.

The onboard phone started to ring through a little speaker built into his chair. He stared at it curiously for a second and then pressed the green button to accept the call.

"Arthur?" Frieda asked as she was connected.

Her voice boomed through the jet's speakers, causing him to wince. He found the volume controls and turned it down to a more acceptable level. He hadn't realized just how peaceful his cell had been without loud noises.

"I'm here," he replied.

"You should be landing in just under an hour. We will have an escort ready to—"

"No escort," he said. "Just a car. I will travel alone."

"You should have someone with you in case—"

"No escort," he reiterated, cutting her off once more.

She was silent for a moment. "Very well," she agreed finally. "Did you find the supplies I left for you?"

He glanced at a cardboard box on the chair beside him with a frown on his face. "I did."

"I know it isn't much," she said, "but I can't make this trip common knowledge. I'm already pushing my luck with the jet."

It was definitely not much: a small caliber revolver, a few vials of holy water, a satellite phone, and a pair of short knives...none of the more powerful implements he'd used while he'd still been a Hunter serving the Council.

Then again, the one absolute thing he'd learned over the years was that those items had been a crutch. The only true weapon he'd had in his battles against evil had been his faith.

Something he'd lost long ago.

"You won't tell the Council?" he asked.

"No," Frieda replied. "They would never approve."

"How many of them wanted me dead when I went into the cell?"

"Arthur..."

"How many still do?" he asked.

She sighed. "They are fools for not trusting you."

"Maybe," he said. "Or maybe you're the fool."

She was silent for a long moment. "When you arrive at the airport we'll have a car waiting. The GPS is already set, and it's the last known coordinates of Rachael Felton's phone. It's up in the mountains out in the middle of nowhere."

"What were they doing there?"

"It isn't clear," Frieda said. "Rachael called us the day before she died and said she and her husband were chasing something powerful, and they said it was time sensitive as though it had an agenda. They picked up Abigail for backup and said they would report back to the Council once everything was taken care of. But they never did."

"So you sent a team?"

"The Council sent a team to check on them," Frieda corrected. "And when they found the bodies…"

"You came to me," he finished.

"The Council is still debating its next steps. They think Rachael acted rashly by not calling for more backup, and they're trying to blame this on her. By the time they make a decision it will be too late."

"All right, Frieda," Arthur said. "I'm doing this for Abi. But you need to make sure my cell is ready for me when I get home."

✳✳✳

As soon as the jet landed, Arthur stretched out his body and breathed in the cool mountain air. He allowed himself a few seconds to savor it before walking toward the waiting car. The airfield was empty except for his jet.

There were a few people watching him in suits, but they said nothing as he approached. He ignored their mixed expressions of awe and hatred and climbed into the waiting car

He had spent seven hours trapped on that jet being flown halfway across the world to the Rocky Mountains. The sun hadn't yet risen in the sky by the time he landed. The red, ominous glow in the clouds warned him that a storm was approaching, but he didn't have time to wait around.

He headed off into the mountains, following the GPS, and for the next several hours lost himself in the simple act of driving. It had been so long since he'd sat behind a steering wheel that it was almost cathartic.

He was forced to park alongside the road in a ditch and make the last leg of his journey on foot. It was a five mile hike into a cold and dark forest. His body burned from the exertion, and the loved the sensation. The walk gave him time to clear his mind and prepare himself for what he might find.

He didn't need the GPS to tell him that he'd arrived at the right location.

The bodies were torn to shreds, dried blood everywhere. Arthur could tell immediately, however, that the Council's foot soldiers had been mistaken about how many people were killed here in this clearing.

18

There were only two bodies.

It was a forgivable error with how mangled and disfigured those two were. He stood in a clearing, miles from civilization in any direction. Organs hung from tree limbs, entrails were ripped apart and scattered across the ground, and both heads were missing.

More than that, neither of the two heads were Abigail's, nor any dismembered body parts her shade of skin. She wasn't lying here mixed in with the dead, which meant she might still be alive.

She might be alive…

He had come here full of hatred, wanting nothing more than to avenge his adopted daughter and destroy whatever had taken her life. Frieda had manipulated him, knowing he would agree to this mission because of his love for Abigail. They both knew he relished the opportunity to punish whatever creature had harmed her.

But, if Abigail was alive and there was even the *slightest* chance of saving her…

The realization gave Arthur pause, and he felt a stirring of something he hadn't experienced in a long time: hope.

The Reverend patted the loaner pistol at his side—a snub nose revolver that looked like a peashooter—and headed through the trees. He had a few other implements with him, including the knife and a vial of holy water, as well as the satellite phone, but he didn't bring much else.

The phone was off for now: anything technological had a tendency to fail around the supernatural and was more of a burden than anything else. He'd considered leaving it behind as well but decided to hang onto it. He was supposed to report in every hour and give Frieda a status update, but that definitely wasn't going to happen. This wasn't about her, and it sure as hell wasn't for her.

Instead, he followed the tracks.

Those tracks weren't even hidden: broken branches, scraps of discarded clothing, and dried blood. Arthur felt like he was being led somewhere rather than chasing something. Never a good sign. After killing two members of Arthur's order, this demon had to know there would be retaliation. Whatever Arthur was dealing with, it wasn't afraid of him at all.

He walked for a few hours, stepping lightly and feeling his body limber up as he went. The air tasted perfect. He'd grown used to the stale oxygen from the caves, piped in through the elevator shaft and having an oily, metallic flavor. This air tasted of trees and nature. He hadn't even known how much he missed clean air, and he could feel it rejuvenating his soul.

He paused at a tree line looking over an empty mining town. It was built into the side of a hill and consisted of around twenty dilapidated buildings. The tracks led him here, and he knew the demon was somewhere in the town, waiting for him.

Squat houses that were rundown, decrepit, and overgrown with vines surrounded a broken down Church. This was an old country-store town, abandoned in the woods and falling apart in the preceding years.

Four spikes adorned with heads were standing in front of the Church. Each had an expression of horror and served as a deterrent: a warning.

He remembered how a sight like this would have bothered him when he was a younger man. Two of the heads were the missing Hunters, and the other two he didn't recognize. When he was younger, knowing that this creature had killed his friends would have made him furious enough to charge headlong into the Church and start blasting everything in sight. The depravity of it would have bothered him.

The only thing that bothered him now was how little he cared.

A mist hung in the air as the sun rose, dew clinging to his boots. He felt a breeze of wind and tasted moisture. It was quiet in the clearing, filled with foreboding.

He walked through the overgrown street toward the Church. Broken shutters and roof tiles littered the dirt road as he went. It felt like a ghost town: empty, uninviting, and threatening.

The sun flitted through the trees overhead. It was eerily quiet, not even birds or insects chirping. They could feel the supernatural presence, the sheer *wrongness* of it, as easily as he could. Even the forest could sense something was amiss.

The Church was bigger up close, built on a hill and dwarfing the buildings around it. Part of the ceiling was caved in and it was covered in mold and vines. He guessed it to have been built in the middle of the nineteenth century. It must have been abandoned not long after.

He stepped past the spikes, barely noticing the grotesque expressions of pain and terror on the faces of his friends. He'd seen worse in his time.

He'd done worse in his time.

He moved to the door and slipped the snub nose revolver from his belt. It felt comfortable in his hand, ready and waiting to deal death.

The door was cracked. Inside, he heard the creaking of a board as someone strode across the floor.

"Whoever I find inside," he said, "I will kill."

A moment passed in silence, and then a silky, smooth voice came back to him. It was a voice he recognized instantly:

"That…"

The Reverend felt a shiver run down his spine and his heart skipped a beat. "No, no, no," he muttered.

The door opened smoothly in front of him and he saw Abigail standing there, a lascivious smile on her face.

"…would be a shame," she finished.

✳✳✳

She was older than he remembered, no longer the little girl he'd rescued so long ago. She had deep black skin, high cheekbones, and brown eyes. She also had a scar on her right cheek that never fully healed, a gift from her earlier life.

But she still looked so young and vulnerable to him, standing in the antechamber of the Church. She was barely older than twenty, little more than a child. As soon as he saw her a thousand emotions he'd kept bottled inside spilled loose, overwhelming him with raw intensity. Fear, love, loss, grief, it rocked him to his core, but one emotion stood above them all.

Shame.

He was ashamed that he hadn't been there for her for these past five years. He'd fallen apart, lost everything, and she'd suffered because of it. He hated himself because he'd allowed this to happen to her. He hadn't been there to protect her like he should have. Like he promised he would be.

Abigail was not his child by birth, but she was the only family he had left.

And now she was possessed by a demon.

What stood before Arthur was only the shell of the girl he loved. Something else was in control. He could feel the rage and hatred emanating from Abigail's lithe body. Her skin was covered in a heat rash, her flesh barely containing the demonic presence within.

Except something was wrong. The process was happening too fast. This demon was destroying Abigail's body at a prodigious rate. Hours: that was all the time she would have before the demon's essence consumed her and finished wrecking her body. Then the demon would be forced to find a new host or return to hell.

"That's why you took the children," he mumbled in horror. "Vessels."

The demon grinned. "These bodies are just so…weak. I took this one this morning, and already I feel her giving out."

"You can't be here," he said.

Arthur's hands were shaking as his mind struggled to understand what he was dealing with.

"Nevertheless, I am."

"I mean you *can't*," Arthur said. "It isn't possible."

He'd never seen or heard of a creature this powerful on the surface before. It made normal demons seem like candles beside a bonfire. Hell spawn destroyed bodies over years, months if they were more taxing than normal, but never weeks or even days.

Hours? That was unthinkable.

"And yet here I am," Abigail said. The demon stepped back, holding the door and gesturing with her arm. "Might I invite you in?"

The Reverend felt a sharp pang of fear rip through his stomach, something he didn't expect. He'd faced terrible things, battled demons, torn cults to the ground. He'd always assumed he'd faced the worst the world had to offer.

He'd been wrong.

And now it was too late to fully appreciate his overconfidence. Frieda's overconfidence. The Council's arrogance. They had all underestimated this, and their response was too small. They should have called in every asset they had available and sent them in. With sheer numbers, they might be able to take something like this down.

By the time this creature was returned to hell, the path of devastation in its wake would be immense. The body count in the thousands.

He couldn't run. He wouldn't make it more than a few steps before the demon brought him down. The gun he was carrying would be useless, except as a distraction. He'd faced the possibility that in coming here he might die, but he'd never felt it was more than a small chance.

Now, the reality was he would die as a failure.

He forced himself to breathe normally and stepped into the Church.

"That's the spirit."

"How are you here?" he asked.

"Maybe you should ask God."

"She and I aren't on speaking terms."

Abigail roared with laughter as though Arthur had said the funniest thing in the world. The demon wiped her eyes, little pieces of skin flaking away.

The Reverend glanced around the Church. Most of the pews were old and rotten, the floor was rough and covered in dust, and a section of the north wall had caved in. Stained glass adorned the windows along the right side, one of which had shattered. Glass shards littered the floor

Upon a raised platform at the front of the Church lay three little girls, unconscious, maybe six years old. They looked unhurt, though it was difficult to tell from this far away.

On the left side of the room lay a rotten corpse covered in flies. The stench filled the air. Skin was sloughing off, and it appeared to have been boiled.

"That one lasted six hours," the demon said, following his gaze. "One of the better ones."

"Who are you?"

"Does it matter?" the demon asked. "Who are you?"

"Arthur Vangeest," he muttered. The demon perked up and grinned.

"*The* Reverend? The legend himself?" It walked around, eyeing him like a prize pig. "You don't look like much."

His mouth tasted like cotton. It felt like his body was wrapped in a coating of lead, weighing him down.

"I heard you went off the reservation. That you were out of commission."

"What do you want?" he asked, ignoring it.

"What does anybody want?" the demon replied. "I just want to live, to experience this world for a while. It's been far too long."

"You're lying."

"Maybe I am. Maybe I'm not."

"I can't allow it."

"You don't have a choice," the demon replied. "But, in the spirit of fairness and out of respect, I'll make you a deal. I will *not* kill indiscriminately. I will only take what I need to survive and accomplish my mission."

"You took children," Arthur replied.

The demon shrugged. "They last longer."

She said it matter-of-factly, as if the explanation was self-evident.

"And the best part," the demon said, "is that I'll let you walk away. You get to live."

The Reverend felt the words sink in, the realization awakening him from a dream. A dream of that had lasted for the past five years; it began with the death of his family and culminated in this moment. It was why he'd taken Frieda's offer, why he was standing here at all.

He turned, stared the demon squarely in the eye, and smiled. All of his fear evaporated.

"You don't get it," he said. "I don't want to live."

He drew the snub nose revolver and fired right in the demon's face, but the demon wasn't there anymore. It moved in a flash, anticipating and countering. It ducked under the shot and quickly stepped to the side, falling into a fighting stance.

Arthur fell into his old self, the fighter, the Hunter, and let his muscles do the work. He spun, dodging an attack, and fired another bullet at the demon.

This shot went wide as well but gave him enough time to slip a short blade out of his boot. He aimed the gun, pulled the trigger, and stabbed at the same time. He caught the demon off guard, drawing a long cut across Abigail's stomach as the demon avoided the shot.

The demon punched back, grazing his chin and sending him staggering. Arthur ducked, stabbed, and twisted his body to avoid a kick from the demon.

It followed with another series of precise punches, but Arthur managed to dance away from all of them. He slashed with the blade and drew another cut on Abigail's forearm, drawing a thin line.

They separated, both panting, and the demon leaped to the far wall. It bounded straight into the air with a superhuman jump, catching a beam and sliding up. It hung from the rafters, legs curled like a praying mantis, hissing down at him.

Arthur felt his heart pounding in his throat. His muscles were loose, and adrenaline coursed through his veins. This was what he lived for, the thrill of it.

"Not what you were expecting?" he asked.

"*Exactly* what I was expecting," the demon replied. "I like to play with my food before dinner."

The demon pounced down at him, and he dove out of the way. He rolled and came up dancing, moving his body gracefully to avoid the demon's attacks. He moved with practiced ease, dodging blows with only millimeters to spare, no wasted motion. The Order thought it was a blessing, a gift from God that he could move so fluidly and quickly.

It wasn't. Years of training and thousands of fights gave him this skill. He'd received his fair share of scars and bruises battling demons and humans, but it had turned him into a practiced machine with one purpose. There was never a divine substitute for the real thing.

Another attack, another dodge. He countered an uppercut by sliding just out of reach, stabbing out with his blade and drawing another cut on Abigail's shoulder. He hated hurting her, but this wasn't her anymore, and anything he could do to weaken the body increased his chances of survival.

The demon grew frustrated and called on its inner nature to gain the upper hand. It lashed out at Arthur with a fist and then telekinetically threw a wooden pew at him. He dodged both attacks, and then spun out of the way of a second pew followed by a roof beam. The building shuddered under the blows, and the floor tilted a few degrees, throwing them both off balance.

He danced back, quick-stepping over the pews and dodging another attack. The demon pursued, using Abigail's body and the Church itself as weapons. It tore down a section of roof and threw it, but Arthur ducked out of the way, diving under a pew. The roof exploded into dust and rained shards of desiccated wood around him.

When Arthur came back up, he cut with his short blade, stabbing the demon in the knee. It hissed in anger, bounding away from him.

It raised a hand and telekinetically threw three pews through the air at him at the same time. They were spread apart to cover a large area. The demon laughed, knowing they would be impossible to dodge.

So Arthur didn't.

With a roar he charged forward, launching his fist into the center pew. It shattered into dust and small fragments with a resounding boom. He walked through the cloud of particles hanging in the air, panting. He felt dust cling to his sweaty skin.

"Impressive," the demon said. "You aren't quite human anymore, are you?"

It circled around Arthur, keeping a safe distance. He saw respect, if not fear, on Abigail's face. He spun slowly, keeping his eyes on the demon and catching his breath.

"Just what are you?" it purred. "You aren't one of us."

"I'm what your kind made me," Arthur said.

The demon glanced at the cuts on its knee and hip. They weren't deep, but that wasn't the point.

"Now I see why they call you a legend," she said.

"You haven't seen anything yet."

"Oh?"

"I have a counter offer," Arthur said. He turned his body away from the demon, cutting his palm with the blade. He did it smoothly, out of her sight. "If you leave now, I won't hunt you through hell."

The demon laughed, but this time, it was less confident. Arthur raised the gun, firing another shot, and the demon charged back in. The stub was empty, so he tossed it aside, ducking an attack and countering.

It only took seconds to realize how outmatched he was in this second engagement. Arthur's adrenaline was wearing out and the demon was still sizing him up. His tricks weren't as impressive this time around, and he was half a step slower.

The demon was fast, pushing Abigail's honed reflexes well beyond human limitations. It didn't need to rest, didn't need breaks. It didn't care what happened to her, whether it shattered her hands or tore her muscles. It was relentless.

Inevitably, a hit landed. It caught Arthur in the ribs, just under the lung. He felt the air rush out and collapsed to one knee. One rib, at least, was cracked.

The demon followed through with a roundhouse kick, catching him on the side of the head. The world went out of focus, and he tried to find his feet.

The demon didn't let him, kicking him in the ribs again and knocking him back down. If the rib hadn't pierced his lung, he would be lucky.

He tried to suck in air but got nothing. He crawled away and heard the demon laughing. His shirt was wet, and he felt blood streaming down the side of his face.

"That's it? Already done?"

Arthur moved toward the dais, leaving bloody handprints behind him. Another kick sent him down, but he kept crawling.

"I expected more!"

His vision closed in, and he could only see through pinholes when he reached the dais.

The demon hit him again and laughed. "Get up! I'm not done with you yet!"

He pulled himself alongside the three girls, gasping.

"You can't save them," the demon said, laughing. "You are nothing. Pathetic and weak. Explain to them that you failed. Tell them that they belong to me now."

He knelt between the girls, muttering. He pressed his palm against their foreheads, smearing his blood from the cut.

"Praying? It's too late for that now," the demon said. It knelt next to him.

"Are you asking God why she abandoned you?"

Arthur ignored the demon and kept muttering in Latin. It listened for a second, then he felt it tense up beside him.

"That isn't a prayer," the demon said.

Arthur stopped, one word short of finishing his litany, and faced the demon. "No," he said. "It isn't. *Hanc.*"

The hit landed a split-second later, a punch to the side of his head that rocked his neck and threw him to the ground. He groaned and rolled, leaning against the dais.

Abigail roared in anger, pacing in front of the girls. Abigail's hand was broken, the bones shattered from hitting Arthur with the full force of her muscles. It hung limp at her side, unnoticed by the demon.

"What have you done?" the demon screamed, gesturing toward the girls.

"The thing about being a legend," Arthur groaned, "is you learn a few tricks.

Abigail screamed and kicked him again.

"You claimed them!"

"And now you can't touch them."

"But you aren't a demon!"

"No," he mumbled. "Not quite."

He rolled and slipped his hand into his pocket.

This was his last shot, and this time, he did pray. Just a quick request. He'd already done everything he could, protecting the girls, and this would be his Hail Mary. He was dead either way.

He slid to a knee, popped the vial in his hand, and scattered liquid into the air. The demon tried to avoid it, but some landed on its skin. It seared where it touched, sizzling like bacon. Arthur climbed to his feet and began chanting, sanctifying. He begged God to ordain Abigail, to protect her.

He prayed, for the first time in many long years, that God would listen.

The demon screamed in rage. "I'll kill her!"

He could feel the change in the air as Abigail's body began closing to the demon, purifying against his presence, and he knew his prayer had been answered. Abigail's body was no longer a safe haven for the demon.

"And then you'll be back in hell," he said.

"She will come, too!"

"Then a counter offer," he said. "Take me instead."

The room fell silent. Arthur could hear sizzling as the holy water burned flesh. He prayed that Abigail would survive.

"You won't fight me?"

"You don't have long to decide. Nowhere else is safe."

The demon calculated, and he knew what it would decide. In him, it would have time; time to find another body.

At least, that's what it thought.

26

It happened in an instant. One second he was Arthur, and the next he was something else. He felt overwhelming pressure inside his temple, and it was more than he ever could have imagined.

It was no wonder it had taken Abigail so easily, he doubted any human could be a match for it longer than a few seconds. It was a hot knife slicing through his brain.

His Hail Mary seemed an even longer shot now. He doubted he could hold it back long enough with sheer willpower. If he failed, it would kill Abigail anyway just out of spite.

All he needed was a few seconds.

He took the short dagger into his right hand and began carving into his left arm, just below the wrist. Blood ran from his first cut.

He started the second line in his skin, and the demon understood what he was doing. He felt it roaring in his mind, trying to subsume him. He nearly caved under the pressure, nearly lost it all, but he understood pain. He understood what true devastation was. The demon was fighting with brutality, trying to overwhelm him with sheer force. It didn't understand that he had passed that threshold long ago.

I killed those people, he whispered in his mind.

He finished his second cut, shaking from the sheer pressure of the demon's strength. Every single pain receptor in his body was being triggered, and it felt like he was standing in a fire. He felt it tearing and clawing for control, shredding his very existence.

There is no forgiveness.

The third cut, drawn at an angle to connect the other two. He felt his will wavering and knew he wouldn't have long. He'd mentally battled demons before, but never like this. It felt like a train crashing into a brick wall.

There is only penance.

He finished the final cut and collapsed, feeling everything drain away. The demon went silent in his mind, and he felt humble respect mixed with unfathomable rage. The sigil in his arm trapped it, and once his body died the demon would have nowhere to go but back to hell.

When it went, he knew, it would take him with it.

But he was ready.

Shaking, he pulled the satellite phone out of his pocket and set it on the ground in front of him. He tapped the only stored number. It rang and was answered almost instantly.

"Arthur?" Frieda said.

"Promise me," he said, sucking in a shuddering breath. Red agony had closed his vision to narrow slits.

"Arthur? What's wrong—?"

"Promise me you'll take care of her," he interrupted.

27

The words hung in the air. A long moment passed and he imagined Frieda on the other end of the line, tense and barely containing her emotions.

"I promise," she said finally.

He looked over at the form of the girl who should have been his daughter. She looked so young lying there on the floor. She seemed dead, but he hoped she was only unconscious.

He prayed she could come back. He thought of the good times he'd spent with her, raising her and teaching her and loving her like a father.

"Tell her I love her," he said. "I always will."

"I'll tell her."

With a smile, he plunged the dagger into his heart.

Chapter 1
Five Months Later

Haatim walked into the Ocotillo Library in Phoenix, Arizona, in the early afternoon and found a table in the back corner. It was the middle of the work week, so it wasn't very crowded inside. That was fine with him; he wasn't in the mood to talk to a lot of people.

He slipped his laptop out of his bag and powered it on, then hooked it up to the Wi-Fi and started browsing. To be honest, there wasn't any particular reason for him to visit the library; he could search the Internet inside his apartment, but he didn't really want to be alone. He'd been alone in his grief for the last few days, and he needed to get out and see other people.

This library had been his second home while he was studying for his graduate degree. It was small and quaint with a lot of old editions of books he liked to leaf through. Just being here was enough to help him relax and clear his mind. All he was trying to do was keep from thinking about his family, especially his—

"Haatim?" someone asked, interrupting his thoughts and pulling him back to his surroundings. He glanced up and saw Kelly Smith standing over his table. She was holding a stack of books and smiling quizzically at him.

Crap. He definitely didn't intend to run into any of the other students he'd gone to school with. Kelly had been in many of the same Theology classes as him, and they'd been pretty good friends through their time in graduate school. Now, both had their Theology degrees, which were about as useless as Humanities degrees in the outside world.

That was before he went back home to India and they lost touch. He hadn't known what had happened to her, and he definitely wasn't expecting her to still be living here.

The look on her face spoke volumes as she sized him up. He knew how must look, disheveled and pathetic with several weeks' worth of stubble on his cheeks. He was also wearing sweatpants and probably looked more ready to take a midday nap than do research in a library.

"Hey, Kelly," he offered.

"Wow, I wasn't expecting to see you back in town," she said. "I thought you'd move back home."

"I did," he replied awkwardly. "What are you doing here?"

"I work here," she answered. "Temporarily, until I can find a teaching job."

What are the odds, he thought with an internal sigh.

"That's awesome," he said instead. "I hope you find something soon."

"Me, too. So how long are you going to be in the country?"

"A few months," he said. "Just back for a while."

She nodded conspiratorially, and he knew what she was about to say. She was going to bring up his sister, which was something he didn't want to talk about it with her. "I heard about your—"

"Where are you planning to teach?" he interrupted.

She frowned. "I put some applications in the area, and I'm hoping to stay local. Mostly just community colleges, just until I can get established. Brad proposed last month."

She held up her hand so he could see the ring. It was big but incredibly plain. "It's nice," Haatim offered. He didn't know anything about wedding rings but felt like it was the right thing to say.

"We don't want to move just yet, so here's hoping I can find something good soon. What about you? Are you planning to teach, too?"

"No," he replied. "I thought about it, but it just doesn't really feel like something I want to do."

"What about your blog? Are you still writing?"

"Yeah," he said. "Still writing."

His blog was called the Hidden Lens, and he wrote about various religions of the world and how they interacted with each other in positive ways. It had consumed him when he first started it, and he'd hoped he could use it as a positive contribution to the world.

But now it just felt…empty.

"Sort of. That's actually why I'm here. I'm trying to find inspiration for something to write about."

"I remember your post about how all religions stemmed from the same prism and how if people could understand that it would fix so many things."

He shrugged. "Farfetched, I know."

"I thought it was great."

"Thanks," he said. "But I just don't feel like writing anything religious right now."

"Oh," she said. "I understand. I heard about what happened on Facebook—"

He interrupted again. He hadn't come to the library for sympathy, but rather to escape his emotions. "I was thinking about taking my blog in a new direction," he said. "I think I'm going to turn it into a crime blog."

"Ah," she said. "So like: writing about famous crimes?"

"Maybe," he replied. "I'm not totally sure yet. Right now, I just need a job."

They stared at each other awkwardly for a few seconds. Finally, she gestured with her stack of books. "Well, I guess I had better get back to work."

"OK," he said. "I should probably start trying to do something productive anyway."

"It was nice seeing you, Haatim," Kelly said.

"You, too."

She disappeared into the aisles and shelves, leaving Haatim alone. He actually felt even worse now after talking to her, which he hadn't thought was possible. It was one thing to know random strangers were looking at him like he was a disheveled bum, but to have someone he'd thought of as a friend for so many years see him like...this...

It was terrible.

He let out a long sigh, realizing that now even the library was a compromised location. He didn't want to talk to Kelly about school or life, and he definitely didn't want to talk to her about his grief. He didn't want her judgment, nor her sympathy.

And he didn't really want to write a crime blog. He just...didn't know what he wanted. Nothing really made sense anymore, and if he was being completely honest, he was just looking for a reason to do nothing with his life.

He started to pack his laptop bag, planning to head home and work from there, when suddenly a man sat on the chair opposite him. He was a short and fat man with a black suit and red tie. He was sweating and had greasy, receding hair.

The man laid his arms on the table and stared at Haatim, breathing heavily. "I need your help."

Haatim was in the middle of putting his laptop away, and he stopped, staring at the man. "Uh, what?"

"You said you are looking for a job."

"You were listening to my conversation?"

"Not intentionally," the man said. "But I need you to do something for me."

"I don't think I'll be able to—"

"I think someone is planning to kill me."

✳✳✳

Haatim almost dropped his laptop. He slid it into his bag and sat up in his chair. "What?"

"There's a woman that has been following me for a few days, and I think she's planning to kill me."

"Why would you think that?"

"I don't know," the guy said. "It's just a feeling I have."

"Then why did you come to a library?" Haatim asked. "Why not go to the police?"

"I did," he said. "Twice. They don't believe me. They said I need evidence." The man leaned back in his chair, and with a shaky hand reached into his vest pocket and pulled out a half-eaten candy bar. He took a bite, chewing with his mouth open. "I'm sorry, I eat whenever I'm anxious."

"What kind of evidence?"

"I don't know," he said. "I don't know what kind of evidence I need, but I need *someone* to take me seriously." He pulled a picture out of his pocket and slid it across the table. "That's her. That's the woman who's been following me. Her name is Abigail."

Haatim glanced at the picture. It was of a black woman, maybe in her mid-twenties, but the image was blurry and out of focus. She was glancing over her shoulder and wearing sunglasses so he couldn't really see her face. He looked back up at the man.

"OK…"

"So you'll help?"

"What exactly are you asking me to do?"

"Just follow her," the man said. "Look, maybe I'm crazy. Or I'm overthinking things. Hell, maybe she just happens to go to a lot of the same places I go."

He stuffed the last of his candy bar in his mouth and kept speaking: "But I need to know for sure. I just want you to keep an eye on her and report back. That's all I ask. Follow her and snap some pictures."

"And if she *is* following you?"

"Then take the pictures to the police," the guy said. "If she is following me or…if…something happens to me."

Haatim hesitated. "Why me?"

"I don't have anyone else to ask," the man said. "I can pay, but it isn't a lot, and it won't cover a real private eye to look into this for me."

Haatim leaned back in his chair, trying to think through what the guy was asking. It sounded ridiculous at face value, and Haatim thought his best option was just to turn the guy down politely and send him on his way.

But, the thing was, he could use the money. He had access to funds through his parents, but he didn't really have any income of his own. He'd planned to find a job by now, but he'd never really gotten around to looking for one.

And it *did* sound somewhat interesting. He'd been hoping to find something worth writing about and take his mind off his depression, and this sounded like something simple to keep him busy. The guy acted a little shady, but who was

Haatim to judge?

He was always telling himself he should step out of his comfort zone. Maybe this was the perfect way to do it.

"I'll do it," he said. "For a couple of days?"

The guy lit up. "You will? Oh, that's fantastic. Thank you so much."

He reached his hand out, and Haatim shook it. The guy's palm was greasy and sweaty, and he rubbed his hand on his sweatpants after.

"What do you need from me?"

Haatim thought for a second. He knew exactly nothing about trying to tail someone except that he would need an expensive camera. "Do you know anywhere that she likes to hang out?"

"A couple of places. I can give you the addresses of different places I've seen her. But, if you follow me, then she's bound to turn up."

"You're that confident that she's following you?"

"Completely," the guy said.

"All right," Haatim said. "I can meet with you tomorrow and we can find someplace for me to start."

"Sure," the guy said. He pulled out a business card and handed it to Haatim. It said his name was George Wertman. "I really appreciate this. You have no idea."

They shook hands again, and the fat man stood up and left the library. Haatim sat at his table for a few more minutes, trying to decide if this was a good idea of a bad one. He didn't really know what he was doing, but honestly, how hard could it be?"

✳✳✳

Haatim was up early the next morning. He shaved off the stubble on his cheeks, combed his hair, and put on some fresh and comfortable clothes. He'd done laundry the night before—the first time in over two weeks—and picked up an expensive camera. It was something he'd charged to his parents, but he doubted they would mind since it was for a productive purpose.

He honestly doubted he would need to tell them anything about the guy he'd met in the library. The more he thought about it, the more he figured the man was just paranoid or racist. Or both. He probably didn't have anyone following him and nothing strange, and if he was going to pay Haatim to do nothing, then Haatim wasn't about to refuse his money.

And now that Haatim had the camera, he actually found the prospect of taking pictures to be exciting. He'd never really thought about being a photographer, but he did think of himself as creative, and maybe this would be just the spark he needed to forget about his grief.

He met George at the library once more, though this time outside on the benches. The man was wearing a different and grimier suit, and he was eating a cheeseburger, fries, and milkshake on a bench when Haatim walked up.

"Gorgeous day," George said, taking an enormous bite from his sandwich and chewing. He dabbed at his forehead, which was drenched in sweat. He looked less nervous than the previous day, but not by much. "Ready to get started?"

Haatim nodded. "I've got my stuff. Just act normal, and I'll follow along and keep an eye out for anything strange."

"I've got a couple of meetings in a few minutes," George said. "So it would be boring for you. But I have a better idea. I spotted her this morning at the park up the road."

"When?"

"Fifteen minutes ago. But I bet she's still there. You could go get a good look at her while I wrap up some business."

"Sure," Haatim said. George handed him the picture he had, but when he did he smeared mustard across it. "I'll be back in a bit."

Haatim climbed back into his car and drove to the park. It was sunny and warm, so there were a lot of kids and their parents out playing. He saw a group tossing a Frisbee and heard people shouting.

He found a parking spot near the back of the lot and scanned the area. It only took him a few seconds to spot Abigail: she was sitting on a park bench and looked like she was just relaxing and enjoying the day. She had on a pair of sunglasses and her hair pulled back in a bun.

Haatim took the new camera and fiddled with the settings. It had a zoom lens, but it wasn't as high resolution as he would have liked. He snapped a couple of pictures but couldn't manage to get a clean one of her face.

After about ten minutes she stood and left the bench in the opposite direction. He checked his pictures, deleting the blurry ones, and headed back to the library. He waited for about an hour for George to show up. This time, he had a hotdog, and there was a ketchup stain on his suit coat.

"Did you find her?" George asked.

"Yes," Haatim replied. He held up the camera and flipped through several of the images, showing George. "That's her?"

"Definitely," George replied. "That's the woman who's been following me."

"What now?"

"If we can get any pictures that incriminate her, I can take them to the police."

"And I can post them on my blog?"

George nodded. "Anything we find you can use."

"All right," Haatim said.

"We won't want to meet again for a couple of days so she doesn't get suspicious," George added. "Once you have all of the pictures, give me a call, and I'll set up a time."

Chapter 2

Haatim Arison sat in his apartment in his underwear, listening to classic rock and working at his desk. He drummed his fingers on the table and stared at the word document open on his laptop, wondering if there was anything he needed to add or rephrase. It was the blog post he'd been working on for the last couple of days as he followed George Wertman around the city.

And it was almost finished. He had confirmed on that first day that George was definitely being followed. At first Haatim wasn't sure why she was stalking him, but at least he'd discovered that George wasn't paranoid.

He had enough now to go to the police and they might or might not arrest the woman. He had some incriminating photos, but nothing illegal. George wanted him to bring the photos to the police, but Haatim had decided he wanted to write a blog post to go along with it. Something he could post to say *he* had helped capture a stalker. George was hesitant at first, but Haatim sold him on the idea.

It was kind of exciting, actually, following this woman around the city and snapping pictures. The crime blog idea had just been something he threw out when talking to Kelly in the library. It was more just to pretend like he was being productive than anything else, but now that he was doing it he had to admit it was kind of fun.

And super easy, too. He'd always imagined being a sleuth or a gumshoe detective and tailing someone. He assumed it would he harder than they made it out in the books and movies, but things had been going really well for him. Plus, he was getting paid, which made it all the sweeter. Maybe it wasn't enough for a career, but this could, at the very least, be a really fun hobby.

His phone started ringing. He glanced down and saw that it was George calling him. He answered it.

"Hello."

"We need to meet," George said. His voice sounded thick, muddled. "I need those pictures."

"All right," Haatim said. "I'm almost done writing my blog post—"

"Just publish your stupid blog," George interrupted. "Finish it now."

"I don't have any good pictures of her," Haatim argued. "They are from too far away, and something is usually covering her face."

"Doesn't matter. We need this to be over with now before she decides to kill me."

Haatim smirked. George was completely paranoid about that possibility, but he had seen no evidence at all that the woman planned to kill the big guy. Of course, Haatim knew telling George that would just set him off, so he decided to just play along. Might as well let him keep his crazy delusions.

"I don't have any pictures of her doing anything illegal," Haatim replied. "Right now, it is just photos of a girl, and I look like a stalker. If I bring these to the police they'll ask why I've been taking so many pictures of her."

"I don't care," George replied.

Haatim hesitated. The more he'd learned about George, the less he liked him. George was arrogant and annoying and came across as a complete jerk and bully. Haatim was also fairly sure George was involved in a lot of illegal activity.

Which meant that maybe Abigail was following him for the same reason he was following her. Maybe she was gathering evidence on George for some unknown employer.

Or, worse, maybe she worked for the police and was keeping an eye on him. It was impossible to tell, but the further things went, the surer he was that trusting George completely was a bad idea.

"Do you have a lot of enemies," he asked. "She *is* following you, but that's all. Maybe she is trying to get evidence on you."

"She's planning to kill me."

"No, she isn't," Haatim said bluntly.

"What do you know about it?" George asked, defensive now.

"I've been following her for two days, and she hasn't done *anything* suspicious."

"And, so what? You're an expert now?"

"I didn't say—"

"Publish your damn blog post and give me the photos."

Haatim pursed his lips. "No."

"No?"

"Not until we have more evidence," he said. "I'm not posting negative things about her until I know more."

George was silent for a long minute. "Give me the photos," he said calmly. "What?"

"Give me *all* of the photos. Tonight. Or I'm going to come get them myself."

Haatim felt a chill run down his spine. The way George said it was eerie. He'd never given George his address, but he had no doubts that the man could figure out where he lived.

Luckily, his apartment was in an upscale part of town and had security. No one would be dumb enough to come out here and make threats like that. His apartment was secure.

Still…Haatim didn't like the idea of pissing this guy off. He didn't want to keep looking over his shoulder when he went outside, and George didn't seem like the kind of guy to forgive easily.

"All right," he said. "Where do you want them?"

"Tomorrow morning. Meet me at the library—eight sharp."

"OK," Haatim said.

George hung up, and Haatim dropped the phone on his desk. He was annoyed and frustrated by the entire situation, but he thought he'd made the right decision. George could deal with his problems on his own, and now it was time for Haatim to extricate himself.

Plus, he'd gotten what he wanted out of the situation. It had been difficult and rewarding tailing Abigail around the city, and it helped clear his mind and bring him back into reality. He'd been sad for so long, but now he could feel that spark again where he wanted to achieve something.

And he did want to post the article on his blog. He just wanted to get it right and not run the risk of calling out an innocent woman he didn't even know.

What he needed was more information or, at least, pictures of her doing something illegal. He also needed cleaner pictures in general and one good headshot of her. That would be the main image on his blog.

He would turn the images over tomorrow, sure, but that meant he still had the night to put his story together and get the images he needed.

His computer started buzzing and popped up a Skype call. He glanced at the name, let out a sigh, and then clicked accept.

"Hi, Mom."

"Haatim? Where are you?"

"Home."

"Why are you in your underwear?"

"It's my apartment," he said. "And I'm not expecting visitors."

She put her hand on her forehead and mumbled a few unmentionable phrases.

"Oh, Haatim," she said finally.

"Did you need something?"

"I just wanted to see how you were doing."

"I'm fine," he replied.

"Are you sure? You haven't called in weeks, and I haven't seen you since you left for Arizona."

"I've only been back for three months."

"I'm worried that you aren't facing your grief properly, Haatim. You should be surrounding yourself with family and friends, not running away."

Haatim was silent for a long moment, struggling with the emotions roiling inside of him. He knew objectively that she was correct, and he did miss his family, but he also couldn't ignore the part of himself that wanted to be alone.

"Was that all you needed?" he asked finally.

"No. Your father also wanted me to ask you if you need—"

"If he wants to ask me something, he can call himself," Haatim interrupted. He kept his voice nonchalant, determined not to sound angry or frustrated. It didn't work. "He doesn't need to use you as a go-between."

"He misses you," she said.

"Does he?" Haatim asked. "He has a funny way of showing it."

"You know he has a hard time expressing his emotions."

"You use that excuse for him far too often," Haatim said. "It would be different if he showed me or Nida *any* affection. Instead, he was always away. He was always off on business trips until Nida died, and then suddenly he wants everyone to think he was the best father in the world."

"He was busy—"

"He never has trouble talking about his emotions when he's preaching," Haatim continued, ranting but unable to stop himself. "He was great at telling *other* people how much he loved us. In fact, I think he might be too good at it."

There was a touch of bitterness in Haatim's voice as he spoke and he forced himself to stop. He felt a strong ache in his chest and tears welling in his eyes.

"A lot of people loved your sister," his mother said softly. "Your father was trying to help assuage their grief."

"That doesn't make her any less dead."

The words hung in the air, and seconds ticked past. A tear rolled down his cheek, and he roughly brushed it away.

"He just wanted the people to know—"

"What did he want to ask me?" Haatim interrupted, determined to change the subject.

"He…he's afraid that because of Nida's death you're losing your faith."

"He's not worried about losing his son? Or upset because his God took his daughter away from him? No, I guess not. He's concerned that I'm losing faith in my religion?"

"You know it's important to him."

"Yeah. Of course. Priorities, right?"

"He just…"

"What kind of God would allow a sixteen-year-old girl to die from cancer? No, I'm sorry mom. Dad can keep his faith. He can shove the entire religion up his—"

"Haatim, you shouldn't speak like this."

"No, Mom, I'm not losing my faith. It's gone. I'm done, and I'm out. You can tell him that if you want. I really don't care."

"Haatim…you know your place is here, with your family."

"I'm not so sure," he replied.

"Your sister wouldn't want you to—"

"Don't bring her into this," Haatim interrupted. "You have no right to bring her into this."

"We lost her, too, Haatim," his mother said, and he could tell she was on the verge of crying.

Haatim was silent for a long moment, fighting down the wave of despair that always hit him when he thought about his little sister. It had been four months since she'd died of stomach cancer, but it hurt just as much as the first moment she was gone.

"Did you lose her?" he asked. "Sometimes I'm not so sure."

"Haatim!" his mother said sharply.

He blew out a deep breath of air. "I'm sorry. That was uncalled for."

He saw her sniffle. "It's OK."

"Look, mom, I need to go. I'm busy, and I have some stuff to take care of."

"We need to talk about this, Haatim," his mother said. "I miss you, and your father misses you."

"I know. You're right. I'll call you tomorrow, OK?"

"Haatim…"

"I promise, Mom, I'll call."

A pause, and then she said: "Very well. Have a good night, Haatim."

"And you have a good day. Bye, mom."

Then she clicked the connection closed. Haatim tapped the mouse on his desk, chewing on his lip and fighting back tears. He let out a coughing sob and knew his eyes were red. His emotions were roiling the same as they always were when he talked to either of his parents. He loved them completely and utterly, but another part blamed them for what happened to his sister.

That wasn't completely true. He didn't blame his mother for anything except her inability to stand up to his father. His father was the one who had refused to seek medical treatment for his sister when her condition worsened. He didn't want to put her through rough clinical trials that would make her last few months miserable, and instead, he put his faith in God's hands.

For all the good that did her.

Haatim pushed the thoughts and the bitterness away. After he graduated from college in Arizona he'd moved back to India to be with his family and get married, but after his sister died he'd fled back to his old stomping grounds in the States. He'd come here to get away from all of that grief and anger.

He glanced back at his computer and the missing place in his article for a photo. Like his life, he felt it wasn't complete and had a vast, empty hole in it.

Haatim got dressed, grabbed his camera, and headed out into the night. It was passed time he got those photographs.

✳✳✳

Abigail Dressler waited in the little diner called Ashley's Burger Joint for her tail to arrive. She sat in a corner booth, keeping her back to the wall so she had a clear view of the street and other patrons eating their meals. She sipped on lukewarm coffee and considered ordering a sandwich. Haatim was a little later than normal, and she was getting bored waiting for him.

She had to take care of some business and wrap things up with George Wertman, but she wanted to make sure Haatim followed her when she did. Normally she would just give him the slip and disappear, but this time, things were different.

Haatim had managed to get closer to her than she'd anticipated. He had snapped some incriminating photos of her, and she'd only found out about them this morning. She had to take care of the images to make sure they wouldn't be floating over her head when she left Arizona.

She hadn't considered Haatim a serious threat and was surprised that he'd managed to track her so efficiently. She was impressed with his skills considering how novice he was to the entire situation. She'd looked into him and confirmed that he wasn't a detective and had no law enforcement affiliation. He was just a kid in over his head.

But that didn't soften her annoyance that he was running late. She had to get to the docks before George managed to flee the city and escape, and she couldn't do that until Haatim had shown up so he could follow her.

Her plan was to lead Haatim somewhere quiet after she dealt with George Wertman, confront him, and explain that he wasn't cut out for this life and then delete all of the images he had of her. Finally, she would send him on his merry way.

No sense killing him if she didn't have to.

She was handling a job on behalf of the Council; mostly, it was just tracking and information gathering against the Ninth Circle, but now her mission had changed to elimination. George was a low-level threat to the Council and they had decided to eliminate him. It wouldn't be difficult.

Which was why they put Abigail on the job: they still didn't trust her with anything important. Not after what happened in the Church. It had been a long time since the incident and she lost Arthur, but they still refused to cut her any slack. At first, she'd been so sore and miserable she didn't care, but now it had been several months and it was getting downright patronizing.

Her phone started buzzing. She slipped it out of her pocket and read the name on the screen: Frieda. Abigail blew out an annoyed breath and accepted the call.

"Yeah?"

"Abi? Where are you?"

"I hate when you call me that. My name is Abigail."

"And I hate when you dodge my calls. I've been trying to get ahold of you for two days."

"I've been busy."

"Doing what?" Frieda asked.

"What you sent me here to do."

"Where are you?"

"In Arizona."

"You aren't finished yet?" Frieda asked.

"I only got the order this morning."

"What order?"

"To eliminate Wertman."

Frieda was silenced. "Who signed it?"

"Doesn't say," Abigail replied. "But it's legitimate."

"I didn't authorize anything."

"Then someone else must have. Do you want me to hold off?"

"No," Frieda said. "Go ahead and take care of it. I'm sure I just missed the memo. Do you need backup?"

"Nope," Abigail said. "Not for George."

"Yeah, it shouldn't be too difficult. George isn't much of a threat."

"That's what pisses me off," Abigail said. "It's been five months, and you're still holding my hand. I'm not a child, and I need some free reign to do my own things."

"It's not me. It's the Council."

"You are *on* the Council," Abigail noted.

"Barely. I don't have much sway. I'm on *your* side. I've been telling them we should trust you for weeks, they just don't listen."

"I need to look into Arthur and find out what happened."

"They don't want you to," Frieda said. "Arthur is entirely off-limits."

"For me?"

"For everyone," Frieda said.

"I don't care."

"You should. I'm working on getting you cleared, but it's hard to stick up for you when you go off the radar like this. You need to answer my calls."

"I do," Abigail said. "When I'm not busy. I'm going to take care of Wertman tonight."

"Good, because we have something else for you to look into."

"I told you I'm not doing anything else for the Council until I track down the demon who took Arthur."

"That isn't how this works," Frieda replied. "You were ordered to stop looking into it."

"I thought you were on my side."

"In most things. This isn't one of them. Just drop it, Abi."

"You know I won't."

"Then you're treading on thin ice," Frieda replied coolly. "And no one is going to rescue you when you fall through."

"Then what am I supposed to do?"

"Forget about him."

"You know I can't do that," Abigail said. "He's been saving me for my entire life."

"Then let him save you now, too."

"No," Abigail said. "This time, I'm saving him."

"The Council is pursuing various avenues—"

"Various avenues?" Abigail interrupted, incredulous. "What avenues, Frieda? The avenue of pretending everything is OK? They barely even admit anything happened at that Church, and you won't even tell me what state it happened in. You know the Council isn't going to look into it."

Frieda hesitated. "Maybe not," she said. "But that doesn't mean you should, Abi. The Council is watching you."

Abigail felt a chill run across her spine. "Watching me?"

Abigail glanced at the street, wondering if she had another tail besides Haatim, her innocent bystander. Maybe someone else was following her, and this tail was good at staying out of sight.

Or, maybe Haatim was playing her, letting her think he was just a clueless bystander…

"After everything that happened, I can't blame them," Frieda said. "You had a demon inside you."

"I know," Abigail said, blowing out a sigh.

"You don't remember anything from before the demon took you?"

"No," Abigail said, annoyed. "We've been over this, Frieda. I don't remember anything from while the demon was in control or a few weeks before."

"OK."

"So they don't trust me?"

"No, they don't," Frieda replied. "And in their defense, you don't have the greatest track record. You can't keep going MIA."

"All right, all right, I get it."

"You'll stop dodging my calls?"

"Yes."

"And you'll stop looking into Arthur? I promised him I would keep you safe."

"And I promised him I would find him," Abigail said. "That's what I'm going to do."

"Abi, the Council might not care what happened to Arthur, but I do. I'm

44

looking into it, and I promise that as soon as I find something you will be the first person I call."

"We should be talking to—"

"No," Frieda said. "That's one line we cannot cross. You saw what it did to Arthur."

Abigail fell silent. She did know, first hand, what it had done to her dearest friend and mentor. It had brought the greatest of all Hunters down, casting a shadow over his entire legacy.

But, that was a small factor in the greater picture. No matter what he had done or what he had become, she was going to rescue him from the clutches of whatever hellspawn was holding him.

With or without Frieda's help.

"Fine," she lied. "I won't look into it."

"Good."

"What does the Council want me to do?"

"We've had reports about unusual activity in the Smokey Mountains. Way out in Tennessee in the middle of nowhere. A small town called Raven's Peak."

"Raven's Peak?"

"You've heard of it?" Frieda asked, surprised.

"No," Abigail said, frowning. She didn't know why, but she thought she might have heard the name before. Maybe someone had mentioned it a long time ago.

"It's tiny, population less than three thousand. Not many have heard of it beyond the people who live there."

"What kind of activity are you talking about?"

"It wasn't clear in our reports, but locals were spreading stories of seeing and hearing strange things."

"That happens all the time," Abigail said. "It's usually nothing."

"Still, we need you to look into it," Frieda replied.

"Why me? This sounds like grunt work."

"Maybe, maybe not."

"There are better things I could be doing, like taking care of high priority targets or tracking down demons that might know something about Arthur."

"How's your wrist?" Frieda asked.

A pointed statement: they both knew her wrist hurt like hell. Abigail had stopped taking pain medicine for it weeks ago, but it was still throbbing and difficult to use for extended periods. It had taken months to heal enough to remove the cast and months more before she could put any pressure on it. Most of her other scars from that fateful day had healed or faded, but her hand was still recovering.

A gift from the demon who had inhabited her body.

"The Council is just trying to keep me busy," Abigail argued.

45

"No doubt," Frieda said. "In any case, I expect you to be there by tomorrow morning."

"Fine," Abigail said. "But I'm going to hold you to your word. If you find *anything* out about where Arthur is, you'll tell me."

"Deal," Frieda said.

Abigail glanced out the window of the small diner. Haatim, her stalker, was leaning against the brick wall across the street, trying his best to act casual.

"I have to go," Abigail said. "My shadow is here."

"Someone is tailing you?"

"A nobody. He was hired to follow me a few days ago."

"By who?"

"You mean it isn't the Council?"

"They haven't sent anyone," Frieda replied. "Yet."

Abigail wasn't sure she believed her, but a direct confrontation over it wouldn't do any good.

"Not sure," Abigail said. "But my theory is he was hired by George to snap some photos of my killing him."

Frieda was silent for a moment. "Do you want me to send a team?"

"No, he isn't a threat," Abigail replied. "Just a guy in way over his head. I'll deal with him after I finish Wertman, then head to Raven's Peak."

"All right," Frieda said. "Call me as soon as you get there and—"

"Oh," Abigail interrupted, curious. "That's interesting."

Abigail had just spotted something else, farther up the road from Haatim.

"What?" Frieda asked. "What is it?"

Abigail watched the two men for a few seconds, confirming her suspicions.

"My tail has a tail," she said.

✳✳✳

The air weighed heavy in the night, heavy and cold. It was a blanket of icy frost wrapping around one's soul, suffocating and overwhelming it, threatening to drag it to the pit of despair and cast it in. The night was full of the sort of emptiness that sapped strength and broke a man's will, filling even the hardiest of hearts with dread.

That was, at least, how Haatim saw it.

Maybe he would admit to being a *little* melodramatic, but that was how he felt right now, walking alone in an empty alley near Fourteenth Avenue. He had a nagging suspicion that something bad was about to happen.

Of course, that probably had something to do with the fact that he was on abandoned streets in the desolate side of town in the middle of the night. The only defensive item he was carrying was an expensive camera that might make a decent bludgeon, so maybe the fact that his suspicions were only *nagging* at him wasn't so bad after all.

The clacking of his hard-soled footsteps was the only sound to be heard this deep in the alley. *Normal people steered clear of this sort of place*, Haatim knew. Sane people stayed away; not consciously, yet entirely and without hesitation. He liked to think he was sane.

But he was starting to wonder if he'd gotten in over his head. He'd never been to a place like this, let alone this early in the morning (or was it considered late at night?). It made the hairs stand up on his arms and neck, his breath come in short panicked gasps, and his knees weak and wobbly. It was so quiet, so damned quiet. He was certain that at any moment something would burst out of the darkness and drag him down to hell.

Which wasn't far from the truth. Or, at least, not nearly far enough.

But Haatim didn't know that.

His footsteps stopped, and a furrow appeared on his dark complexioned brow.

"He—Hello?" Haatim whispered, shredding the stillness of the air with his dulcet tones. "Hello?" and then under his breath: "Where the *hell* did she go?"

He scratched at his arm as he looked around. He had an open sore just below the elbow, discolored and ugly. It was something he'd gotten a few days ago, though he didn't remember exactly what had happened. It just refused to heal. It was also itchy and painful.

Haatim heard a scurrying sound and almost jumped out of his shoes, letting out a choked cry. He looked over and saw a rat, completely oblivious to him, running along the wall. It disappeared behind a trash can.

He let out a breath he hadn't realized he was holding and laughed at himself. *Terrified of a rat, huh?*

There was no one else in the alley. The woman he had been following had disappeared. Vanished. He'd been following her for several hours now, ever since she left Ashley's Burger Joint. He had his camera and was hoping to snap a close-up shot of her, but he'd never gotten a clear glimpse of her face.

That was because he'd been keeping his distance, and now he was kicking himself for his caution. He could have gotten a half-decent shot earlier in the night but decided against it. He'd been hoping to find out where she was heading, so held off.

And now he'd lost her.

He cursed his bad luck and realized he would need to go home empty handed. He'd parked a few blocks back and one or two streets over. He wasn't great with directions and knew he'd spend a while searching before he finally found his car.

He heard the sound of someone shouting from up ahead. It sounded like it was spilling out of a window several stories up in one of the buildings. He walked forward, curious. It sounded like it might be George who was yelling.

Suddenly he heard the sound of shattering glass and saw something heavy come flying out the third story window of one of the abandoned buildings. It thudded to the ground about four meters in front of him with a sickening wet sound and laid there.

Haatim stared at it, fiddling with his camera. It looked like a body, and he racked his brain trying to think of something else it could be. It definitely wasn't a person, and even if it was then that person *definitely* wasn't dead.

But it sure looked like George, and he wasn't moving. His face looked like bits of skin had flaked off, and his eyes were open, staring up at the sky. He looked even fatter than Haatim remembered.

Couldn't be him. That would be insane because Haatim had *just* spoken to him on the phone. And, if it was him, then that meant Haatim had just followed his murderer out here into the middle of an abandoned alleyway—

He felt his hands shaking and realized he'd stopped breathing. He sucked in a ragged breath and tried to clear his mind. This wasn't right. None of this was right. He shouldn't be here, and he had to leave before the woman who just killed George realized he was here.

He turned to go find his car.

A man stood in the mouth of the alley, a silhouette in the streetlights.

At first, Haatim thought it was an illusion or maybe a trick of the light, a trick the way walking into a dimly lit room can turn a coat rack into a bear or a shadow into a monster. His heart started racing, and he told it to calm down. He was overreacting and panicking, neither of which was necessary.

Then Haatim had a startling realization: panic might actually *be* necessary. He was trekking alone behind a broken down Starbucks off Fifteenth Avenue at two in the morning. He hadn't heard or seen a car travel past in over twenty minutes, and the only significant light source was coming from the cross-street.

And on *that* street was a man whose face he couldn't see who was casually blocking his exit.

Maybe the man couldn't see him. Maybe it was just a homeless guy looking for a dry place to spend the night, or someone wandering by who happened to pause in the streetlight to check his watch.

Not likely.

Haatim decided he would turn around and walk (casually) the other direction. He would have to walk past George, but the alley was wide, and he could step around him. He would exit the alley onto a side street, then cross back over to Fourteenth and double back to find his car.

Haatim started moving again, executing this new plan. He ignored his sweaty palms and loosened his grip on the camera. It was expensive (worth stealing, he remembered) and he didn't want it to break.

48

Lost in his thoughts, he stepped into a pothole filled with dirty rainwater. It filled his shoe and soaked his pants leg to the calf. He let out a groan, his shoe sloshing as he took a step. The water felt greasy and disgusting.

But he wasn't about to stop, though; not for some puddle water. There was no sense panicking. No sense at all in panicking or overreacting or overthinking things. And there was definitely, definitely, *definitely* no sense in looking back to see if he was being followed.

Haatim looked back.

The man was well into the alleyway pursuing him, only about forty meters behind and closing the gap. He walked with long, even strides. Methodical.

Some might even say murderous.

Haatim gulped and pressed on, quickening his pace. He turned forward just in time to see another man step into the alley in front of him, blocking that way, too.

He heard a whimpering sound, realized it was coming from him, and then the weight of what was happening sank in. This wasn't coincidental. These two weren't here on a pleasant early morning stroll. They were here for him.

A foot scuffed on the pavement behind Haatim. Muscles tensed in his body he didn't even know he had.

He hadn't imagined this. Never thought that something like *this* could happen. Not to him. He'd just come out here hoping to snap a photograph of an intriguing woman…who was apparently also a murderer.

He decided at that moment that if he survived, he would sign up for the first class he saw where they taught people how best to kick a guy in the testicles and put him down, or how to get in close and poke eyes.

If he survived.

Run.

The thought was sudden and powerful. Maybe he could surprise his pursuer and escape to the road. Heaven willing, a police car might drive past.

Haatim ran. The steps behind him grew louder as his pursuer picked up the pace as well. The man in front spread out his arms in an awkward linebacker stance, like an overweight uncle looking for a hug. Haatim ran to about four steps away from the man and then sidestepped. Years of cricket made him fairly agile.

The man lurched after him, missing his arm but catching the shoulder strap on his camera. Haatim stumbled, caught in the strap with his hand still clutching the precious device.

He didn't let go, not at first (it was a $1,000 camera!) but after a split second rationality set in. He slipped the strap off his shoulder and released his grip. He could get a new camera, and if that was the only thing he lost in this misadventure he would count himself lucky.

He turned, free of the strap, and took another step. Something caught his leg, and he staggered to the ground. He wriggled forward, glancing back.

The man who'd originally been chasing him was about twenty meters behind at a full sprint. The closer man had fallen to a knee, one hand on Haatim's pants leg. The camera banged painfully against the ground, and Haatim couldn't help but wince. He looked at the man's face.

And then time stopped.

The man was dead.

He was *dead*.

Or, at least, he should have been. One of his eyes was missing. Not missing like *"argh matey,"* but missing, missing. Dried blood caked the left side of his face, and Haatim could see . . . tendrils or something hanging limp in the socket. Whatever it was that attached the eyeball to the brain. Those looked to have been severed.

But the gash in his throat was the worst of it. It was deep, caked in blood, and wide. The throat was torn open, and he could see bone protruding from the wound. The smell coming off him was fetid and rotten.

And the man was grinning. A wide, toothy grin with yellow-stained crooked teeth.

Haatim vomited. There was no warning, just suddenly he was vomiting. It got on his shirt and his pants, and he could care less.

With panicked, nimble fingers he undid the clasp on his jeans and wriggled free. His left shoe caught on the pants and he kicked that off, too. Free of his constraint he slid a step farther back and rolled to his feet. Off balance, he stumbled out of the alley and fled.

He kept going. He sprinted back to his car, running faster than he ever had before. Someone was screaming. It took him a second to realize that it was him. He forced himself to stop and promptly began panting. Blood pumped in his ears, and he felt light-headed and dizzy. He threw himself into the car and looked back over his shoulder.

No one was there. The street behind was empty and silent. He felt woozy, and it seemed like he was staring down a long tunnel. His mind couldn't focus, and he realized he wasn't getting enough oxygen.

He looked around frantically for his keys, breathing in short frantic bursts, and remembered they were in his pants. The feeling of dizziness intensified.

My pants are back in the alley...

...with the dead guy.

And the world went blank.

Chapter 3

Reality came into hazy focus.

A room.

His living room.

He didn't know why, but that didn't feel right. Why was Haatim in his living room? How had he gotten back to his apartment? Where had he been, because he vaguely knew that he hadn't been here? He had a strange suspicion that this wasn't where he was before he passed out, lying on his leather couch.

And was that . . .

. . . bacon?

It all hit him at once: the night, George flying out of the window, his camera, and the attack. He sat up, gasping for air. His body felt rigid, and he let out a grunt of pain as his muscles cramped.

He focused on breathing, but he could feel himself panicking: he'd been in his car, and he hadn't had pants on, and George was dead, and someone was after him, and he was about to be mugged or killed, and it was a dead guy, and he lost his camera and he vomited and—

"You're awake!" a voice called cheerfully from the kitchen.

Haatim screamed.

"Shh. Don't wake your neighbors.'

It was a woman's voice. He looked up, cowering, and saw the lithe black woman—Abigail—he'd been following for the last few days standing in his kitchen, drying her hands on his blue kitchen towel. This was the first time he'd gotten a close-up and unobstructed view of her: she had shoulder-length curly hair and high cheekbones. There was a scar on her right cheek, maybe an inch and a half long.

She was in her early twenties, maybe, but hard to tell with most of the lights off in his apartment. She was wearing skinny jeans and a faded gray T-Shirt that read *"Avalon Wolves Rock!"* with a wolf's head on it.

"Who—who—who—who—"

"Are you pretending to be an owl?"

Haatim felt his mouth hanging open, trying to process what she was saying.

"OK," she offered with a shrug. "I guess it wasn't *that* funny."

Haatim gulped. "Why . . . " he started "...why are you in my kitchen?"

"Because I was hungry?"

Haatim couldn't think of a reply. He looked down and saw that he was in his underwear.

"Why am I . . . ?" he trailed off.

"Almost naked? Because you vomited all over yourself. I threw your clothes into the bedroom and shut the door. Seriously, you don't have a washing machine or anything?"

He looked again at his underwear, feeling his face flush.

"I didn't take *those* off," she said with a laugh. "But I can't stand the smell of vomit. You didn't seem to mind, either. You just sort of moaned and thrashed while I did it."

"I uh . . . I don't have any money," he said. "Or not a lot, but you can have . . . "

She frowned. "You think I'm here to rob you? Why would I bring you home, drop you on your couch, strip your puke-covered clothes off you, and *then* cook us both breakfast if I was going to rob you?"

"Then what do you want?"

"You have been following me," she said. She stated it directly, making it clear it wasn't a question.

He winced as if she had punched him. "I wasn't."

"You're going to try that route? I advise against it."

He winced again. "I was hired to."

"So you think you're a detective?"

"Sort of."

She shrugged. "Not a very good one."

"I'm a blogger."

"Ah," she said, her face solemn. "I'm very sorry."

"Why would you think I'm a detective?"

"You've been photographing me."

"For my blog."

"You mean for George Wertman, right?"

"Him, too. He's the guy who hired me."

"I've read your blog. You've never done a single story like this."

"The opportunity was sort of sprung on me," he said.

She smiled sadly and shook her head. "You have no idea how right you are."

She turned and disappeared into the kitchen. He could hear sizzling and the microwave was running. "How do you like your eggs?" she called out.

"Excuse me?"

She appeared around the corner again. "Eggs? How do you like them?"

"I'm not hungry," he said, shaking his head. "How did I get here?"

"In a car. Your car, I hope. Otherwise, someone is going to be pissed tomorrow when their space is empty."

"What happened?"

"You passed out. I thought *that* much was obvious."

"I mean, what happened after that? How did I get here? Did you drive?"

She paused, staring at him with pursed lips. "You ask a lot of dumb questions. You know that?"

"Excuse me?"

"You keep asking questions that would be obvious to any sane person who examined this logically. Do I look like I have a driver with me? Maybe someone waiting out front to chauffeur us around? No, after you hyperventilated I shoved your ass into the passenger seat and climbed in."

"How did you know where I live?"

"Your driver's license," she said.

"My driver's license . . . "

He sucked in a breath. He started to feel dizzy.

"Whoa there, stay with me. Let's not do that again."

"Guy . . . he was dead . . . "

"It was a costume," the woman said. "Just a costume."

Haatim kept gasping for air, having trouble focusing.

Suddenly she banged her hand on the wall, startling Haatim. He shook his head, back in reality.

"Just a costume," she reiterated. "The guy uses it to scare people."

Haatim hesitated. "It didn't seem like a costume."

She shrugged. "I don't care what it seemed like. In any case, I retrieved your wallet and keys and brought you back here."

Then she disappeared back into the kitchen. After a second, he heard humming.

He stood up, still a little off balance, and staggered over to his bedroom. The smell of stale vomit wafted out as soon as he opened the door and he swallowed back a bit of bile. Without breathing more than necessary he kicked his dirty clothes toward the basket in the corner of the room and pulled a shirt and some pants on.

He stared longingly at the bedroom window for a few minutes after he was dressed. He could slip out, find a police officer, and tell them some strange person was in his kitchen, someone he'd never met before who had apparently driven him home and undressed him in his apartment.

But he decided against it. For one thing, he didn't know what was going on, and it seemed like maybe she had saved his life. Another problem was that he'd been following her for a few days now, collecting evidence on his computer and the document he'd been writing mention of her more than a few times. *"Sorry officer, this person I've been cyber stalking for a few days broke into my apartment and cooked breakfast in my kitchen,"* didn't sound very convincing.

But, the real reason he decided against it was that his bedroom window was

53

really small. He wasn't in as good of shape as he used to be and doubted he could slip through.

✳✳✳

With a deep and—he hoped—calming breath, he headed back to his living room. He felt better now that he had clean clothes on, and the pain and tightness in his body had mostly gone away.

The woman was sitting on one of his barstools, munching a piece of toast and scrolling through a phone. She paid him no attention at all.

It was the first time he saw her in good lighting up close. She was actually quite beautiful, he admitted, with full lips and smooth black skin. He'd suspected she was gorgeous, and she certainly didn't look like a murderer.

But, he now knew, looks could be deceiving.

Not looking up, she pushed another plate of food toward him. It had bacon, eggs, and a piece of toast on it.

"Eat."

"I'm not hungry."

"Wasn't an offer," she said, taking another bite of her toast.

He picked up a piece of bacon and twirled it in his fingers. Just thinking of the grease in his stomach made him queasy. He dropped it back onto the plate and glanced at her again.

"Wait a second, isn't that my phone?" he asked.

"Yep."

"Hey give it—"

She looked up at him sharply. He stopped reaching and folded his hands in his lap.

"Uh . . . how did you get my passcode?"

"Seriously?" she asked. "It's the first four digits of your birthday. About as secure as a broken lock."

He wasn't sure he wanted to ask, but he did anyway: "How did you know my birthday?"

"I looked you up Monday," she said. Haatim did some quick math. That would have been the same day he was first asked to check into her when he'd met George at the library.

On Monday, he'd spotted her in a nearby park sitting on a bench. He only snapped a few pictures from his car on that day. He hadn't even gotten close to her, so how the hell had she known he was tailing her?

"Plus, every time you log on in the morning to check your email, you hold the phone up in clear sight of the window."

A flood of emotions hit him all at once. He couldn't decide if he was disheartened that she'd known he was following her from that very first day or that she had been spying on *him* and he hadn't noticed.

Or . . .

"Wait . . . I check my email in the bathroom."

She didn't look up. "Yep."

"OK, OK, what the hell is going on?" he asked, flushing again. "Who the hell *are* you?"

She hit the power button on his phone and slid it across the table to him. "Why didn't you publish your article?"

"Excuse me."

"You have plenty of evidence against me. Why didn't you take it to the authorities or post it like George wanted you to?"

"I wasn't supposed to take it to the police. George was going to do that."

"Oh, come on. I saw the pictures on your camera. They would have stuck me with a restraining order if you'd shown them even a few of these. Maybe not enough for a conviction, but certainly enough to raise suspicion."

"I wanted to get an up-close picture," he said awkwardly, "to post on my blog."

"Is that the only reason?"

He paused. "Yes."

"You hesitated."

"Yes," he repeated firmly. "You've been through my phone. Probably my laptop, too. You read the post I wrote. It's almost ready to submit. I just needed a final picture for the front page and I was going to publish."

"And then you would give the photos to the authorities and have me arrested?"

"Yes," he said. Then his eyes widened as he realized what he had just said. "I mean no. No. No way. I wouldn't turn you in. No. Probably not. Maybe. I don't know."

"Relax," she said. "You never would have made it that far."

He started to ask her what she meant, then decided against it.

"In any case, you've pissed a lot of people off sitting on this evidence, and they decided to take it from you."

"What? Who?"

"The people who work for the guy I just killed."

Haatim was silent for a long minute, having no idea what to say.

"You're wondering why I killed him."

"I . . ." he trailed off.

"He was a sex trafficker and money launderer."

"Then shouldn't the police deal with someone like him?"

"I *am* the police for someone like him," she said. "Sort of."

"The police don't execute people."

"Trust me, George was already dead. In either case, when you didn't give him the stuff he wanted, he decided to take it from you. Now that he's dead, his people want to use it."

"It's just some pictures. I didn't even catch you doing anything illegal."

"That doesn't matter," she said. "It's why they were after you in the alley."

He felt a chill run down his spine. "What do you mean?"

"They're planning to kill you and make it look like I discovered that you were tailing me."

"What? Why?"

"They want to frame me for two murders and hopefully, have me arrested. You're just a piece of the puzzle. When the police find out you are dead they will search your laptop, and then they'll find the pictures you took of me and come looking."

She took a piece of bacon from his plate and popped it in her mouth. Haatim stared blankly, trying to work his way through what she had just said.

"You really should eat," she said. "After earlier you need something in your stomach. It'll help steady you."

"I'm not hungry."

"Is this Applewood? I *love* Applewood bacon!"

"Why are you here, then?"

She was silent, studying him. "I had been watching George for two weeks, trying to be obvious about it. This morning, I got the order to take him out."

"By who?"

"Doesn't matter. I'm here now because I need to delete those pictures and make sure you aren't planning to do anything stupid, like go to the police."

"Never," Haatim agreed immediately. It seemed like the safest thing to say.

"The only thing is: I didn't realize *they* had the same idea and would come looking for you. That means you're valuable to them, and I don't want them to get their hands on you."

"So you're protecting me from them?"

"You could say that," she said. "But I'm also protecting myself from the cops finding those pictures. I need for you to delete everything on your computer and on your cloud backups, I'm heading out of town tonight, and I can't afford to leave any loose ends."

"Loose ends?"

"You are my loose end," she said. "But you won't be any danger once I've destroyed the images and taken the computer. If you aren't holding evidence against me then you won't be worth anything to them. There won't be any more reason for them to kill you."

"So you're stealing my computer?"

"And your phone," she said. "After you delete all mention of me."

"Do I have a choice?"

She shrugged. "You always have a choice; but, in this case, there is a correct way for things to go."

Haatim stared at her for a second and then went over to grab his laptop. "All right. It's only a few files and the document I was writing."

"I know," she said. "You should stick with that blog, just not as a crime journalist. You have some real talent, and that other stuff you write about God and forgiveness is really interesting."

He sighed. "Thanks. I think."

He opened the laptop and logged in. He hated to delete all of the pictures he'd collected over the last few days, but he didn't have much choice. It was just frustrating because he'd worked so hard gathering them to begin with.

Of course, even with that at stake, he found himself believing what Abigail had told him. The men in the alley hadn't seemed interested in chatting with him, and he hadn't trusted George by the end. The idea that he might have been part of a set-up was terrifying but not nearly as far-fetched as he would have liked.

"This is a really nice place," she said after a few minutes. "You know, that reminds me of something I've been wondering: how do you afford a place like this?"

"What do you mean?"

"You don't seem to have a full-time job, and you just graduated from college with a *very* expensive degree, yet you are living in a ritzy upscale neighborhood on one of its nicer floors. How the hell do you pay for it?"

He shrugged. "My parents help."

"That's what I assumed, but when I looked into them there weren't many details," she said. "I couldn't find any information about your father."

"He doesn't like the Internet," Haatim said.

"Still," she replied, "I assumed there would be *something* listed about him if he could afford a place like this. But, no, there was nothing."

Haatim was silent, staring at the table.

"What?" Abigail asked. "What aren't you telling me?"

"What do you mean?"

"You're hiding something. Is it about your father?"

He hesitated.

"You hesitated," she said. "Tell me. I'm not going to ask again."

"The thing is, my father and I have different last names and—"

He was interrupted by the buzzing of a cellphone on vibrate. Abigail slipped a phone out of her pocket and glanced at it. She read the name on the front and then looked at him.

"I have to take this. Keep deleting."

"I will," he said.

"No funny stuff."

"Wouldn't dream of it," he replied.

She stood and disappeared into the bathroom, closing the door behind her. Haatim waited a few seconds and then tiptoed across the floor. He pressed his ear against the wood and listened.

"No, but it's almost taken care of," he heard her say, voice muffled by the thick door. "Just some personal business, and I'll be on the road in an hour or two at the most. Yeah, Frieda, I got it: Raven's Peak, I know. No, I won't. I gave you my word, didn't I?"

There was a moment of silence. Haatim leaned closer, straining to hear.

"Don't worry, I'll take care of it. Look, Frieda, I have to go. I'm in the middle of something, but I promise I'll be on the road heading out of town in just a short while."

Haatim tiptoed back to the counter only seconds before the bathroom door opened. He sat down next to his laptop and typed, pretending to ignore her. Abigail walked back to the other side of the counter, sliding her phone away and frowning.

"Almost done?" she asked.

"Almost," he said. "Just one last group of photos to delete."

"All right," she said, checking her watch. "I'm in kind of a hurry."

"OK," he said, scratching at his arm.

He heard a sharp intake of breath from the other side of the table. He sensed her tensing up and froze, slowly turning to look at her.

"What?" he asked.

"Uh oh," she said.

"Uh oh?" he echoed.

"Let me see your arm."

Haatim held it up.   She turned it to get a clear view of the cut, shaking her head.

"What is it?" he asked.

"When did you get this?"

"A few days ago," he said. "I think. Just a scratch, but it just hasn't closed."

"It isn't a normal scrape."

"Then what is it?"

She hesitated. "Something else."

"Then what does it mean?" he asked.

"It means," she explained. "That things just got a lot more complicated."

Chapter 4

"Complicated how?" Haatim asked. The intensity on Abigail's face had just gone up dramatically. Anything that unsettled her, he realized, was definitely not good for him.

"I need to get you out of here right now," she said. "I was wrong. They didn't just want you for the pictures."

"What do you mean?"

"They'll be back," she said.

"The people in the alley?"

"Yes," she said. "Probably with more this time. We need to get moving."

"I thought you said I wasn't worth anything to them without the pictures."

"I didn't think you were," she said. "Turns out, you're worth a whole hell of a lot."

"What aren't you telling me?"

"A lot," she said. "But right now, I don't have time to explain. Are you done deleting? We need to go."

She stood up and slipped a revolver out of her belt. She slipped open the chamber, making sure it was loaded.

"Yeah," he said. He closed the laptop. "Everything is deleted."

"Good," she replied. She flipped his laptop over and slammed the grip of her gun into the battery component, smashing it. The case cracked and he could see the shattered components inside

"Hey!" he said.

She ignored him and kept pounding, destroying everything down to small fragments. She focused on the hard drive, destroying it beyond easy recovery.

"Now your phone," she said, reaching out to him.

"So you can smash it?"

"Yes," she said. "We don't have much time. Give it to me."

"Not without some answers," he argued. "What the hell is going on?"

"I already told you," she replied. "They will be coming for you. They might already be on the way"

"*Who* is after me?" he asked. "And why? What changed?"

"We don't have time—"

"Who was that guy in the alley?" Haatim interrupted. He didn't really want to know the answer, but he couldn't stop himself from speaking. "The one with the torn throat and missing eye? He looked like he was...he was...?"

"He was what?"

Haatim couldn't bring himself to say '*dead*'. The guy couldn't have been dead. That was just ridiculous.

"Just a costume. He was wearing it to try and scare you so you would hesitate and he could grab you."

"I don't believe you. Tell me what's really going on."

"Haatim, we *really* don't have time for this."

"I'm not going anywhere with you until you tell me what the hell is going on. No more lies."

She sighed. "No more lies?"

Haatim stared at her.

"Fine," she said. "You pissed off an organization called the Ninth Circle."

"The what?"

"The Ninth Circle," she reiterated. "They have been hunting me for years and generally causing problems in the world. It's mostly comprised of psychopaths and demon worshippers, but a few members are lesser demons living in human hosts and corpses."

Haatim coughed. "Corpses?"

She ignored him. "They run an underground black market ring of slaves and guns, and they have been trying to get to *me* because I have been crippling their organization for years. I have sent dozens of them back to hell and George was just my latest target."

She finished speaking and looked at him, pursing her lips.

Haatim continued staring. "Uh . . . what?"

"See? Doesn't *"the guy was just wearing a costume"* sound so much better now?"

"But that's ridiculous," Haatim said, shaking his head. He forced himself to laugh. "You want me to believe that demons can control dead bodies?"

"I don't care what you *believe*," she said. "You just asked me not to lie."

"Demons aren't real."

"For someone who writes about religious unity across the world and the complete love and forgiveness of God, you sure seem close-minded about the supernatural."

"I don't believe in God," he replied. "Not anymore."

Abigail fell silent. "Then what was all that stuff you wrote on your blog?" she asked finally.

"That was before..." he trailed off.

"All right then. Do you believe in guys carrying guns who want to shoot you?"

"What do they want with me? And why are you helping me?"

"Because the fate they have in mind for you is far worse than just death," she answered.

"What do you mean?"

"It isn't important," she said. "Just know that I won't let them hurt you if you do exactly what I say."

"OK," he said. "OK, fine. I'll trust you for now."

"Good. But we need to leave *right* now."

The lights flickered.

Abigail was up in a flash, looking around. "Damn it all."

"What was that?"

"It means we're too late," she said. "We've been here too long. They are here."

Haatim felt a shiver run down his spine. "They are here?"

She didn't get the chance to reply. A crash suddenly overwhelmed Haatim's senses. He tried to react and duck behind the counter, but he wasn't quite quick enough. The front door blew in, scattering fragments of wood in all directions. Haatim felt a burning sensation on his arm as he crouched.

The first explosion was followed by a series of echoing gunshots. Some came from the hallway, and others barked from only a few meters away. They were loud, a lot louder than he expected having never heard a real gunshot, and he plugged his ears. His right arm felt wet as he closed his eyes.

The gunshots dissipated after a few seconds, and he felt a hand on his shoulder. He screamed in pain.

"Relax. It's just a scratch."

"What happened?"

"Shrapnel," Abigail said. "Wood. Not a bullet. It isn't bad. Come on."

She didn't give him time to respond but began dragging him toward the door. All around him, the furniture in his apartment was torn to shreds from the explosion. The walls were covered in holes and fractured pieces of debris.

He half stumbled and was half dragged to the front. The body of a skinny man lay across the entryway on his stomach, an enormous hole through his back. Blood and gore were all over the walls and carpet, dripping down the paint.

Another man was in the hallway, his left shoulder drenched in blood with more dribbling out each time his heart pumped. There was a hole in the wall a few meters above him with a trail of blood streaming down to where he lay.

This man wasn't dead.

Abigail dragged Haatim into the hall past the two, looking both directions. The dying man coughed and sputtered, whispering something under his breath in what sounded like Latin.

"Are there stairs nearby?" she asked. From the look on her face, it wasn't the first time she'd spoken to him.

"Uh…"

Haatim was staring at the man leaning against the wall, watching blood spurt out of his torn shoulder. The man was gasping and sputtering as he chanted, the words too low to make out. It was like a train wreck: Haatim couldn't look away.

Haatim felt himself being shaken. "Hey! Stay with me. Are there stairs near here?"

"Um…" he said, thinking. He had lived here for four years and knew the building by heart, but right now he simply couldn't remember anything. "Elevators are to the right."

"No elevators. We don't want to get trapped. We need stairs."

He shook his head, forcing his mind to focus. "Down there, we take a left," he said, pointing. Abigail didn't hesitate; she took off down the hall at a quick pace.

She let go of Haatim, holding her revolver at the ready. He stared at the dying man for a few more seconds, nauseous and terrified. He didn't know what was going on and had no clue what he was supposed to do. Part of him wanted to go back into his bedroom, crawl under the sheets, and hide until all of this went away.

But he knew it wouldn't work. This wasn't a dream. This was real, and if he wanted to survive he needed to act. He turned and sprinted down the hall, chasing after Abigail.

This is crazy. This is crazy.

The thoughts bounced around in his mind, and he felt like he was operating on autopilot. They came to the stairwell, and she threw open the door. He heard shouting from behind, back near the elevators, and then they were stepping onto the landing. Gunshots sounded in the distance, and he heard the crack of wood as bullets smashed into the wall behind him.

Abigail ran down the stairs with impressive grace, hitting every few steps lightly and rounding each corner to the next landing. Haatim plodded along behind her, gasping for air and leaning heavily against the railing as he tried to keep up.

"Where are we going?" he asked after they were down a few flights.

"Your car."

"And then where?"

"A safe place," she said. "Stop talking and breathe."

Haatim did just that, frantically trying to maintain pace with her as they passed landing after landing. He lived on the twelfth floor, which meant they had a long way to go to reach the lobby.

His entire body ached from exhaustion, and he quickly lost count of how many floors they had passed. It became claustrophobic and the air in the stairwell tasted stale. He focused on putting one leg in front of the other without tripping. It seemed like an eternity before they reached the ground level.

The front desk was empty as they spilled into the lobby, and the entire room was quiet. His lungs were burning as he sucked in ragged breaths of fresh air.

Two security guards were laid out near the front desk: one had a gash on his forehead and the other's arm was bent in an odd direction. Abigail stepped over to them and put her fingers on his neck.

"Are they...?" he asked.

"Just unconscious," she replied.

Haatim saw a desk clerk behind the desk. "Looks like she is, too," he said.

Abigail crouched and cocked her head to the side.

"Three out front," she said. "And four more behind us on the stairs."

"They attacked the door guards," Haatim said, shaking his head. "That's insane."

"They want you," she said. "They won't stop until they get you."

She reached into a pocket and drew out a handful of bullets; she reloaded the spent shells in her revolver, spilling the empties onto the ground. They made a *tink tink* sound as they bounced across the marble flooring.

"Is it because of my arm?" he asked.

"Yes," she said. "I was planning on taking you outside the city and dumping you a few counties away, but it's going to be difficult if they want you this badly."

"What do we do——?"

Bullets ripped through the glass ahead of them.

"Get down!" she shouted, grabbing Haatim and pulling him behind the front desk. He heard shouting coming from the street outside and the staircase behind him. "Damn it!"

"This is crazy. This is crazy," he said, panting in terror.

"Way more than I expected," she muttered. "I can't believe they sent this many."

"This is crazy..."

She ignored him. "George was the one who touched your arm, right?"

"Who?"

"George," she said. "The guy who hired you. He was the one who left that mark?"

"Yeah, I think so. He brushed me when he first hired me. I didn't notice a cut until the next day."

Another round of gunshots as the shooters out front fired into the desk. They ducked farther behind the thick wood, staying out of sight.

"OK," she said. "But I still don't understand why they would work this hard to get you. What makes *you* so valuable?"

Haatim grabbed her shoulder and turned her to face him. "What did he do to me?"

"He claimed you."

"Claimed me for what?"

Abigail grimaced. "His replacement vessel."

Chapter 5

"What the hell does that mean?"

Another gun barked, this time from behind them near the stairwell. Abigail pushed Haatim farther into their hiding space, rounding a corner out of sight of the stairwell. She leaned over the top and fired back, forcing their pursuer to retreat.

Abigail reached into her pocket and pulled a long and thin vial out. It was filled with a purplish liquid and had black specks floating on the surface. More gunshots hit the area above Haatim, showering fragments of wood and concrete on him.

"This sure as hell wasn't how I was planning to spend my night," Abigail bemoaned.

"What did you mean when you said *'replacement vessel'*?" Haatim reiterated.

"I meant exactly what it sounds like. I came here to send the demon Abaddon back to hell, but I guess he has his own contingency plan. These are his followers."

More bullets thudded into the area around them and Haatim was finding it difficult to concentrate. He was more terrified than he'd ever been before in his entire life. The shots were getting louder, which meant the shooters were getting closer. Abigail leaned over the counter and fired again, but she wasn't really aiming.

"His followers?"

"The cult. You're Abaddon's easy step back into this world, so they'll do anything to capture you."

"Demons aren't real," Haatim muttered. "They can't be real."

"Tell that to the guys trying to shoot us. All they want is your body. Dead or alive, you're valuable to the cult right now. But don't worry: you're worth way more alive."

She popped the cap off the vial and offered it to Haatim.

"Drink this."

"What is it?" he asked.

"It's something to keep you safe," she said.

"But, what is it?"

"Trust me, Haatim."

Haatim looked at her for a second and then accepted the vial. He eyed it for a second, and then took a sip. "Ack, that tastes terrible."

"I know. It's poison."

He spit it out in shock. "*Poison?*"

"So the demon can't possess you right away," she said. "With this running in your system, your body will be dangerous for the demon. But don't worry; it takes several hours for the full effect."

"To do what?" he asked.

A spasm ripped through his stomach, and he doubled over in pain. He let out a sharp gasp, and it felt like his intestines were being ripped open from the inside. He coughed and saw reddish-purple liquid on his fingers.

"To kill you," she explained.

Haatim doubled over in pain again. "Oh God, it hurts."

"That goes away," she said. Then she added: "Sometimes."

"What did you do to me?"

"Just think of it this way," Abigail said. "Your shoulder doesn't hurt anymore, does it?"

More bullets ripped into the walls, sending shards of dust into the air. Haatim could hear more shouting, but it sounded distorted now, like listening to it through tinny speakers. The only thing he could focus on was how badly his stomach hurt.

"I can't get both of us out of here," Abigail explained. "So I'm going to have to come back for you."

He groaned, clutching his stomach and making little gasping noises.

"Haatim," Abigail said, squeezing his arm. "Focus. I *need* you to focus. They are going to grab you and bring you somewhere. Whatever you do... what*ever* you do, don't eat or drink anything. And don't, under any circumstances, make any deals. You got that?"

"Wha...What?" he asked.

"They're going to lie and attempt to manipulate you, but you can't trust them. I'm going to come and get you, but I can't help if the demon is already in control. The poison will keep you safe until I get there."

The pain rippled through his body again, and he fell to his knees gasping.

"Oh, God," he muttered, spitting more purple mucus onto the ground. He could still hear gunshots barking, but they sounded farther away now, like in a dream. "Oh, God."

"Stay with me. No deals, Haatim!" she said. She grabbed his shoulder. "Hey, focus. Stay with me!"

That was the last thing Haatim heard before falling unconscious for a second time that night.

***

Frieda was awake and getting dressed when she heard the knock on her door.

"Come in," she said.

The door opened, spilling light from the hotel hallway into her dim room. Her personal assistant, Martha, padded silently into the room, carrying a silver tray and wearing a frown. Martha had worked with Frieda for over ten years as her assistant, but Martha hated being awoken in the middle of the night.

On the tray sat a glass of orange juice, a granola bar, a pair of glasses, and a tablet. Frieda finished pulling up her stockings and skirt, smoothed out her blouse, and then picked up the tablet. She flicked it on and began scanning through the images.

"What do we know?"

"Gunmen broke into the building. Several people are dead, and there is a full police investigation on the scene."

"This happened on the twelfth floor?"

"That isn't confirmed," Martha said. "But, Aram called the meeting and it is the complex where Haatim is living."

Aram Malhotra was a powerful member of the Council. He had been a member for far longer than Frieda, and he often reminded her of it.

"When was the attack?"

"Forty minutes ago," Martha answered. "We have operatives on the way, but it'll be at least three hours to get on scene and start analyzing."

"Is the rest of the Council assembled?"

"Waiting for you."

Frieda sighed and handed Martha the tablet. She picked up the glasses and slipped them on. She saw an image flash to life and suddenly the various members of the Council were filling up the room around her, holograms generated by the lenses. Martha tapped the tablet and then nodded, signaling that her mic was live.

"I apologize for my late arrival, but I only just received word about what has happened. Thank you for your quick response to this matter of some urgency," she said.

"What has happened?" one member asked. "There was no briefing."

Frieda bit back her annoyance. Aram had called this meeting on behalf of his family, but he was forcing her to deliver the news to the Council. It was technically her responsibility to handle matters like these, but it put her in an awkward position.

Which had, of course, been his intention.

"Forty minutes ago there was an attack on an apartment complex in

Phoenix, Arizona," she continued. "We believe it was orchestrated by the Ninth Circle."

She heard muttering as she broke the news.

"We are looking into the situation and will send full reports and briefings as soon as we have more information."

"What about my son?" Aram asked. All of the other Council members fell silent.

"We are looking into the possibility that he was the target of this attack," Frieda said. "But until we know more—"

"You *know* he was the target," Aram interrupted angrily. "And I want to know what you're planning to do about it."

"They are targeting *us* now?" one of Aram's friends, Frederick Davenport, said. "Our defense network has grown so weak that they feel unchallenged. They are growing more brazen by the day, and our inaction is costing us our families."

Frieda knew the remarks were targeted at her: she was responsible for the Order of Hunters and maintaining the Council's security.

"We are looking into the possibility—"

"They should be our top priority," Frederick interrupted. Frieda knew it was for show and that Aram and Frederick had scripted this out. "We shouldn't be wasting resources on other endeavors. Not until the Ninth Circle has been eliminated."

"I agree," Aram said. "I demand a vote to focus our efforts on the Ninth Circle, and I demand that you send assets to rescue and protect my son."

Frieda frowned. "The vote has been noted but will be postponed until after this crisis is taken care of. Abigail is in the region, and I will send her to—"

"Abigail Dressler?" Aram interrupted incredulously. "You would put the life of my son in *her* hands?'

"She is the only asset in the vicinity."

"I wouldn't trust her to take out the garbage," Aram said. "No, I demand that you send someone else."

Frieda bit back her annoyance. "I can send Oleg Petrov. He is several hours away but could be there by morning."

"Fine," Aram said. "Send him. And I expect hourly status updates until my son is safely back with his family!"

"Of course," Frieda said.

She gestured with her hand to Martha, and the connection went blank. She took off the glasses and tossed them angrily onto the tray. "These are *my* assets," she complained.

"I am aware," Martha agreed.

"I am in charge of the Hunters, not Aram. The nerve of that man, telling me what I will and won't do with *my* soldiers."

"I understand completely, ma'am," Martha said. "He seemed

…disingenuous."

"I know," Frieda said. "He's hiding something, and he knows more than he's willing to say. I don't know what game he's playing, but I need to find out."

"Shall I contact Oleg?"

"He's on an operation," Frieda lamented with a sigh. "But yes, contact him and tell him it is urgent. Fill him in on any questions he might have."

"Would you like that I contact Abigail as well?"

"No," Frieda said. "I'll call Abigail myself."

✳✳✳

Haatim awoke with a start, jerking his body against leather restraints and feeling a burst of panic. His mind was foggy and disoriented, and he struggled vainly to find his bearings. He felt sick to his stomach and ached all over like he'd just finished running a marathon while simultaneously writing a graduate-level term paper.

"Where…where am I?" he muttered. His mouth was dry and tasted of cotton. He swallowed, struggling to open his eyes. It felt unnaturally bright, and he blinked several times. It didn't help, though, and his vision was still blurry. "Where is this?"

"Shh," a voice said. He felt a hand on his forehead, gently brushing his hair. "Shh. You're safe now."

The voice was soft and feminine, hypnotic.

"Where am I?" he asked again.

"You're in St. Mary's Hospital," the woman said. Haatim blinked to clear his vision and saw a young woman standing next to his bed wearing green scrubs. She had red hair and lots of freckles. "Room 222."

"How did I get here?"

"You were dropped off last night."

"Why am I tied down?"

"You had a bad reaction to the drugs in your system and became violent. We had to restrain you."

"The *what's* in my system?"

She glanced at a clipboard on a bedside table and smiled at him. "You overdosed on narcotics late last evening. The police found you unconscious in an alley and brought you here."

She stepped closer and undid the braces holding Haatim's legs, then she moved to his hands and began unclipping those as well. He could smell her perfume: a sickly-sweet fruity concoction masking something else. Something that smelled vaguely like rotting meat. He couldn't tell if it was coming from the nurse or something else in the room, though.

After a second, she finished freeing him and stepped back. The smell disappeared, and he wondered if he had imagined it. She smiled at him.

He rubbed his wrists and looked himself over. He was in a green and white hospital gown that looked and felt grimy. He saw his pants and shirt—no less grimy, but at least they were his—resting on a nearby chair.

"Better?" she asked

Haatim nodded. "Much. Thanks. Is it OK if I get changed?"

"Certainly," she said. "I'll be in the hall if you need me. Let me know when you have finished."

"All right," he said. She stepped out and closed the door. He stripped off the gown and put his own clothes back on. He wished he had something clean to wear, but it was better than nothing.

"I'm done," he said.

She stepped back into the room and smiled at him. "Great. I just have a couple of questions before we call the doctor. What do you remember from last night?"

"I don't remember anything, but I definitely don't do any narcotics."

"The police believe that a dosage was administered without your knowledge or permission."

"You mean I was drugged?"

"Yes," she said. "Do you remember anything that happened yesterday evening?"

Haatim racked his memory but kept coming back to one thing: "I was *drugged?*" he echoed, shaking his head. It was throbbing and felt like it might explode at any moment. "That doesn't sound right. Yeah, I remember some things. I mean, I think so…"

He trailed off, trying to piece his memories together. His thoughts were fragmented: he only had bits and pieces.

"I remember going out to the coffee shop, and then…"

He hesitated, remembering Abigail. He'd been following her and had caught up with her; something had fallen out a window, and she had told him something at his apartment and—

He suddenly remembered the attack at his apartment complex. It came back as a flood: he'd been running down the stairs and into the lobby of his apartment with Abigail, and someone had been shooting at them.

"No, I wasn't drugged," he said, speaking quickly. "I was *poisoned.* My apartment was shot up, and we were being chased into the lobby and…"

He trailed off, seeing her puzzled expression.

"Attacked?" she said. "No, I don't believe so. You seemed rather out of it when they brought you in. Delirious and raving."

"But my apartment…" he said. "The people chasing us . . . "

"I can assure you, if something like that had happened, we would have heard about it on the news. Where do you live?"

"At the corner of Rochester and Bixby," he said.

She looked surprised. "Oh."

Haatim was used to that kind of response when people found out where his apartment was located. Those units weren't cheap by any means and catered primarily to wealthy individuals with expensive lofts. He didn't have a huge apartment, but it wasn't shabby, either, and it was definitely expensive

But it wasn't something he paid for. His father footed the bill for his accommodations these last few months. He was furious with Haatim's decision to return to the States, but he had still rented the apartment for him.

"Well," the nurse added, finally. "There was certainly nothing on the news about gunshots in *that* neighborhood, and you're a long way from home."

"Where is this?"

"Mohave County," she replied.

That was nowhere near his apartment. It meant he was, at least, a few hours northwest of home. Haatim shook his head, trying to focus his thoughts and make sense of the situation.

Haatim hesitated. "No, that can't be right. We were being shot at, and we rushed down the stairs and…"

He trailed off again.

"And?" the woman prompted.

"And I was given something to drink, and I blacked out."

"That's the last thing you remember?"

"I barely remember it," he said. "It's foggy, and I don't recall anything clearly."

"I wouldn't expect you to. You were dosed with some pretty heavy sedatives and amphetamines. There's no telling what you experienced while they were in your system."

She turned toward the doorway. "Doctor?" she called. A moment later a tall man in a lab coat and blue scrubs strode into the room. She handed him the clipboard, and he walked up to the bed with a small smile. He was gaunt and balding.

"Well, well. Our patient has finally woken up," the doctor said.

"He's doing quite a bit better," the nurse added.

"How are you feeling?" the doctor asked.

"I…" Haatim said. "I'm OK, I guess."

"That's excellent," the doctor said, making a note on the clipboard. "Most excellent. Do you have any residual effects from the drugs you were administered? Any nausea, dizziness, or lightheadedness?"

"No," Haatim said. "My head is killing me, but otherwise, I feel fine."

"How about your stomach? Is it OK?"

"I think so," he said.

"Then are there any other problems to report?"

"Other than the fact that everything I remember from yesterday is hazy," Haatim began. "No, I don't think so."

"It's somewhat expected with how many different chemicals were in your bloodstream. They can alter your perceptions dramatically."

Haatim let out a sigh. "Tell me about it."

The doctor noted on the clipboard again. "In any case, I think we can discharge you in a few hours. All of our tests came back negative, and I think you're going to be all right."

"Good," Haatim said, lying back on the bed. He felt relaxed and sleepy, and all he wanted to do was take a nap.

He found it hard to believe that he'd simply imagined the events of the previous night. But then again they were pretty outrageous when he actually stopped to think about them. Maybe he'd just been on a really bad psychedelic trip and imagined most of it.

It sounded way more plausible than demon's being real and hunting him. Actually, the more he thought about it, the more reasonable it all sounded. He'd been tracking Abigail, and when he caught up with her she'd drugged him to give him the slip.

"Can you sign this here?" the doctor asked, holding out the clipboard and a pen.

"Sure," Haatim said, reaching out. As he moved his right arm he felt a sudden burst of pain in his shoulder and cried out. He collapsed back on the bed, groaning. "What was that?"

"An injury," the doctor said. "Something you sustained last night."

Haatim felt the wound with his right hand. It was bandaged and hurt like hell. He suddenly remembered the door exploding in his apartment and the feeling of the wet blood as shrapnel ripped through his skin. It was vivid and clear and powerful, and it felt very real.

"How did I get it?" he asked.

"We believe you fell down and struck your shoulder against something sharp."

Something in Haatim's mind screamed that wasn't true. He rubbed the injury, trying to piece things together.

"All right," he said, not entirely convinced.

The doctor gestured with the clipboard again. "Please sign."

He hesitated. "Do you mind if I sign a little later. After the pain goes away."

"We can give you some painkillers—"

"No," he interrupted, "no more drugs. I just need a few minutes to relax and recover."

The doctor frowned at him for a second and then nodded. He pulled the clipboard back. "Very well. I believe we'll have to gather some other paperwork for you as well, so we might as well get it all at the same time and spare your shoulder the worst of it. Nurse...?"

"I'll grab him his lunch while I get the discharge paperwork ready," the nurse said.

"Very good," the doctor said.

The nurse stepped out of the room, and he heard her feet clacking down the hall. The echo was loud as it filtered back to them, a lot louder than he could have expected from a hospital hallway.

The doctor turned back to Haatim. "We were able to pump the drugs out of your stomach, but if we knew what in particular you were administered we could do more to stop what's already in your system. Do you know what it was?"

"No," he said.

"She didn't mention anything before giving it to you?"

"She said..." Haatim started then trailed off. "Wait. How did you know it was a 'she'?"

The doctor blinked. "Lucky guess," he said. "I think you must have mentioned that it was a woman while you were raving last night."

Haatim frowned. "She said it was poison."

"Ah," the doctor replied, unfazed. "What kind?"

"I don't know," Haatim said. "But it wasn't. You said it was drugs, right?"

"It is most likely a narcotic of some kind," the doctor said. "But it could have been mixed with something else. Belladonna, maybe."

"Nightshade?"

"Yes."

"I don't think so."

"What about Agrimony or Hyssop?"

"I don't know what those are. You can't find it in the tests?"

"No," the doctor said. "And we need to know what it was so we can release you."

Haatim absently rubbed his arm, shaking his head. It took him a second to realize the skin was smooth; the cut was gone, as was any trace he'd ever had a wound there. "What about the scratch that was here?"

"What scratch?"

"The one on my arm," Haatim explained. "It's been there for several days."

"There was no scratch."

"Are you sure?" Haatim said. "I remember it from before being drugged. It wouldn't go away."

"I'm telling you," the doctor replied. "There was no scratch."

The nurse stepped back into the room. She was carrying what looked like a prison tray with disgusting looking food slopped into the various compartments. Just looking at it made Haatim's stomach turn.

"I'm not hungry," he said.

"Nonsense," the nurse replied, smiling. "You need to get some food into your stomach to help soak up all the bad things. After you eat this, you'll feel right as rain."

"No thanks," he said.

The nurse looked at him, her smile fading, and then set the tray on the bedside table.

"I'll leave it here, in case you change your mind," she said. Then she disappeared out of the room, leaving him alone with the doctor once more.

"She's right, you know," the doctor said, still scanning his chart and making notes. "You should eat something."

"I will once I get out of here," Haatim said, "but I'm just not hungry right now."

"It's understandable," the doctor replied. "Not many people really enjoy hospital food."

Haatim shrugged, still groggy and hoping to clear his mind. Something felt wrong about the hospital, but he couldn't place his finger on exactly what it was.

"How about I make you a deal," the doctor said suddenly, still looking at the chart.

Haatim felt the hairs stand up on his neck. "Excuse me?"

"A deal," the doctor said, finally looking up at him. "I'll pick you up some food from any restaurant you like, but you have to promise you'll assist me with a few other matters."

Haatim felt his pulse quicken. The words sounded innocent enough, but something in his mind was screaming at him that they were wrong. Something about this entire situation was wrong.

"What?" he asked, pretending he didn't understand. "What do you mean?"

"What kind of sandwich would you like me to get you? Or maybe a burrito or something else? I can get you whatever you require."

"I…um…" Haatim stuttered. "Why is it so quiet?"

That was what had been bothering him. It was far too quiet for a hospital. There should have been people talking in the halls, equipment beeping and TVs playing in other patients' rooms.

Instead, he heard nothing: just silent emptiness.

"What is this?" he asked, sitting up and pulling to the edge of the bed. His body felt sluggish.

The doctor walked casually over and pushed him back down, his expression calm. Then he walked over to a cabinet on the wall and slid it open.

"There is an easy way to do things, Haatim, and a hard way," the doctor said, pulling out a syringe and bottle. He poked the needle in and started filling it. "And the hard way is considerably more painful."

Haatim felt a flood of adrenaline and terror. He jumped out of the bed and started running for the exit. Two men appeared in the doorway, blocking his exit.

They were the same two who had been chasing him the previous night in the alley. Now, in the hospital lighting, he could see them much more clearly.

The living one had greasy black hair and sallow skin. His eyes looked lifeless, like a doll's eyes. The other one, though, was what caught Haatim's attention. The skin of his face was a shade of green, and some of it had sloughed away.

Maggots were crawling in the eye socket and the good one looked dry and dead. The gash on his throat was still there, caked in dry blood with skin hanging loosely on the collar of his coat.

But the smell…that was the worst of it by far. It smelled like Haatim had stepped into a room filled with rotting and burned pork. Flies buzzed around the man, landing unnoticed on his clothes and skin.

Haatim scrambled back, making little panting noises, and bumped against the side of the bed. The doctor appeared next to him and jabbed a needle into his neck.

"This should kick start the effects of the poison and speed up the process. Abigail didn't give you a very large dose, so it may work its way out of your system on its own. We can complete the ritual once you are recovered."

Strong hands pushed Haatim back on the bed. He felt the drug starting to work with a burning sensation in his stomach. It built and within seconds had turned into white hot pain. Haatim screamed as agony ripped through his body.

"And if the poison manages to kill you," the doctor said with a shrug. "Then I'm sure we can still find some use for you."

Chapter 6

Haatim lay on the hospital bed, gasping in agony as heat ripped through his stomach. It seemed like hours had passed since the doctor had injected him, but he rationally knew it had only been minutes. It felt like his insides were being turned into mush.

They hadn't given him any medication to help dull the pain, only something to keep him docile. He could feel everything; he simply couldn't react to it.

He wasn't tied down anymore, but that didn't matter. The two guards were still in his room, the dead one and the one with sallow skin, but the doctor and nurse were still gone. The two guards stood on opposite sides of his bed, watching him struggle with immutable expressions. He had tried pleading with them to no avail. They were cold, lifeless.

After what felt like an eternity, the doctor came back into the room, carrying his clipboard. He frowned down at Haatim and looked at the two men.

"No improvement?" he asked

"None," sallow-skin said.

"A pity," the doctor replied. "All our efforts will be in vain."

"Should we finish him off?"

"No. Let the medicine run its course. Once he's dead we can send his head back to his father. Not the ideal situation, but it is what it is."

"Why...?" Haatim gasped. "Why are you doing this?"

The doctor looked at him. "I'm not doing anything. Your friend poisoned you. I'm simply helping the process along. Unfortunately, it seems that the dose you received *will* prove fatal."

"Please...a hospital..."

"This *is* a hospital," the doctor said, gesturing his arms at the room around them. "Or, at least as close to a hospital as you will get before you expire."

Haatim groaned in pain.

"What?" the doctor said. "You feel let down by the situation? I feel worse. All of my work these past months will have been for naught."

"I know, right?" a voice called from the doorway.

Everyone froze, and slowly they all turned to look at the doorway. Even Haatim managed to cock his head far enough to get a decent view.

Abigail was leaning casually against the door frame, arms folded and a smirk on her face. "You think you found the *perfect* vessel to bring your dark lord back from hell, but it just never works out, does it?"

"You!" the doctor said, dropping the clipboard.

"Me?" she asked innocently. "Relax Christoph, if you brought your lord back here now I would just have to kill him again."

The doctor—Christoph—charged forward with a yell. Abigail exploded into motion, dropping into a crouch and quick-stepping forward to confront him. The two bodyguards were right behind Christoph, entering the fray only seconds later.

The doctor swung wildly at her, waving his arms like they were batons. Abigail ducked under the first attack, sidestepped the second, and then kicked him in the back of the knee. The joint bent down at an uncomfortable angle, snapping with a sharp crack. Haatim winced as he watched the bone shatter.

He saw a blur of motion as Abigail twirled and ducked, avoiding the other two combatants as they launched attacks at her. She was so fast that he could barely follow her movements. At some point, she drew her revolver, and he heard the bark of a gunshot.

The sound filled his ears, leaving behind a ringing. He saw the dead man stumble back into the wall, yet somehow he managed to stay standing despite being shot in the chest at point blank range.

Abigail used the momentary lull to attack her other opponent, launching a flurry of blows that drove sallow-skin into the corner of the room. She finished with a kick to his chest, knocking him into the corner. He sunk into the drywall, partially restrained by it.

When she turned back, the dead man was charging her, attempting to ram her into the wall next to his friend. Abigail dropped to the floor, twined her legs between his, and tripped him. He fell face forward into the drywall, shattering it and staggering through.

Behind the newly created hole, Haatim could see a cavernous space stretching into the distance. Little dots of light from windows decorated the sides throughout at various heights. It was dark, and it looked like boxes were stacked on pallets inside the cavernous space.

It looked like a warehouse, empty and silent with all of the lights turned off. *What the hell...?*

Abigail didn't hesitate: she jumped to her feet, stepped onto the dead man's back, and fired a bullet into the back of his head. Then she spun and aimed the revolver at sallow-skin; he had just pulled himself free from the corner.

"These bullets are blessed," she said. "Go home willingly, or when I pull this trigger you'll be stuck there for a *very* long time."

The man hesitated, and then suddenly his body collapsed to the floor. Abigail lowered the gun and turned to Haatim. She slid a new vial out of her pocket and hurried over to him.

"Drink this," she said.

"Why?"

"It's the antidote."

"I should . . . trust you?" he mumbled, gasping in pain.

"Good," she said. "You're learning. But you'll be dead soon, so what further harm could I do?"

Haatim stared at her, then at the room around them. The walls were shattered, three bodies lay on the ground, and most of the medical equipment was broken.

"A lot, apparently," he offered.

"Just drink it."

Haatim accepted the vial. He took a sip and nearly spat it back out. It was easily the most disgusting thing he'd ever tasted.

"Is that burned grass and asphalt?"

"I don't know," she said. "I just buy it."

The burning sensation and agony subsided almost immediately, and Haatim was able to breathe again. He let out a deep sigh, almost crying with relief.

He sat up on the bed. The doctor was still lying on the ground, clutching his knee and moaning. Abigail saw Haatim staring and added:

"He'll be all right. The demon fled as soon as I shattered the man's knee. We'll call an ambulance when we leave and they'll get him fixed up."

"You mean, that wasn't *him*? It wasn't that man doing those things?"

"That was the demon controlling him," she explained. "Don't look so horrified. He isn't an innocent bystander by any means. He's a member of the Ninth Circle and gave himself willingly. The demon is only a lesser creature I know of as Christoph. I've met up with him and his sister many times in the past."

"That's..." Haatim said, then just shook his head.

"Crazy?" she finished. "I know."

"Why would anyone—"

Abigail made an "shh" sound, silencing Haatim, and glanced around the room. He fell silent, watching her.

"Was anyone else here?"

"A woman," Haatim said. "The nurse."

"The nurse?"

Haatim gestured toward the doorway, where he saw the leg of someone hiding around the corner. She was wearing the blue nurse's scrubs he had seen earlier.

"Her," Haatim said, gesturing to the door. "The nurse."

Abigail's eyes went wide: "Delaphene," she said.

Suddenly, the leg disappeared. He heard scuffling footsteps outside as the woman ran away. Abigail sprinted after her, disappearing through the doorway and beyond.

Haatim was left alone. He staggered out of the bed, tripping and stumbling over the bodies, and followed her out the hospital room. By the time he made it into the faux hallway, Abigail was halfway across the warehouse, chasing the nurse toward the exit. Their footsteps echoed loudly in the warehouse, scuffing across the floor.

He looked around and saw that his "hospital room" was actually a small fabricated contraption in the center of the warehouse, surrounded by old and rotting boxes and rundown equipment. They had built up just enough of a façade to make it appear legitimate to someone lying in the hospital bed, but nothing else.

He pushed one of the walls, which was painted to look like a hospital corridor, and it fell over with a resounding crash. The sound echoed, and Haatim let out a shuddering breath.

"This just keeps getting better and better."

Chapter 7

Abigail rushed out after the demon, sprinting with long, even strides. The woman she was chasing was fast, and the demon inside of her was pushing the nurse's body to peak capacity, which made it difficult to keep up.

The woman climbed atop a stack of wooden pallets and boxes and started running across them. Abigail was a few steps behind as she scrambled to follow, ripping plastic wrapping loose as she went.

The nurse jumped down the far side of the stack, landing with a thud on the concrete below, and ran unencumbered for the exit. Abigail was about forty steps behind and gaining ground. They exploded out the double doors into blazing morning sunlight, and Abigail's prey turned into a blur for a few seconds.

Abigail's eyes adjusted to the sunlight, and she kept sprinting. She had her gun still and knew she could make the shot, but she didn't want to risk killing her target. Not this target, at least.

This was the best chance she had to get some information about Arthur.

"Stop!" she shouted. "I only want to ask a few questions."

The demon ignored her and kept running. They were on the outskirts of the city in a rundown warehousing district. Across the street were dilapidated rent-controlled apartments that had seen better years.

They ran across the empty street into an alleyway between two apartment buildings. The demon leaped atop a large green dumpster and then sprang up to the fire escape, an inhuman leap Abigail knew she couldn't make. Then it pulled itself over the railing and started climbing up the stairs to the roof.

Abigail followed, stepping lightly onto the dumpster and kicking off the wall to push herself high enough to catch the railing. She couldn't jump as high as the demon even with the added step and only caught the bottom of the rail. The extra distance forced her to climb her way up onto the landing.

The demon was already rounding the third staircase by the time Abigail was on the first, and she knew she was losing time. Instead of climbing over the railing and chasing up the stairs, she balanced herself on the rusty handrail and sprung upward from a crouch, catching the metal rail on the second floor of the fire escape.

She rolled over the side onto the staircase and started chasing after the demon. Her wrist hurt, but she ignored the pain. Her feet twanged against the wire-frame flooring, and she felt it wobbling beneath her, but it didn't give out. After a few moments, she burst onto the roof behind her prey.

The demon sprinted across the cement roof, dodging vents and refuse. A pair of pigeons were scared up as it past, hooting as they took flight and disappeared into the sky. Abigail gained a little ground with long strides, but not enough.

There was a stairwell leading back into the building, but that wasn't where the demon was heading. It was sprinting for the edge of the roof. Abigail chased, only a few steps behind.

Delaphene kept going and Abigail steeled herself, forcing her tired muscles to push even harder. The demon reached the edge of the roof and leaped out, landing on the next building over. The second roof was about four meters away and three or so meters down. The demon hit the cement in a roll and came to its feet sprinting.

Abigail reached the edge and jumped out into the air, pushing off as hard as she could. There was a moment when she was floating in the air, wondering if this had been a bad decision and she should have just let Delaphene escape. It was a long distance between buildings, and she was six flights in the air.

She crashed against the side of the second building, fingers clinging to the cement siding. She kicked her feet, catching small holes in the bricks, and scrambled up the side.

The demon was almost across the second roof already, heading for the next building over. Abigail found her footing and cursed.

"Damn it," she growled, brushing loose hairs out of her face. With a growl, she took off after it.

***

Haatim half walked and half ran out of the warehouse, uncomfortable in the heavy silence now that the two women were gone. He didn't like staying in the vast emptiness with the echoing moans of the doctor, especially without Abigail nearby.

The entire cavernous chamber felt empty and abandoned, entirely uninviting. He came to the stack of boxes where Abigail and the nurse had climbed over and decided that finding a way around was a better plan. He had to walk his way over six aisles to find an opening. The place felt like a maze, and it stank of rotten things and death.

He felt like he needed to get some fresh air.

He reached the exit and stumbled into the sunlight beyond. He basked in it, closing his eyes and just breathing. His head hurt, his body was sore, and he was still terrified and confused, but at least he could breathe easily again.

He finally relaxed and glanced around for Abigail, wondering where she had disappeared to. She was nowhere in sight, but he couldn't decide if that was a good or bad thing. Maybe that was the last time he would ever see her.

The only problem was that he didn't know where he was. Or how to get home. Or what he would find when he got home. Or if it was even safe to go home. Or...

He trailed off, hearing someone shouting from up above. It sounded like a woman on the roof, but he couldn't tell if it was Abigail, the nurse, or someone else. He walked down the street in that direction, looking up at the rooftops and squinting. Several other people were coming outside their own buildings and looking around in confusion.

"What's going on?" a man asked Haatim, cupping his hands over his eyes and looking at the roof. He was only wearing a pair of white briefs; his big belly hung over the top of them.

"No clue," Haatim replied, moving farther down the street and away from the man. He could understand people being curious, but this guy took it too far in his tightey-whiteys.

He passed an open alleyway and kept moving down the street, still staring up. There was another shout, farther ahead, and he hurried forward. He paused at the entrance to another alley.

There was a fire escape on the right brick wall that climbed all the way to the roof. There was also a large amount of discarded garbage and broken boxes littering the ground. It reminded him of the alley where he'd lost his pants. He had a momentary flashback to the previous night's events and was thankful that at least the sun was out this time.

He waited, straining to hear or see anything, and suddenly a person sprang from the building on his left and landed on the fire escape to the right. It looked like the nurse, though it was hard to tell from her height above him. She landed nimbly on the fire-escape landing and started circling the stairs, running down.

A few seconds later he saw another woman—this one looked like Abigail—leap from the left roof as well. She didn't aim for the top landing but instead caught the rail and swung her body down like a gymnast to the level below, catching the nurse by surprise and kicking her in the chest. The nurse blasted into the glass window, shattering it and flying into the room beyond.

Glass rained down in the alley in front of Haatim, forcing him to step back and cover his face with his arms.

He looked back just in time to see Abigail land nimbly on the landing and jump through the shattered window, disappearing into the apartment building behind the nurse.

Haatim just stared, jaw hanging open. "Holy crap."

***

Abigail wove nimbly around the furniture in the apartment, chasing her prey farther into the room. These were shoddy accommodations with poor construction, and mostly unoccupied. The room they had landed in was only half finished and abandoned by the contractors, filled with rat droppings and dusty furniture and poorly installed insulation.

The nurse was cut now and bleeding in multiple places from smashing through the window. The demon could push her body to the brink of pain and exhaustion, but once it started shutting down there was nothing to be done. It was only a few steps ahead of Abigail now, stumbling along.

Abigail followed it out of the apartment into the hallway. She heard a scream behind her, along with the barking of a dog, but she had the demon in her sights now. She sprinted after it, closing the distance.

The demon ran to the closed door of another apartment, throwing its shoulder against it. The door didn't budge, so the demon tried again. It fell open on the second hit, and the demon stumbled inside. Abigail followed, barely steps behind. On the couch sat an elderly couple watching *Gilligan's Island*. They looked up in shock as the two burst inside.

The demon ran past their couch, stumbling and heading for the hallway leading into the kitchen. Abigail ran up the side of the couch, quick-stepping past the old woman, and dove off. She hit the demon in the back, tackling it to the ground and pinning it.

The demon thrashed and screamed, but Abigail rolled behind it and put it in a headlock. She clamped down on the neck, cutting off the demon's air supply. They struggled for a few more seconds before the demon finally fell limp.

Abigail laid back, panting and trying to catch her breath. She heard rushing footsteps in the hall and drew her gun, aiming at the door.

A second later Haatim rounded the corner, wild-eyed. She relaxed, lowering the gun, and let out a chuckle.

"Glad you could make it."

***

"What the hell is going on?" the old man asked, standing up slowly from the couch. His back creaked, and he looked more confused than angry.

"We're police," Abigail explained, climbing to her feet. She presented a badge from her pocket, flashing it to the man and his wife. "We were in the process of apprehending this woman when she tried to flee. Sorry for the disturbance."

The man turned and eyed Haatim for a long minute before nodding. "OK," he said.

"More officers will be here in a few minutes, and the state will assess the damage to your apartment for the cost of repairs."

This perked the man up, and he nodded again.

"Here," Abigail said, gesturing to Haatim and sliding the ID away. "Come help me get her out of here. We'll take her back to the precinct."

Haatim hesitated for a second and then went over. They picked the nurse up and started carrying her back out of the apartment. A lot of people were in the hallway now, leaning out of doorways to watch. Down the hall, the dog was still barking.

They carried the limp woman over to the elevator and inside. Once the door had slid shut he heard Abigail let out a sigh of relief. She pushed the lobby button and leaned against the wall.

"Police badge?" he asked.

"It's fake," she said. "And a bad one at that. We need to hurry. The real police will be here soon."

"What are we doing with her?"

"*I'm* going to take her somewhere safe," Abigail said, giving him a look.

"Then what am I going to do?"

"You're going to go home."

"What?" he asked, feeling a sudden tightness in his chest. "Home? What if they are still searching for me?"

"They aren't," Abigail said.

"How do you know?"

"Because we eliminated this cell. No one is left in the city to come after you."

"Cell?"

"This local group," she explained. "The organization is decentralized. No head of the snake to cut off, or I would have finished it years ago."

"You hunt them?"

"Yep," she said.

"Why?"

She looked at him but didn't answer. The elevator reached the ground floor and opened. Together they grabbed the woman and carried her out the front of the apartment building.

"I don't want to go home," Haatim said.

"You have to."

"After what happened? I just..."

Abigail looked at him, frowning. "One problem at a time. Stay with her," Abigail said, gesturing at the nurse.

85

She ran back down the street toward the warehouse and disappeared around the corner. Haatim let the body slump to the ground and drew in a few calming breaths. His hands were still shaking but he was starting to feel like his old self again.

A minute later a car pulled up next to Haatim.

His car.

"That's mine," he said as Abigail climbed out of the passenger seat.

"I'm borrowing it," she replied.

"Then I'm coming with you."

"Like hell you are," she said. She circled around the vehicle and opened the backseat, then they carried the nurse over. "You aren't coming with me."

"I'm not going home," he said. Then, quieter, he added: "I can't."

"Then where do you want me to drop you off? Do you have any family in the area?"

He shook his head.

"Any close friends you can stay with?"

"No," he said.

"No family *or* friends," she said with a sigh.

"None," he replied. "My parents don't even live in the US."

She hesitated, and he saw a curious expression on her face. She opened her mouth, but it was a long minute before she said anything. "You were going to tell me earlier what your father's name was," she said. "Back in your apartment."

"Aram Malhotra."

He saw her tense up and frown. She said, "OK."

"What? Why does his name matter?"

"It doesn't," she lied. "Get in."

Haatim thought to ask her why her demeanor had changed when he told her his father's name but decided against it. Right now he just didn't want to be alone.

"All right," he said, climbing into the passenger seat.

"You can come with me," she said, turning the car on. "But you do exactly what I say when I say it. Got it?"

"Got it."

Chapter 8

Abigail drove out of the city and north on the highway, thoroughly exhausted from the day's ordeal but not yet able to relax. Haatim sat in the passenger seat, a blank expression on his face as he tried to process everything that was happening to him.

It wasn't easy, she knew. His eyes had been opened to a world he hadn't even known existed, and it wasn't exactly a slow and simple integration. Abigail had the benefit of being introduced to this life at an early age. When Arthur had rescued her she had been a child, and she already knew that there were some things in this world that didn't make any sense.

And most of them were trying to kill her.

"Where are we going?" Haatim asked.

"Somewhere safe," she replied. "You should get some sleep. Your body is going to need some time to recover."

"What happened to your hand?" he asked.

She glanced down at it. It was covered in scars and swelling in the joints, but she hadn't wrapped it or worn a brace in weeks. It looked hideous and hurt like hell, but she couldn't really remember a time when it hadn't during these last few months.

The swelling was new, and she realized she'd probably damaged it in the fight.

"I broke it," she said. "A few months ago. Still swells up from time to time. I'm not supposed to put any pressure on it."

"Looks like you broke it pretty bad."

"I was in a cast for four months."

"Ouch," Haatim said. "What happened?"

Abigail was silent for a long minute. "You should get some sleep. We have a long way to go."

He reclined the passenger seat and let out a sigh. "I don't know if I'll ever be able to sleep again."

Naturally, he was out in only a few minutes. Abigail tapped him a couple of times, just to make sure he was totally gone, and then she pulled out her phone. There were three missed calls, all from Frieda, and a series of text messages telling her to respond immediately.

She clicked Frieda's number and waited for it to connect. Frieda answered on the first click.

"Hello?" Abigail said, yawning and making it sound like she just woke up.

"Abi? Where are you?"

"My hotel room," she lied.

"Are you still in Arizona?"

"What? No, I left last night. I'm in Arkansas. Almost to Raven's Peak like you said."

"I've been calling all night."

"I was sleeping, had my phone turned off."

"Were you at Rochester and Bixby last night?"

"No. Why?"

"No reason," Frieda said.

"Did something happen?"

"Don't play dumb, Abigail."

"I'm not," Abigail said. "I left about midnight."

"What about your tail? You said someone was following you?"

"Yeah, I dealt with it. Deleted the photos and sent him on his way."

"Did you get his name?"

"I think he said it was Robert. He was nobody."

Frieda was silent for a long moment, and Abigail wasn't sure if she bought the lie or not.

"OK," Frieda said finally. Abigail fought the urge to let out a relieved sigh. That was, at least, until Frieda continued: "Honestly, even if you did have him, I would rather not know just yet."

"Have who?"

"Haatim. If I knew that he was with you, I would be obligated to report that information to the Council. I don't want to cross that bridge until I can look into a few things on my end. I would hope you wouldn't tell me you had him if he was safe. And I definitely would hope you didn't tell anyone else. Do you know what I mean?"

Abigail was silent for a long minute, cursing Frieda in her mind. The silence grew awkward, and she decided to change the subject:

"OK. Anyway, I should be at Raven's Peak before too long and I'll let you know what I find out."

"OK, sounds good. Thanks, Abigail."

"No problem," she said. She hung up the phone and bit her lip. "Sometimes that woman really pisses me off."

It was annoying that Frieda knew she had Haatim, but she was curious what game Frieda was playing at. She didn't want the Council to know where Haatim was, which was crazy. Frieda had always been fiercely loyal to the Council. Maybe there was dysfunction in the ranks. Abigail couldn't decide whether she cared.

Still, she could honor Frieda's unspoken request and hang on to Haatim for a while. Whatever Frieda was doing, it was probably important, and having Frieda owe her a favor could be a huge benefit in the long run.

But, first things first: she glanced in the rearview mirror at the unconscious shape in the backseat of the car. Delaphene, a lesser demon notorious for being an information broker. Abigail hadn't even known Delaphene was in the city or a part of that cell and could hardly believe her good fortune at finding her.

This demon might know something about where Arthur was, and how she could bring him back. Fate, it seemed, had dropped a new avenue of pursuit into her lap.

***

Haatim woke up to a tapping on his arm. He yawned and glanced around. The clock on the dashboard said it was early in the afternoon, and he was still thoroughly exhausted.

"Are we there?"

"Not yet," she said. "Just a gas and restroom break. We have a long way to go before we stop again, so if you need to stretch your legs you better do it now."

Haatim nodded and climbed out of the car. He yawned again and stretched his arms. "Do you need anything?"

"Get me a coke," she said, climbing out and opening the gas hatch on the side. "And some beef jerky."

He nodded and headed into the gas station. His first stop was to the restroom to relieve his bladder, and then he headed out and purchased drinks and snacks. When he got back to the car Abigail was closing up the gas tank.

"My turn," she said, disappearing into the store. Haatim climbed into the passenger seat and leaned back, hoping to fall asleep again.

He heard a muffled buzzing sound as his pocket started to vibrate. He slid his phone out and looked at it curiously. He'd forgotten he still had it with everything that was going on.

Abigail had wanted to take it from him and destroy it, but she'd never gotten the chance. He looked curiously at the number and let out a groan. He clicked accept:

"Crap, Mom, I know I promised to call you back I've just been—"

"Haatim! Thank God!" she interrupted. Her voice sounded thick, like she'd been crying. "Thank God you're all right."

"Yeah," he said awkwardly. "I'm fine."

"Your father and I were so worried when we heard about the attack at your apartment."

Haatim sighed. If there was anything his mom was really good at, it was worrying.

"No, Mom, I'm fine," he said. "I wasn't even home when it happened."

"Where are you?"

"Don't worry. I'm fine. The police got me a hotel room and everything is OK," he lied. He didn't want his mom to be concerned about him, especially since he wasn't exactly sure what was going on or what he was going to do next.

"Do you need us to send you anything? Where is the hotel at?"

"No, Mom. I'm good for now."

"Give me the address and I will—"

"I'm fine, Mom," he said, cutting her off. "I am safe and healthy, and you don't need to worry about me. I promise."

"All right, Haatim," she said. He could tell she wasn't convinced, but she didn't push the issue.

"I need to go, but I promise I'll call you back soon."

"OK. I love you."

"I love you, too, Mom," Haatim said. He hung up the phone and turned it off. The battery was nearly empty, and he didn't know when he would be able to charge it. He slipped it into his pocket and leaned back in his seat.

A few minutes later Abigail returned to the car, slipping into the driver's seat. He glanced over at her and yawned. "How much farther?"

"Not too far," she replied. "A few more hours, maybe less."

She started the engine and pulled out of the gas station. She merged back onto the highway and Haatim stared out the window, watching the countryside roll past.

"Why did you agree to take me with you?" he asked finally.

"Like you said: you have nowhere else to go," she replied.

"You only agreed after I told you my father's name," he argued. "Do you know him?"

She was silent for a long moment. "Why did you stop believing in God?"

"I asked you first."

"I know *of* your father," Abigail said. "Never met him, I just know the name. Your turn."

Haatim had to think about how to answer her question. He'd never really given himself time to think about it himself: "My father is an Acharya," he explained. "A spiritual leader. He was someone looked up to in his community. Growing up, I thought I was going to follow in his footsteps. I studied Theology and learned about world religions."

"And then you stopped believing in God?" Abigail said.

"I never stopped believing God existed," Haatim said. "I stopped believing God was good."

"What happened?"

90

"My sister died," Haatim explained. "She wasn't even seventeen when cancer took her. It was horrible during the last few months, watching her suffer and being unable to help."

"So you lost your faith?"

"How can I have faith in something like that? It's almost worse if God *does* exist because then it means everything wrong about our world is intentional."

"You don't believe in free will and that people can make their own decisions? If we mess up, it's our own fault."

"How can people make decisions when facts are withheld? How is a kid born into poverty without parents supposed to be able to make the same decisions as a kid born into wealth with a silver spoon in his mouth?"

"So it took your sister's death to awaken you to the inequalities of the world?"

Haatim hesitated. "I think I always had questions and concerns, but I guess I just ignored them. I thought if I showed people how to be happy with what they had, that things would be OK. But, when my sister died..."

"It was harder to pretend things were fair in the world," she finished. "I can understand that."

"How do you know about my father?"

Abigail glanced over at him. "You have no idea, do you?"

"What?"

"At first, I thought it was just an act and that maybe you were toying with me, but now I think you genuinely don't know."

"What are you talking about?"

Abigail hesitated. "Look, if you are who I think you are, then it isn't my place to say."

Haatim groaned in exasperation. "Say what?"

Without answering, Abigail reached over and flicked the radio on. She turned up the volume, making it clear that their conversation was over. Haatim stared at her for a long while before looking back out the window, but she refused to make eye contact.

"Do you have any idea how frustrating you are?" he mumbled, resting his chin on his hand.

"Yep."

✳✳✳

Haatim had never seen as much dust in his entire life as when they opened the door to the old cabin. It hung thick in the air and covered all of the furniture in the decrepit building.

It was a massive single story affair made out of logs and beams that looked like it was built in the eighteenth century. It looked sturdy and old, hidden in the mountains of Colorado and far away from civilization in all directions.

The cabin was surrounded by bristlecone pine trees and thick foliage in every direction with no other roads or houses nearby. The perfect little hideaway, Haatim realized.

They had traveled on a dirt road for the last eight miles of the trip, bouncing and jostling across uneven terrain. He wasn't the sort of person to get car sick, but even he was more than a little happy to finally be out of that car.

Abigail had spoken little after his questioning, and after a while, Haatim had managed to fall into an uncomfortable doze once more. His head still hurt, as well as his stomach, but he was starting to feel better overall. Healthier. They picked up a late lunch at a fast food restaurant, and he felt like he was recovering.

"Dusty," Haatim said. He immediately sneezed. Then he sneezed again, and a third time for good measure.

"God bless you," Abigail said. "Hang on, I'll go open some windows."

Haatim waited out on the front porch as she stepped into the foyer and then disappeared into the living room. He heard the grinding of warped wood as she slid windows open, and then the sound of a generator kicking on from the opposite side of the house. That was followed by the whirring of a fan somewhere inside the old log cabin.

A moment later, Abigail reappeared. "We don't have a lot of fuel, but I don't think we'll be here very long."

"Where are we?"

"My cabin," she explained, going back inside.

"I meant what state?"

"Denial," she offered.

Haatim hesitated, then frowned. "Ha, ha, very funny. I meant are we still in Arizona?"

"I know what you meant," she said. "We're in Colorado. Come on."

He followed her inside, trying to breathe through his mouth and avoid the dust clouds. It didn't help, and he sneezed again. "Doesn't look like you've been here for some time."

"I haven't," she said. "Not since..."

She trailed off, and Haatim saw a troubled look cross her face.

"Not in a long time," she agreed. "Help me clear out the living room before we bring Delaphene in."

"Delaphene?"

"The nurse," she said. "It's her name, or, at least, the one she uses. I don't know her real one."

They set to cleaning up the main room. It was an impressive job, given the state of things, which made him glad she didn't want them to clean the entire house. There were a lot of scattered boxes filled with old papers and trinkets.

Little crosses and jewelry, stones and glass sculptures, and millions of other things he barely recognized.

A lot of those trinkets looked like the cheap things Haatim had seen at county fairs when he was younger. The sort of garbage they sold to hapless tourists with too much money and not enough discretion.

Haatim found a broom and rag in the kitchen and set to clearing out the dust. Abigail stacked the boxes, occasionally leafing through the papers inside them. "What are we doing way out here?"

"Just a quick stop before we head on to Raven's Peak," she said. "For some answers."

"We couldn't ask her in Arizona?"

"Not in the way I intend on asking her."

"Are you trying to find out why they are trying to kill me?"

"They aren't anymore," she said. "Or, at least, her cell of the Ninth Circle isn't. You don't have to worry about them anymore."

"Then what are you planning to ask her about?"

"Something important to me," she said. Her tone signaled to him that was the end of that particular line of conversation.

"I've never been to Colorado before," he said after a while. "Is this where you live?"

"No," she said.

"Is this where you grew up?" he asked.

"No."

Haatim waited for her to elaborate, but she didn't. They kept working in silence, getting the room fairly well-cleaned-up. Haatim swept all of the dust and crud out the front door and Abigail took the sheets of plastic off the furniture.

"All right," she said. "That's good. Now, help me bring her in."

Haatim hesitated, and then shook his head.

"What is it?" Abigail asked.

"I want to know why?" Haatim replied. "Why did you bring her all the way out here? So you could torture her?"

"No," Abigail said.

"You're lying."

"So what if I am?"

"I'm not going to help you hurt someone."

"I don't need your help," Abigail said, "and I sure as hell don't need your approval."

"I won't let you do this."

"Then try and stop me," she said. "But keep in mind that we're not dealing with a human, but a demon. And one that was going to use you to summon her master back into the world. She would cut you up into little pieces without a second's hesitation."

"What about the person the demon is living inside?"

"What about her?"

"She's innocent. You said yourself that she's being possessed."

"Willingly," Abigail said. "I know this particular demon, and I know the vessel she resides in. They get along quite well."

"It doesn't matter," Haatim said. "If we torture *her*, we are no better than the demon."

"There is no 'we,'" Abigail said. "*I'm* doing this with or without you."

"Then it makes *you* as bad as them," he argued.

She shrugged. "Maybe," she said. "And maybe not. If it makes you feel better, I'm not going to torture the human. I have a few implements and poultices that only cause the demon to feel pain."

Haatim thought about it. "I'm not sure that makes it any better."

"It's the best you're going to get," she replied. "And, at the end of this, I'm sending the demon back to hell. Then *you* can decide if the vessel is worth saving. Deal?"

"Fine," Haatim said.

"Now help me carry her in."

He headed outside with Abigail, and together they brought the unconscious nurse into the living room. They tied her to a chair, wrapping duct tape around her wrists and ankles to hold her down.

"Now what?" he asked. "Should we wake her up?"

"Now we wait," she said. "Do you want a drink? I think there's some water in the kitchen."

"I'm OK," he replied.

"Suit yourself," she said, sitting on the couch. She laid back, setting her head on the armrest and closing her eyes.

"What are we waiting for?"

"For her to wake up," Abigail said. "I'm going to take a nap. You keep an eye on her. Just wake me up when she starts moving."

✳✳✳

The nurse woke up about an hour after they tied her to the chair, stirring slowly and moaning before anything else. The noise caught Haatim off-guard, drawing him out of a doze.

He was lost in his thoughts, piecing through the events of the last day or so; he was trying to figure out what he was going to do now that everything in his life had fallen apart: how was he supposed to move on?

He was relaxing in an old leather armchair and nearly fell out of it when the nurse's head jerked up. She let out a gasping cough and looked around, wild-eyed and delirious. Her matted hair clung to her face, and she was clearly dazed.

"Where…?" she started to say.

Haatim stood up to wake Abigail, but quickly realized he didn't have to. Abigail was already up, watching the nurse with a calm expression on her face. She sat up on the couch and rubbed her fingers through her hair, letting out a yawn.

She looked exhausted, and for the first time, Haatim could see how young she was. She couldn't be over twenty-three or four years old, and at the very least she was several years younger than himself.

"She's awake," Haatim said awkwardly.

"I can see that."

"What now?"

Abigail looked at him. "Maybe you should wait outside," she said. "While I talk to her."

He hesitated. "You aren't going to…?"

"No," Abigail said. "Not unless she forces me to."

The nurse rocked in her chair and threw a look of pure hatred at Abigail.

"I'm going to rip your eyeballs out, then jam them so far up your ass you'll see your intestines," the nurse said.

Silence hung in the air, and Haatim felt his mouth hanging open. He finally glanced over and saw Abigail staring at him, a bemused expression on her face. He quickly closed his mouth.

"Do you need any help?" he asked.

"No," she said. "But it might be best if you took a walk in the woods while you were out there."

✳✳✳

Once Haatim had left and Abigail was certain he was out of earshot, she turned to the demon. "Hello, Delaphene."

The demon stared at her for a long moment, frowning. "Hello, Abi. It's been a long time."

"I think you scared my friend."

"I'm surprised he's still with you," she said. "I thought by now the Council would have dragged him home to his father."

Abigail was silent.

Delaphene raised an eyebrow. "They don't know you have him? Oh, that is quite delicious."

"Why were you after him? It's very brazen of you to go after a family member of someone sitting on the Council."

"His father had a deal with our Lord that the Council didn't know about.

95

He didn't hold up his end of the bargain, so we were going to show him just how costly it was to betray us. Then we found out you were in town. Two birds, so to speak."

"You're lying."

"Am I?"

"No member of the Council would make a deal with Abaddon."

Delaphene pursed her lips. "Oh, my sweet innocent Abi. And here you thought *we* were the bad ones. What are you planning to do with Haatim?"

Abigail didn't know. She'd never known Aram Malhotra to have children, and she'd certainly never expected him to go to such great lengths to keep them from understanding this side of their lives. She'd always assumed children were indoctrinated into the life, carrying on the legacy of their parents. But, Haatim was clueless and detached from it all.

Maybe that was for the best, and Abigail envied him a little for his naiveté. She'd often wondered how her life might have been if she wasn't kidnapped by the cult and rescued by Arthur. What might have happened if she was allowed to live a normal life?

Still, for the most part, she enjoyed her life and was proud of the work she did on behalf of the Council. They were saving lives…yet, if what Delaphene was saying was true and Aram was compromised…

"You could just give Haatim back to me," Delaphene offered. "I can find some use for him."

"You? I'm pretty sure he thinks you're a cold and heartless monster," Abigail said. "He'll never know that underneath the evil and ugly exterior you're really just a fluffy puppy."

"Say that again and I *really* will kill you."

"And how are you planning on doing that?"

"This won't be our last encounter," the demon said. "And I have a *very* long memory."

"Good," Abigail said. "Then you should remember this."

She held up a dried plant with purple flowers, twirling it in her fingers.

"*Verbena*," Delaphene breathed, narrowing her eyes.

"Excellent. You *do* remember. I haven't used Isis's Tears in a long time, so this should be a lot of fun."

"What are you going to do with it?"

"That depends on how forthcoming you are with information," Abigail said.

Delaphene hesitated. "If the Council knew—"

"What they don't know won't hurt them," Abigail said. "And if a word of this finds its way back to the Council, I will dedicate my life to making your time in hell as miserable as possible. My memory is long, too."

Another moment of silence as the demon considered its options. "One condition."

"You aren't exactly in a bargaining position—"

"Don't send me back," Delaphene said. "Not yet. I'm not ready to go."

Abigail paused as if considering the proposition.

"We'll cross that bridge when we come to it," Abigail said. "For now, it's time to be helpful.

"Fine, ask your questions."

"Why were you trying to bring Abaddon back?"

"He ordered us to."

"I just sent him home," Abigail said. "Is he a *glutton* for punishment?"

"Very funny," Delaphene said. "Because gluttony…never mind. He has business to attend to, and he thought it would be amusing to confront the Council in Haatim's body."

"Seems risky," Abigail said. "Going after the son of a Council member."

"We have been watching him and several others for months now. The last time he lived in Arizona, he had two Council guards watching over him to keep him safe. This time, he didn't."

It made sense because aside from Delaphene's cell she hadn't noticed anyone keeping tabs on Haatim. There hadn't been anyone from the Council in the city aside from herself, as far as she knew.

"The only thing we didn't account for was *you*," Delaphene added. "Abaddon knew you were about to execute him, so he didn't want to risk taking Haatim as a vessel right away. He thought he could keep Haatim close and use him to get you off the streets."

"All Haatim had to do was take the bait."

"And he did," Delaphene said. "Yet he hesitated when he was supposed to turn the evidence over. I suppose his conscience got the better of him."

"Lucky for him," Abigail said. "I might have killed him myself if he went through with your plan."

Delaphene shrugged. "Little loss there. We underestimated just how resourceful you could be. Arthur trained you well, it seems."

Abigail frowned.

"Oh, a sensitive subject? And why wouldn't it be, with Arthur languishing in hell—"

"What business is Abaddon on?"

Delaphene stared at her. "I can't say."

"Who sent him on it?"

"You *know* I can't say, Abi. And even if I could, I wouldn't."

"Don't say it's because they'll do worse to you than I will," Abigail said softly.

Delaphene laughed. "Not worse, just for a *hell* of a lot longer. Is that all of your questions?"

Abigail hesitated. "Where is Arthur?"

"Ah," Delaphene whispered, smiling. "I wondered how long it would take to get to that."

"I know you don't like him—"

"Like him?" Delaphene interrupted. "He destroyed *everything* I built. He brought my entire organization crashing down. And, worst of all, he stole *you* from me."

"I was never yours."

"You will *always* be mine," Delaphene replied, and the conviction in her voice sent a shiver down Abigail's spine. "It will just take some time for you to realize it."

Abigail remembered being a little girl who was terrified of Delaphene and the others. She remembered the horrors and devastation that had been her life: they kept her locked in the closet when they weren't abusing her...

When they weren't corrupting her.

But she wasn't that girl anymore. She'd been freed and shown a better way, and now her life was dedicated to sparing other people from that same fate. She'd come to terms with her past, and she was not going to be ruled by fear.

Abigail stood calmly and slid a knife free from her belt. She walked to Delaphene's chair and knelt in front of it. The nurse had a concerned expression on her face now. She rocked the chair, trying to move it away, but it didn't budge.

Abigail slid the knife forward and drew a small cut on the demon's arm, a little over two inches long. Then she snapped off a few of the dry flower petals from the dried Verbena and began grinding them between her fingers. She chanted softly, closing her eyes.

"No," Delaphene muttered, trying to rock the chair again. "No, don't, please. It was just a joke. Please."

Abigail reached forward, scattering the crumbled flower into the wound. The effect was instantaneous, a sizzling bubbling from the cut as though she'd hit the skin with a blow torch.

Delaphene screamed in pain, thrashing so hard veins popped out on her neck. She rocked in the chair, trying to rip her arm loose.

Abigail waited about ten seconds before walking to the table, grabbing a towel, and wiping the petals off the demon's arm. It took a few seconds before the sizzling sound subsided and the demon stopped screaming. The nurse sat in the chair panting, head hung low and hair matted against her face.

"It doesn't hurt the human," Abigail said, holding up the remainder of the plant. "But I can't say the same for the parasite inside."

"They said you had changed," Delaphene mumbled. Her eyes were bloodshot from popped blood vessels.

"They were right. Tell me where Arthur is."

"I'll tell you the same thing I told the last person who asked me that," Delaphene mumbled. "I *don't* know."

Abigail froze, the knife shaking in her hand. The demon looked up at her slowly, realizing its mistake.

Abigail mumbled: "The last one?"

✳✳✳

"Who was it?" Abigail asked, stepping forward. "Don't lie to me."

"I don't know," Delaphene replied.

"Was it Frieda?"

"No."

"Greathouse?"

"No," Delaphene said. "It wasn't someone I know, which means you sure as hell don't know who it is."

"What did the person look like?"

"I never saw clearly," the demon said.

"But they *were* asking about Arthur?"

"Yes," Delaphene said in exasperation. "She wanted to know where Arthur had been taken. I told her that I don't know because it's somewhere we don't go. It's somewhere…outside. Beneath. I don't know exactly how to describe it. The things down there are *our* demons."

"Does Abaddon know who it was?"

"No," Delaphene said. "But it is something which concerns him. The things down there…they don't wake up very often, and they certainly don't come up for air. Whatever is going on…it's big, and it's only going to get worse."

"If you're lying to me…"

"I'm not," Delaphene replied quickly. "Look, for what it's worth, I don't think this other woman is trying to find Arthur to rescue him. I'm pretty sure she has something else in mind."

"Like what?"

"Like finding out what took him to make a deal with them."

Abigail was silent for a long minute, thinking about the possibilities of that statement. She remembered the creature that had been inside her all those months ago, the way it had utterly dominated her. The sort of power it could grant to a human being was…

Unthinkable.

"Does the Council know?"

"I don't speak to the Council," Delaphene said. "Maybe you should ask them."

"I can't," Abigail said.

"Of course, you can't," the demon said. "Because nothing you're doing right now is sanctioned, is it? They don't know you're looking into this, and they definitely don't know you're talking to me, right? They think you're a good little soldier, behaving orders like you are supposed to. They don't understand you, Abi."

"Oh, and you do?"

"Most assuredly, I do," Delaphene said. "I chose you for a reason. I saw your potential when you were a little girl. I knew what you could become. I had great plans for you, Abi, before Arthur stole you from me."

"I'm nothing like you."

"You're *exactly* like me," Delaphene countered. "Look around us. Look where we are. This is Arthur's home. His sanctuary. And you are using it to treat with a demon. The foremost tenet of your Order is that you will *not* deal with demons, and yet here we are."

"Be quiet."

"You dishonor him—"

"Shut up," Abigail said angrily, but Delaphene was ignoring her.

"You are betraying *everything* Arthur stood for in your pursuit to rescue him—"

"I said *shut up!*" Abigail said, stepping forward and backhanding Delaphene across the face.

She'd known it was a bad idea to bring Delaphene out here. She had too much history with this demon; never mind how connected Delaphene was to the underworld and what kind of information she had access to, she was dangerous. The problem was: Delaphene knew just how to push her buttons.

The demon stared at her, a red handprint on her left cheek.

"That anger," Delaphene said, smiling knowingly. "That's the part I miss the most."

✳✳✳

"Answer my questions, and nothing else," Abigail said, forcing herself to calm down and take deep breaths.

"I did," Delaphene said. "I told you everything that I know."

"You are withholding something," Abigail said. "You think you know me? Well, I definitely know you, too. I know when you're holding out."

"I'm not."

Abigail held up the leaf. "The last time I left it only for a few seconds. This time, I'll leave it for an hour."

Delaphene hesitated. "That would kill me."

"Little loss there."

"Bravo," Delaphene muttered finally. "I suppose there is *one* other thing you could try. It's a trick I heard about long ago, and I've been wondering if it might help track Arthur down: intersect the link."

"The link?"

"The one Arthur created with the girls. Their scars never faded, did they?"

Abigail shook her head. "No, they didn't."

Normally, the scars of a claiming wouldn't last more than a day. Two at the most. But the scars on the three little girls had lasted through all of the months since Arthur first claimed them in the Church. Various doctors had tried to heal the sores, but they stayed open, uninfected but ugly marks on their foreheads.

"The link is still open," Delaphene said.

"What good does that do me?"

"There is a way to bridge the connection. I can show you how to do it. You *might* be able to see where his soul has gone, and, who knows, you might even be able to bring him back."

Abigail thought about it for a second. "Show me."

"Only if you agree to tell me where he is if you find him."

"Not a chance," Abigail said. "But, I will let you keep this body for a while longer if you help me."

"Deal," Delaphene said. She rocked a little in the chair. "Do you want to remove these bindings so we can shake on it?"

✳✳✳

By the time Haatim returned to the cabin Abigail was on the porch waiting for him. He had turned his phone on, but there was no signal out here, so he'd just turned it back off and slipped it into his pocket. They were in the middle of nowhere, so he hadn't been expecting much.

Abigail looked unhappy and exhausted, leaning against the railing of the porch and staring out into the wilderness. She didn't react to his approach.

"Is it...?" he started to say. "Should I walk some more?"

"No," she said, "it's taken care of."

"Did you...?"

Abigail looked at him. "No, I didn't kill her. Like you said, the human is innocent," she said. Then she shrugged. "Mostly, and with a loose definition of innocent."

"Then what did you do?"

"I found out some interesting things, and we have one more stop to make before we leave Colorado."

"To do what?"

She walked over to the car and gestured for him to get in. He followed her over and then glanced back at the cabin.

"What about the...?"

101

"The demon?" she finished.

"Yeah."

"I promised her I would let her stay in that body for a while longer. I never said I would let her leave the cabin. I locked her in one of the cages, and I'll let her go when we get back."

"Cages?"

"Prison cells," she explained. "There are three down in the basement. Don't worry, she has plenty of food and water."

Haatim climbed into the passenger seat. Abigail turned it on and started rolling back down the dirt road. "Why are prison cells in your cabin?"

"For situations like this."

"Does this happen often?"

"More often than you'd expect," she replied. She started the car and drove out onto the dirt road. It was slow going with all of the potholes and uneven sections.

Haatim glanced over at Abigail.

"What?" Abigail asked.

Haatim hesitated. "Is she really a demon?"

"You saw what she is," she replied. "Your own senses are your best judge, not me."

"I don't know what I saw," Haatim argued, shaking his head. "But, I mean, seeing something strange that I can't explain and seeing a *demon* are entirely different things."

"True."

"So why do you call it a demon?"

Abigail shrugged. "Habit," she said.

"What do you mean?"

"What people call it depends on how they grew up. Different religions call them different things. Some people just consider them evil creatures and refuse to associate them with any religion. Some even worship them. I personally just think of them as demons."

"Like hellspawn?"

"You could call them that," she agreed. "Except not hell in any religious sense. Hell is an idea. The reality is ambiguous."

"So, you call them demons because you are Catholic?"

"Not me," she said. "My mentor was. The man who taught me about all of this stuff. He considered them demons, and it stuck with me."

"So it's the lens through which you view the world," Haatim mused.

Abigail shrugged. "Sure."

"How are things like that real?"

"No one thinks they are until they know better," she said. "People are naturally ingrained to disbelieve in things like that."

"Are vampires real?"

"In a sense," Abigail said. "But we haven't seen one in a long time. Same thing with werewolves and other creatures. Most of them have some basis in reality, but their stories have been blown out of proportion."

"With social media things like this should be impossible keep hidden."

"It's actually easier," Abigail said. "Doctored footage and trending topics mean people will believe anything they are told. It's never been easier to spread propaganda."

Haatim fell silent, wondering about that. On the one hand, it was hard to believe that demons and supernatural creatures could remain hidden, but, on the other hand, it did sound plausible. Just looking at world politics made it easy to believe that people could be tricked.

"Where are we going now?" he asked.

"You'll see when we get there," she replied. "It isn't too far away and should only take a couple of minutes."

"To do what?"

"Nothing too major," Abigail said, glancing over at him. "On a side note: how do you feel about kidnapping?"

Chapter 9

The car came to a stop next to the curb, idling just outside the playground on Miller Street. Haatim glanced out the window at all of the gathered children, running around and playing on the swings and climbing objects scattered throughout.

Along the western end of the park was a line of park benches filled with parents, chatting and watching their children play. They were laughing and amicable right now, but Haatim knew they could turn dangerous at a moment's notice.

He tried to sink lower into his seat and become invisible, praying no one looked in his direction.

"I thought you were joking," he said.

"About what?"

"About kidnapping kids."

"I would never joke about that," Abigail replied solemnly. "We only need one child. And we aren't kidnapping her; I just need to talk to her for a few minutes without her mother noticing."

"Is that why we are here?" Haatim asked.

Abigail ignored Haatim and pulled a picture out of her pocket. She studied it for a second, then flipped the car off and scanned the playground.

"There," she said, pointing toward the swings.

"Don't point," he said, pulling her arm down and out of sight of the windows.

"What?"

"If you point, it looks like we're picking a kid out," Haatim said. "And that just seems creepy."

Haatim looked over and saw a pack of children gathered around the swings. They were shouting and laughing; he watched one catapult himself off a swing from a modest height and land roughly on the ground.

"Which one?"

"That little girl, third swing from the left."

Haatim squinted to get a better view. "The one with the blonde hair and a Band-Aid on her forehead?"

105

Abigail nodded. "She has a sore under that Band-Aid much like the one you had on your arm."

"You mean the one that wouldn't heal?" Haatim asked, rubbing his elbow where the torn skin had been. "You said it had something to do with the demon marking me."

"Exactly."

"But mine went away," Haatim said.

"They fade after a few days," Abigail replied. "A week at the most. Eventually, the bond wears thin and breaks, and the host is no longer vulnerable."

"When did she get hers?"

"Six months ago."

"And she still has it?"

Abigail nodded. "It never faded."

"What claimed her then?" Haatim asked. "Something powerful to make it last so long?"

Abigail was silent for a long moment, watching the little girl play.

"My father."

✳✳✳

"What?"

Abigail looked at him. "It doesn't matter."

"It sure as hell does matter," Haatim argued. "What do you mean your father claimed her?"

"He isn't a demon."

"Is that supposed to reassure me?"

"He also isn't my real father."

"Still not helping," Haatim said. "I'm not getting out of this car until you tell me what's going on."

"His name was Arthur. He was a mentor of mine. He raised me from a little girl and trained me."

"So he adopted you?"

"Never officially, but I always considered him family. He is the one who trained me to be a Hunter."

"Hunter?"

"It's exactly how it sounds," she said. "Only, the things I hunt typically hunt me back."

"So your father claimed this girl? How?"

"I don't know," Abigail said.

"I thought only demons could do that."

"I thought so, too."

"Do you think he might have—?"

"I don't know what he did or how he did it. All I know is that he *did*, and because he did I am alive today."

Haatim hesitated. "Is that why he isn't here? You don't trust him anymore?"

"No," Abigail said. "He was taken."

"Taken how?"

"I don't know."

"Where was he taken?"

"I don't know," Abigail repeated. She gestured her hand at the little blonde girl again. "That's why I need to talk to *her*."

"You think she knows?"

"In a sense."

"Who is she?"

"Someone important," she said. "And someone I need to speak to privately."

"I don't think that's a good idea," Haatim said. "You do realize we are parked outside of a playground full of kids, and we have no children of our own. We are the epitome of dangerous creeps right now."

"Nevertheless," Abigail said. "She's the only one of the three who lives in Colorado."

She pointed out the window toward a bench along the western edge of the park, a good eighty meters from the blonde girl. "That is her mother."

Haatim sighed and looked where she was pointing. "Green blouse or blue?"

"Green."

"OK."

"I need you to distract her?"

"What?" Haatim asked.

"Only for a few minutes," Abigail explained. "I just need to check the girl's scar."

"For what?"

"I need to see if the link is still active and if I can use it to find Arthur."

"Why can't we just ask her mom if we can talk to her for a few minutes?"

"It isn't that simple."

"Sure it is. I'll just say: 'Hey, you know that scar on your daughter's forehead? My friend thinks she knows what it is, and she might be able to make it go away. Can we just talk to her for a few seconds?'"

"There are people involved who can't know we were here," she said.

"What people?"

"I can't get into that right now," she said. "We don't have time."

Haatim pursed his lips. Part of him believed her because he'd already seen so much that didn't make any sense. But another part was curious and wanted to know everything. It was in his nature, and he hated the feeling of being left out of the loop.

107

"Fine," he said. "I'll help you. But you have to do something for me."

"You don't get to—"

"After we do this, you tell me everything," he interrupted.

Abigail was silent for a long moment. "Everything?"

"Everything," he reiterated. "Or I'll go tell those cops by the hotdog stand what you're planning."

She frowned, looking out the window at the young girl playing on the swings. Finally, she nodded: "Deal. When we're done, you can ask me anything, and I'll tell you the truth."

Haatim opened the car door. Halfway out, he paused and glanced back at Abigail.

"If I get arrested, you will bail me out, right?"

Abigail stared at him. "Possibly."

With a resigned sigh, Haatim left the car and started walking toward the women on the park bench.

✳✳✳

There is a severe limitation to this plan, Haatim decided as he walked: he was wearing the same clothes he'd had on since yesterday, the shorts and baggy t-shirt he'd thrown on. The clothes were dirty, and he looked disheveled; he also had a five o'clock shadow and bags under his eyes. Anyone who saw him might assume he was a bum begging for change.

Which *could* have been a worthwhile plan for distraction if it wasn't for the fact that there were several policeman stationed at miscellaneous points throughout the park. They wouldn't hesitate to grab him and cart him away if they thought he was a beggar disturbing the peace.

He wasn't sure what else he could do to get their attention, though. Maybe he could pretend to be a salesman of some sort, except he had nothing to sell; if he happened to have had a copy of the Quran with him he could keep their attention by pretending to convert them. Never mind that he wasn't Muslim; their own prejudices and assumptions would make the illusion reality.

Another angle he considered was pretending to be a street entertainer. He'd learned how to juggle—poorly—years ago and knew a few passable jokes. It might be enough to keep their attention for more than a few minutes, especially if he was able to entertain the children. If he caught the attention of the kids, then the parents would inevitably keep their eyes on him as well.

As he closed in on the group, he decided that street performer was his best option. He spotted an acorn tree nearby and scooped up a handful of them, testing their balance. They were light but heavy enough to keep in the air. He started juggling, missing his rhythm on the first few tries but finally managing to keep them in the air effectively.

A few children noticed and started pointing at him. They watched for a few seconds before coming closer. Haatim moved toward the women on the benches, pretending not to notice them, and kept juggling.

One of the curious kids moved shyly up to Haatim, a little girl with red hair and freckles.

"Would you like me to teach you how to do this?" Haatim asked, catching the acorns in his hands and holding a few out to the girl.

"Uh huh," she said, walking a few steps closer. She gingerly came up to him and accepted the acorns, then scrambled back to a safe distance from Haatim. That was fine with him, he didn't want anyone to think he was being aggressive.

He held one of his own up to show her and then tossed it in the air and caught it. "All you need to do is catch and release."

The little girl threw it up and then missed it on the way down. It hit the ground and bounced and she giggled. She scooped it back up and tried again.

"Hey," he said to another little boy who was nearby. "What do you call a fake noodle?"

The kid scrunched up his face to think and then shook his head. "I don't know."

"An impasta!" he said. The kid burst out laughing, and a few more kids moved closer.

He looked at another kid, raising his voice to get more attention. "What did the pencil say to the other pencil? You're looking sharp today!"

A few kids laughed. More kids came closer as they saw the little girl attempting to juggle. Curiosity got the better of them. Some picked up acorns of their own and tried to juggle, and others simply watched. Haatim knew he had their full attention.

Which meant he also had the attention of their mothers and fathers, who wore expressions ranging from mild amusement to worry and annoyance on their faces. They chatted amicably with one another but kept their eyes locked on him. He knew how he must look, disheveled and pitiful and invariably out-of-place. They stared at him like hawks, disinterested for now but ready to pounce at a moment's notice.

He also saw the woman in the green blouse watching him, which meant she wasn't watching her own daughter, and Abigail would have a free moment. He smiled at the group of parents. "Why did the picture go to jail? Because it was framed!"

"I can't do it," the little girl said, holding up her acorns. She was getting frustrated, tossing them up in the air and missing them on the way down.

"It takes a lot of practice," Haatim said, juggling the remaining acorns once more. "You just have to catch and release."

He realized that a few uniformed officers had also taken notice of his little charade. Harmless or not, he looked like a guy trying to distract young children without a clown costume on. Like the mothers on their benches, they were content to watch for now, but he knew their patience wouldn't last forever.

"Catch and release," he said, again, turning to show the other children what he was doing. Under his breath, he added: "I *really* hope all the cops do is catch and release. Whatever you are doing, Abigail, you'd better hurry."

✳✳✳

Abigail waited until Haatim had the full attention of the gathered children and parents before approaching the little blonde girl, Sara. She had been keeping an eye on Sara for the last several months, ever since she was returned to her family after the events at the Church. Abigail wanted to make sure the girl was safe with her family and no one came looking for her.

The Council had given her strict orders to stay away. They didn't want her anywhere near Sara, so she'd kept her distance. But she wasn't about to abandon the girl completely: after everything Arthur had done to keep the three girls safe from the demon, she was hell-bent and determined that nothing else would get to them.

Abigail hadn't dreamed, however, that the girl would be able to help her find Arthur. The mark on her forehead had never faded, and she'd thought it was just a coincidence of circumstance. The Council theorized that when the demon took Arthur's soul to hell, the mark had been left behind by the severed connection and would heal on its own eventually.

But now she knew that the bond was still open, something that linked Sara to whatever entity had stolen Arthur's soul. The realization that Abigail might be able to use this to find Arthur made her giddy with excitement but also filled with nervous worry. During the last six months, she'd never come this close to finding Arthur.

After all this time, she'd finally be able to rescue him. And, if he didn't want to come back with her to Earth, she could, at least, send him to the final rest he had earned in his time serving the Council and Order.

Abigail walked across the park, weaving around children and doing her best to look inconspicuous. She was wearing tight fitting black pants and a sweater several sizes too big for her that served to conceal her weapons, so she hoped she didn't stick out too much.

She slipped a little crystal out of her pocket. It was dense and heavy, a lot heavier than would be expected for a gem its size. She knew if she stared into its depths she would immediately feel sleepy, and she would be inclined to answer any questions posed to her honestly. It was like taking a triple dose of Xanax.

She walked near the little girl and said: "Excuse me, are you Sara?"

Sara turned and looked at her. She saw the stone in Abigail's hand and stared at it curiously. The effect was instantaneous, a glazed look in the little girl's eyes and a drooping in her expression.

"Yes. I'm Sara."

The girl moved closer, studying the little crystal with fascination.

"That's good," Abigail said. "I need to talk to you for just a minute, OK?"

"OK. What is that?"

"It's a special crystal. Would you mind looking at it for a while longer?"

"Sure. What does it do?"

"It is something to protect you. It will keep you safe."

"Keep me safe?" Sara asked sleepily. "From what?"

"From monsters," Abigail said.

Sara looked up suddenly, a look of terror on her face and all of the fuzziness gone. "Monsters? Like the Mean One?"

Abigail nodded. She doubted Sara remembered much about that day when Arthur saved her, but remembering anything would be terrifying for her. "Like the Mean One. He's the one who left the mark on your forehead, right?"

Sara absently touched the Band-Aid on her forehead, glancing back down at the crystal in her hand. Her expression became vacant and her tone monotone once again.

"Mommy says it's an infection."

"Do you want me to make it go away?"

Sara nodded.

"Take this," Abigail said. She handed Sara the crystal. "And hold onto it very tight, OK?"

"OK," Sara said. She continued staring at the little object, dazed.

Abigail reached up and gently removed the Band-Aid from Sara's forehead, exposing the wound. It was still moist and about half a penny in size.

"I hope this works," she muttered to herself, taking a deep breath.

Delaphene had said it would be uncomfortable to bridge a connection like this. Intelligent people didn't do it. Abigail certainly had never done anything like it because it was anathema to the laws of the Council to mess with any demonic creations.

The ritual would allow Abigail to step into the bond connecting the girl and Arthur, only that connection belonged to the demon holding Arthur now. It would be awkward and disorienting at the very least because of how foreign it would be for Abigail. Or, at least, that was how Delaphene had described it.

Abigail chanted out the harsh words the demon had taught her back in the cabin. They were in one of the Deep languages, known only to a handful of Council members and forbidden from ever being spoken aloud. But Abigail was in the midst of breaking far worse rules, so that didn't concern her: desperate times called for desperate measures.

111

As soon as she was done chanting, she felt her fingers tingling with energy. Like electricity, waiting to be discharged. She steeled herself, ready for the pain or discomfort that would come as she released the energy.

With a reassuring smile at Sara, she pressed her thumb against the open wound on the little girl's forehead. She'd dealt with pain before; she could handle this.

She was wrong.

***

It started with a warm sensation in her chest, a sort of awareness as she entered the connection. It was huge, like someone hovering over her shoulder, but she knew there was no one actually there in the park with her. The presence was filled with amusement, as though more surprised than concerned that she was there.

Then it attacked.

It was like a hot iron was stabbed into her gut. It burned so bad it took her breath away; she felt like she was suffocating; like the pressure would rupture and collapse her lungs.

Then the heat spread like wildfire across her skin, triggering every pain receptor she had. It was as if she were suddenly standing in a bonfire and she could feel it torching her skin. But the pain didn't diminish as her pain receptors were destroyed, but rather it intensified, overwhelming her. She tried to cry out, but she couldn't breathe.

Yet the worst part of all: she understood that whatever was on the other end of the connection was holding back. It was toying with her, swatting at her like she was only an insect. It didn't take her seriously but rather was simply hurting her for the pleasure of it.

She fought back, all hope of winning this encounter gone. She gave up her plan of using this connection to save Arthur, or even find out where he was being held.

Now all she wanted to do was escape. She had always thought that she would be an apt competitor in a battle of wills, but this was a fight for her life. She had never experienced anything this powerful, and she knew this creature was beyond anything she'd ever faced…

Except…

There was a familiarity to it, as if a drape had been pulled aside in her own mind. She remembered *this* demon possessing her, how it had used her body, broken her will and dominated her. She remembered how pathetic and weak it thought she was.

She remembered…

The demeanor of the demon changed in a flash, and she felt a spark of worry emanate from it. She sensed that it didn't want her to remember.

After the events in the Church, all of her memories were gone. The demon had stripped them away, replacing them and overwriting them in her mind. The Council therapists couldn't recover the memories, and they all assumed the demon had destroyed them.

But it hadn't.

She had a startling realization that she had known the demon's *name*; when she first confronted it in the forest six months ago, before it had taken her body, she had known its true name. The demon hid the memory from her…

Inside her own mind…

Suddenly, the demon was gone, the connection severed. She fell to the ground, gasping. It felt like she'd been trapped there for an eternity, but it had only been seconds. She sucked in ragged breaths of air, her skin tingling and burning but physically unharmed. The demon couldn't do real damage to her while she was here, only mental, but that had been enough.

She grasped in her mind for the name, but now that she was alone the memories were fuzzy. She felt them receding and dissipating. She nearly started crying in frustration that she'd come so close to unlocking her memories, yet they were still buried and hidden from her.

Sara was looking at her, a concerned expression on her young face.

"Are you OK?"

Abigail nodded slowly. She was anything but *OK*, but she said: "Yeah, I'm fine."

Sara frowned. "Are you sure?"

"Yeah," Abigail said. She pushed the pain and weakness away. "Look, your scrape is gone."

Sara touched her forehead and started grinning. The skin was smooth, the seeping wound closed.

"It is," she said excitedly. "I need to go show my mommy!"

Then Sara took off, running across the park to her mother. She dropped the little crystal behind her, unnoticed, and it bounced on the paved walkway. Abigail scooped it up and slid it back into her pocket, still kneeling on the ground.

It took her a long minute before she was able to climb to her feet. The pain was fading, and she was covered in a sheen of sweat. Everything hurt. She headed back to the car, staggering a little as she went.

By the time she got there, Haatim had returned from distracting the mothers and was waiting for her. He glanced her over, a concerned expression on his face:

"You OK?"

"No," she said. "But I will be."

"Did you find what you were looking for?"

Abigail shook her head. "No, but I know where I can find it now."

"Where?"

"Inside my head. Come on, we need to get moving. We're already late."

"All right, then," Haatim said. "But I'm driving."

Interlude - Raven's Peak

Bret wandered through the trees, bored and aimless. It was a cold and cloudy day; the sky looked like it was going to rain soon. He swatted at the branches and yawned, wishing his mom would just give up on this stupid vacation and take him back home. He would much rather be back at home playing video games than wandering out here in the middle of the forest with nothing to do.

He'd just passed his twelfth birthday, and of course, his dad hadn't been there to celebrate it. He hadn't even found the time to come out here on the family camping trip *he* planned with his son. He was too busy with work.

Bret's mom brought him to the Smokey Mountains anyway, having already reserved the cabin. "Camping" in her vernacular meant staying in a secluded cabin, but one that still had all of the same amenities they had at home. Bret didn't mind; he didn't really like sleeping on the ground, either.

"Bret!" he heard his mom shout. He couldn't see her through the trees anymore, but their rented cabin wasn't very far away. "Where are you?"

"I'm out here," he shouted back.

"OK, sweetie. Don't wander too far."

"I won't," he said. "I'll be back in a bit!"

He kept walking, weaving around the tall trees and underbrush. It was quiet out here, peaceful and relaxing. The only sounds were those of birds and rustling leaves, and that was something he realized that he actually liked. He could have done without the mosquitos and other insects, though.

Lost in his thoughts, he tripped on a long metal object sticking out of the dirt. He caught himself on a tree, scratching up his hand on the bark, and managed to keep his feet. He hissed in pain and then angrily kicked the thing that had almost tripped him.

His foot partially dislodged the object, and he saw the edges of a thin sheet of metal. It was half-buried in the dirt, and when he dug it out he saw that it was an old signpost. Written on it were the words: ***Raven's Peak***.

Which didn't make any sense to Bret. Raven's Peak was the little town they had driven through on their way to the campgrounds. It was over an hour back the way they had come, not out here in the campgrounds. It was definitely strange to find the sign all the way out here.

115

Strange, but not unexplainable. Maybe someone had brought it out here and dropped it off, perhaps as a prank.

He kept walking, curious if he might find something else hidden out here.

After a few more minutes, he saw the squat roof of a building in the distance front of him. It was hidden in the trees, built on the side of a hill and tucked away.

A new thought occurred to Bret: maybe *this* was the original Raven's Peak, and the newer town they had driven through was built later. He knew about old mining towns and how most of them had been abandoned over the years as the coal industry shrunk, he was just surprised to see all of this out here.

Places like this, if it was the original town, were usually tourist destinations. The campgrounds could rake in good money with visitors wanting to see a town built in the nineteenth century, but he hadn't heard anything about old ruins being out here.

Maybe no one remembered anything was out here at all, but that didn't sound reasonable. The idea that no one knew about something like this so close to the campgrounds didn't seem realistic. More likely, it was just that the town was trying to keep tourists away.

If nothing else, it made his trip out here a lot more interesting.

As he got closer, he started to see other structures. He wondered if maybe he was the first person to come this far out here in many long years, and the thought excited him. He imagined himself as an explorer discovering a lost civilization.

All of them were old and falling apart. Many were built on stilts to stay level on the uneven terrain. He counted twenty buildings in all, as well as the foundation of eight or nine more; they were of varying sizes and levels of disrepair.

Near the center of the small town was the largest structure of them all, and it looked like an old Church or municipal building. Part of the roof was caved in, and he could only see the back from this side. He walked slowly past the other buildings, glancing inside the ones that weren't too high off the ground but afraid to climb up any of the walkways.

It felt like a ghost town, and he was filled with excitement and trepidation at the same time.

He certainly hadn't expected to find something like this out here: an old abandoned town in the mountains, built of brick and wood. How cool was that?

He kept moving forward, circling around the enormous building to get a glimpse of the front door. Definitely a Church, he decided. The walls were made up of faded and chipped paint; vines crawled up to the roof and mud caked the outside. Out front were four large poles, arranged to flank the entrance and stuck deep into the ground.

He looked at the poles curiously, wondering what they were for. They didn't look like decoration and were covered in a reddish-black stain. He took a few steps closer to the door. This building looked sturdier than many of the others, and maybe he could take a peek inside.

Just a quick little peek.

The beams creaked under his footsteps as he climbed up the stairs. Gingerly, he reached forward and pushed the old oaken door open. Inside was utter chaos: broken wood, dust, and glass lay strewn about the floor.

Splotches of red covered the floor in various places, like wine had been spilled and left to dry, staining the wood. A raised dais near the front was also covered in debris, and behind it was that hole in the ceiling he saw earlier. And—

Suddenly something moved in the left corner of the Church.

It wasn't empty.

Bret stumbled back onto the front walkway and ran toward the stairs. Something was in there, he realized, and it had just woken up. He heard footsteps coming toward him form inside the Church, boards creaking underfoot.

Bret jumped down the stairs and started sprinting, not looking back. He heard a screeching sound unlike nothing he'd ever heard, followed by cackling laughter. The door blasted open, but he was too scared to look back.

He fled farther into the town, away from whatever was behind him. He weaved around a few more buildings, feeling his pulse race, and saw a hole in the hillside up ahead. It looked like a carved doorway leading underground.

The mining tunnels.

It was pitch black inside, eerily so, but he didn't see a lot of other options. He ducked inside, scraping his leg on the way in. Ahead, he saw a huge metal grate blocking his way. It was about four meters into the tunnel and barely visible. It was also locked, but there was enough room underneath it for him to wriggle inside.

He crawled past the grate and turned around, looking back the way he had come. Chilly air flowed up from the tunnels behind him, causing him to shiver. Inside here it felt thirty degrees colder than outside.

Past the grate he could see out the mine entrance and the buildings beyond. It looked quiet, peaceful, and he strained to hear anything. The darkness weighed on him like a blanket; the only sounds were his breathing and the soft dripping of water somewhere down the tunnels behind him.

He watched, hands shaking, waiting for someone or something to come into view. Whoever had been after him, they wouldn't be able to fit through the grate like he had. He would hide until they had given up trying to find him and leave, and then he could slip out and find his—

There was a soft tickle on his neck as a shiver ran up his spine. He realized in horror that there was something behind him.

He could feel a presence in the darkness. He turned and looked but saw nothing. Only a black so pure he couldn't see more than a few inches in front of his face.

But *something* was there. He knew it in his heart and in his gut. He could feel it watching him and waiting.

Bret's bottom lip started quivering, and he felt tears stream down his face. He'd never been so terrified in his entire life. He started to back up, slowly moving toward the grate as quietly as he could with his hands stretched out in front of him.

Suddenly there was a rattling sound from the mine entrance. Something was shaking the grate. He spun, crying out, but there was nothing there. Only emptiness and the buildings beyond. *What is going on?*

The gate rattled again.

And then he heard laughing. Not in the tunnel, but in his head. The same cackling laughter he'd heard in the Church.

He slipped on the wet ground and fell, hitting his head against the stone. Dazed, he tried to stand up but felt the presence holding him down. Not physically, but when he tried to move it felt like he was wearing leaden weights. His body wouldn't respond to his commands.

"Don't fight it," the presence said in his mind. It was a throaty voice, thick and full of phlegm.

Bret cried, blubbering now and shifting with short jerky movements. He crawled toward the grate, but it felt like it was miles away. He was terrified

"Oh, we're going to have so much fun together," the voice said.

And then he felt something clamp over his face, and the world went dark.

✳✳✳

A loud knock on the door woke Kurt from his stupor. He awoke groggily and heard the sound of rain spattering against the window. It was cold and dark in the room, and he wondered how long he'd been out of it.

"...the hell was that?" Alex mumbled, lying on the opposite couch in the living room of their rental cabin.

They'd both started pounding drinks a few hours earlier and ended up passing out. Kurt was pretty sure some of their friends had been drinking, too, but they must have bailed and headed to their rooms upstairs.

Kurt sat up and rubbed his eyes, yawning. "I don't know," he said. "Sounded like the door."

Another knock, this one louder and more frantic. It was definitely coming from the front door of the cabin, and whoever it was, they weren't very patient.

"Way out here?" Alex mumbled. "We're in the middle of nowhere. Who the hell would come knocking?"

He sat up, beer cans falling to the floor around him. He was drunk, though it was barely the middle of the afternoon.

"Maybe the cops," Kurt offered.

"Not funny."

"Can one of you get that?" Becky shouted from upstairs. She was probably in her room with Derrick, smoking a blunt and giggling at his dumb jokes.

Kurt groaned and rubbed his forehead. "I'll get it," he shouted back, staggering to his feet. He wasn't drunk anymore, but he was still floating on cloud nine after they hit the gravity bong earlier. Alex had filled the bathtub with water to do it, and Kurt's lungs were still burning.

Now he felt vaguely muddled; not particularly out of control, just tired and hungry. He stumbled across the hardwood floor to the door of their cabin, fiddled with the lock, and then jerked it open.

A woman stood just outside on the deck. She was in her mid-to-late thirties and pretty in a mousy sort of way. She had on a brown rain jacket and was glancing around anxiously. It was raining out past the patio, but only a light drizzle. Kurt felt a breeze roll by him, raising goose bumps on his skin.

"Uh…hello," he said awkwardly. He rubbed his arms, fighting off the chill.

"I need your help," the woman said. She glanced past Kurt, into the room, as though looking for something or someone else. "I can't find my son."

"What?"

"My son," she reiterated. "I think he's lost out in the woods."

She wasn't crying, but Kurt could tell she was holding on by a thread. The slightest provocation would send her collapsing into a puddle on the floor.

"You're the ones who rented the other cabin," he said, trying vainly to remember her name. They'd met her and her son when they first showed up, even helped bring their suitcases in, but her name escaped him.

She nodded. "Yes, we rented Hawk Cabin. My son went wandering, and I haven't seen him. I think he's lost."

"Lost?" Kurt said, scratching his chin. He gestured vaguely toward the endless woods around them. "Like, out there?"

Alex stepped up beside Kurt and put a hand on his shoulder. "How long has he been out in the woods?"

"Uh, an hour. Maybe a little longer. I told him to stay close but he kept wandering farther away. I was on a conference call for work, and when it ended I couldn't see him anymore."

"OK. We'll go find him."

"We will?" Kurt asked. Alex had already turned back into the cabin and was heading over to the stairs. He was wide awake and sober now, totally in control of the situation. Alex was just one of those guys, the type-A personality assholes that made Kurt sick to his stomach when they started bossing people around.

"Everyone, wake up!" he shouted up the stairs. "Get dressed and get down here."

Rustling from upstairs, followed by shouted questions. Alex didn't answer them, he just stood by the stairs and waited. Kurt knew they would all obey. Alex was the de facto leader of their group, and whatever he said was what happened. He was why they had rented the cabin in the first place.

Kurt stood in the doorway and then finally remembered that the woman was still standing outside on the porch.

"Uh. Do you want to come in?"

She nodded and he stepped aside, letting her through.

"I'm Kurt," he said.

"Desiree," she said, shaking his offered hand.

It only took a few minutes for the entire group to assemble. Becky, Alex, Mary, Aniya, and Derrick. They gathered in the living room, looking around at each other curiously. Derrick sat down and started putting his shoes on.

"A kid is missing," Alex explained. He waved at the mom, and she stepped a little closer. "Where did you see him last?"

She pointed out behind the two cabins. "Outside in the woods back there. I was on a conference call with work, and when it ended…"

"All right," Alex said, nodding. "What's his name?"

"Bret."

"Let's head out in groups of two and find him. He couldn't have gotten far. Mary, you're with me."

"Should we bring some supplies?" Mary asked.

"Shouldn't need it," Alex answered. "Tim, Aniya, you guys fan out to the south, and Becky and Kurt have the north. Let's go before it really starts raining."

They headed outside, grabbing coats and umbrellas on the way. Desiree followed them, still looking concerned.

"What should I do?" she asked.

"Stay here in case your son comes back," Alex said. He turned back to his group. "Stick together and walk an hour out and then back. Don't go any more than you're comfortable and don't get lost. If we don't find him, we'll call in a rescue team."

They all glanced at each other, hesitant but unwilling to object. Slowly, the pairs shuffled out into the woods, filtering through the trees in their little teams.

Kurt reluctantly followed Becky into the cold rain. He'd brought a coat, but he didn't have an umbrella. Probably for the best, because the wind was really starting to pick up and would probably just rip it out of his hands.

They walked for ten minutes through the drizzle, and Kurt could feel his wet coat slapping against his legs. He hated being rushed out like that, never mind that a kid might be in danger. He should have at least been given a chance to put long pants on.

Hell, he shouldn't be out here at all.

"This is stupid," he said.

Becky glanced over at him, then looked back ahead. She didn't seem too thrilled to be paired with him.

"It's cold and wet and this is dumb," he added.

"We're searching for a lost kid," Becky said. "How is that dumb?"

"He isn't my kid."

"You don't have any kids," she said. Then she added, quieter: "Probably never will, either."

He laughed, then ended up coughing instead. "No, I definitely won't. Little snot and poop factories. I don't get why anyone would want them."

She fell silent again, scanning the woods. They walked like that for a few more minutes, the only sound the rain pattering against their rain jackets. Hers was yellow, his clear, and the bottoms of his pants were damp where they weren't covered.

"Shouldn't we call the police or something?" he asked finally, sick of the silence.

"It would take hours for them to get out here," she said.

"But they could organize a search party or something."

"We *are* a search party," Becky replied. She cupped her hand around her mouth and shouted: "Bret!"

Kurt winced, feeling a shock of discomfort as she shouted. There was something wrong about it, like it wasn't a good idea. "Don't do that."

She looked over at him, narrowing her eyes. "Do what?"

"Call out," he said. He looked around at the trees and wilderness, feeling very uncomfortable.

"Why not? We need to find this kid."

"Yeah, I know, but…"

He trailed off. "But what?" she prompted.

Kurt hesitated, then shook his head helplessly. He didn't know why, but it felt like a bad idea. Like there was something out there, and he didn't want it to know he was here.

But that was silly. There was nothing out there, just the trees and some lost kid. "Never mind," he said, then added louder: "Hey Bret, you out here?"

"You check over that way," Becky said. "And I'll go this way."

"All right," he said.

"Just don't get out of range where you can't hear me."

"I got it," he said, annoyed.

He turned and walked away from Becky. He pushed branches out of his face, feeling droplets of rain splash his cheeks. They'd only been out here about ten minutes, and already he wanted to get back inside near the fireplace in Owl Cabin.

He heard Becky start shouting for the kid from off to his left. He made sure to keep her in sight and then turned and called out:

121

"Bret!" he shouted, then listened. Nothing but the pitter-patter of rain.

He kept walking, glancing back from time to time to make sure Becky was still with him. He could see her yellow coat moving in parallel to him about eighty meters away. Every once in while she would shout, but, for the most part, it was quiet.

Another few minutes slipped past. Kurt thought about just heading back to the cabin without Becky. He could sneak away and return to the warmth while the rest of the group froze out here. Becky would be pissed, and Alex would be pissed when she told him, but what did that matter? He would care less if they were happy or not.

He didn't go back, though. Not because he felt bad for the lost kid, but because he didn't have the greatest sense of direction. He knew that if he lost sight of Becky he probably couldn't find the cabin again.

That just annoyed him even more.

This wasn't how he'd planned to spend his break between classes. Alex had organized this trip, even footing the bill: he came from money, and he liked everyone to know it.

And that was fine with Kurt. A free place to crash and get high had sounded like heaven. That was before the mosquitos, the crappy Internet connection, and the complete lack of civilization.

And now this.

"Bret!" he shouted, cupping his hands around his mouth.

"I'm here."

Kurt froze, halfway into his next stride. The voice came from behind him. He turned slowly, feeling a shiver run up his spine, and saw a boy standing about three meters away. The boy's clothes were soaked, and his hair was matted to his face, but he looked completely calm and relaxed.

But, his eyes...*man*, there was something wrong with them. They were open with water running around them, and they were blank. It looked like a doll's eyes, like the kid was looking at him and through him at the same time.

They stood still for a long moment, staring at each other. Finally, Kurt said. "You...uh...you got lost?"

"No," the boy replied.

"You're Bret, right?"

"Yes."

Silence hung in the air. It felt like the temperature dropped thirty degrees in the last forty-or-so seconds, and Kurt felt his body shivering. The kid hadn't moved a single muscle, except for his mouth, and he looked more like a statue than a child.

And those eyes...

"I should get you back home."

"In time," Bret replied.

What the hell does that mean?

"Let's go," he said, then took a step to his left, planning to search for Becky.

"They don't like you, you know."

The words stopped him. "Who?"

"The ones you're with," Bret said. "The ones you think are your friends."

"What do you...?" he started to say, and then trailed off. Part of him was thinking: *of course, they don't like me*, as a sort of self-deprecating joke, the way Kurt usually brushed off insults or challenges. He'd heard hurtful things all his life.

Except this was different. There was a seriousness, a matter-of-fact quality to what the kid was saying that was unsettling. He was stating it, not voicing an opinion.

A fact that felt like a sledgehammer had just hit Kurt in the stomach.

"They never liked you," the kid said. "They only wanted you in their group because you could get them mushrooms and weed."

Kurt shook his head: How would this kid know about mushrooms?

But the words rang true, completely and utterly true in a way that nothing else in his life had ever felt true. They were using him. They didn't like him and had never liked him.

He stared at the little kid, feeling like he could trust him. "That's all they wanted?" he asked.

"That's it," Bret said.

Kurt felt a little voice screaming in his mind that something was wrong. Something was terribly and utterly wrong. But the larger part of him understood the depth of this new reality.

"You know what you must do?" Bret asked after another pause. He spoke softly, his pre-pubescent voice barely louder than the rain.

Kurt nodded. "I know."

"Tonight."

"I understand."

"You won't let me down?"

"Never," Kurt said, shaking his head. He'd never been so sure of anything in his entire life.

"Good," Bret said, the wisp of a smile on his young lips. "Then take me home.

***

They were the last group back to the cabin. Everyone else was gathered on the porch and waiting for them, and as soon as the mother saw Bret she broke out in tears.

"Bret!" she gasped, rushing over and scooping her son up. "You scared me."

123

He didn't reply but allowed her to pick him up and spin him around.

Alex looked over at the other two. "Thought we might have to send a search party out for you two as well," he said jokingly.

Kurt forced himself to laugh, but all he could feel was seething hatred for Alex. The bastard had always pretended to be his friend, but Kurt could see through his lies. He knew the truth.

"Kurt found him," Becky said.

"Oh really?" Alex replied. He seemed surprised. Of course, he would be, the two-faced jackal.

"Yes," Kurt said. "I did."

The mother set her son down and walked over. She took Kurt's hand, and he could see the tears streaming down her face despite the rain. "Thank you," she said. "Thank you so much."

"It's no problem," he said.

"I should give you something for helping me find him," she said, digging into her purse. "I owe you so much."

"No," Kurt said. He forced another smile. "We couldn't possibly take your money."

A few of the other members of the group, especially Alex, seemed surprised by the response. "He's right," Alex said finally. "We're just happy we could help."

"Thank you."

She started walking to her car, pulling her son along. They watched her go and then headed inside the cabin.

"Thank God that's over," Becky said, shaking out of her raincoat and brushing her fingers through her hair.

"You're telling me," Alex said. He hung his coat up and then patted Kurt on the back. "Great job, man. I knew you had it in you."

The touch made Kurt's skin crawl, but he kept smiling. "It was nothing."

"No, I'm serious. When you dig down deep, you're a great guy."

Kurt brushed the compliment away, feeling sick to his stomach. "You know what," he said. "It's been a pretty rough day, but it ended well. How about tonight I dip into my private stash and we all have a little party?"

"Seriously?" Mary asked. Kurt knew she wouldn't pass up an opportunity like this. "Hell yeah, I'm in."

"Me, too," Tim added. Kurt knew that if Tim was in, his girlfriend Aniya would be as well.

"Not me," Becky said, shaking her head. "I'm exhausted and cold. Think I'm going to tuck in for the night."

"All right," Alex said. "Let's get some tunes going and get this party started!"

***

Becky felt a hand clamp over her mouth and awoke with a start.

She panicked and thrashed around, but she felt something heavy settle overtop her body, pinning her down. It was pitch black, disorienting, and it took her a few seconds to remember where she was: she'd gone to bed in her room in the cabin. The last thing she'd been thinking about was how much she wanted to turn off that God-awful music blaring downstairs.

She could still hear the music, but it wasn't as loud anymore. She must have finally fallen asleep at some point. She tried to sit up again, but she felt the weight on top of her adjust, forcing her back down. The hand stayed firmly clamped on her mouth, though she could make little gasping noises.

"Shh," a voice said in the darkness from just above. "It's OK."

Becky recognized the whisper as Kurt and thrashed again. He held her firmly, and when she finally gave up, he started gently brushing her hair.

"It's OK. It's all going to be OK."

He gently brushed her forehead, making soft cooing noises, and her eyes adjusted to the dim lighting. She saw Kurt leaning over her bed, using his body weight to keep her down. He looked wild-eyed and crazy, smiling at her.

"I wanted to get to you first," he said. "The others are downstairs and could probably sleep through a hurricane right now, but you didn't accept any of my drugs. So I have to take care of you first."

Take care of me?

Becky started fighting again, then adjusted her mouth to bite Kurt in the hand. He didn't flinch as she bit down, and after a second she could taste blood as she tore through his skin.

But he still didn't move. He stayed still, letting her bite into his skin without even a flinch. It wasn't the response she had been expecting.

"Are you done?" he asked when she finally unclenched her teeth. She watched as he picked something off the bed, and she could make out the shape: it was a knife. "I used to dream about you."

He said it casually, holding the knife up and studying it.

"I was in love with you throughout all of my freshman year, and you wouldn't even give me the time of day. You barely even knew I existed. Hell, you still barely notice me.

"But that changes today, doesn't it? I bet right now I have your full and undivided attention. Too bad it's just too late, huh?"

He gently ran the flat of the blade across her neck, caressing her skin with it. The metal was cold, and she flinched away from it.

"A pity," he said. She could taste his blood and heard herself making soft whimpering sounds.

Gently, ever so gently, he sliced the knife into her neck. She felt heat and pain and cried out, the sound muffled by his hand. He pushed it farther in, severing her jugular vein on the left side of her neck and sliding all the way across.

She felt her life blood spilling out, drenching her clothes and the blankets and immediately felt weak and lightheaded. She tried to sit up, but her body was already too weak.

He released her, sitting up, and she clamped a hand over her neck, gasping and dizzy. She tried to cry out for help, but the sound was raspy and gurgling.

"You should be proud," he whispered to her, kissing her softly on the cheek. "You were my first."

Then he stood from the bed, leaving her alone, and headed for the door. She watched him leave, life slipping away, and heard him whistling a cheerful tune as he exited her room.

Chapter 10

"What happened back there?" Haatim asked once Abigail was finally awake. She shook her head to clear her thoughts and rubbed the hair out of her face. "What happened in the park with that little girl? When you got back to the car you looked terrible."

"Don't you know you should never tell a woman she looks terrible?"

"Somehow, with you, I don't think that rule applies."

Abigail chuckled. "No, I suppose not. Do you have any Tylenol?"

"Aspirin. In the glove box."

Abigail flipped it open and dug through miscellaneous papers until she found a little bottle. She popped two pills into her mouth and swallowed them, hoping it would at least take the edge off.

As soon as she had climbed into the passenger seat of Haatim's little Chevy she passed out. He'd tried striking up a conversation once she woke up, but she wasn't able to respond. Her mind and body hurt and she could barely move. It was as if she'd just run a marathon while taking an exam.

She realized she was putting her life into Haatim's hands, which was something she didn't like doing. The only person she'd ever trusted was Arthur, and after she helped lock him away in that black site prison she'd found it difficult to trust anyone again.

But she hadn't had a lot of options at the time. Her head felt like it was going to explode, and she needed to sleep, which meant she prayed Haatim would keep her safe and get her to Raven's Peak.

And now Haatim had woken her up several hours later, stopping at a gas station for another restroom and food break. He bought them some cheeseburgers, but she wasn't hungry.

She bit into her sandwich, barely tasting anything except the grease, and stared out the window. It was dark out, a little after eight at night, and they were about fifty miles outside of Raven's Peak.

"A lot," she answered finally. "A lot happened, but not all of it was good."

She remembered bridging the connection, but the sensations were fading. It was like her memories of the event were slippery.

She knew one thing for certain: everything she needed to know to rescue

Arthur was locked in her mind.

But she'd also learned something else. When the demon first took her in the Church six months ago, it had been by surprise, and she'd assumed she could handle the demon if she had time to prepare for a confrontation. Whatever it was that had taken Arthur, it was strong. A lot stronger than anything she'd ever dealt with before.

She knew she couldn't go toe-to-toe with it even on her best day with months to get ready. Knowing she was helpless against it elicited an emotion in her she wasn't used to experiencing.

Fear.

She wasn't going to stop trying to find and rescue Arthur, but now the odds of being successful had dropped dramatically.

"You looked like you were hit by a train," Haatim said. He was devouring his sandwich, barely breathing between bites. "Or like you'd been to hell and back."

"Just about," Abigail said with a laugh.

"You said you knew what we needed to do next?"

Abigail stared at him. "We?"

"Yeah," he said. "Me and you."

"There is no 'me and you,'" she said. "There's just me."

"I helped you get to the girl and talk to her."

"And I saved your life," she said. "We're even."

"Not quite," Haatim said. "You promised you would tell me what was going on after. It's after, so start talking."

Abigail sighed. She knew telling him anything would be dangerous: she wasn't allowed to initiate anyone without Council approval. If they found out—worse, if Haatim's *father* found out that she'd been the one to tell him—she'd definitely be punished.

But, she also felt he had a right to know: if there were things out in the world trying to kill him, he should, at least, understand why.

"What do you want to know?"

"You said it wasn't your place to tell me about my father earlier. What did you mean?"

"Your father is on the Council," Abigail said.

"What Council?"

"The Council of Chaldea," she explained. "It's a multi-religious and multi-national organization dedicated to protecting the world from the supernatural."

"What are you talking about?"

"I'm explaining to you who your father really is. It seems you were never told, and this was a side of his life he kept from you. There are thirty members on the Council."

"And you're one of them?"

"No," she said. "I'm a Hunter. I was trained to battle the demons on behalf of the Council, but I belong to the Ordo Daemonium Venator. We protect and serve the men and women like your father. There are…were…fifty-three of us and we answer to a woman named Frieda Gotlieb."

Haatim stared at her. "You're saying my dad is part of a secret organization dedicated to defending the world against evil?"

"We're more concerned with defending against fear and panic caused by evil. But yeah, basically."

A long minute passed. "We need to get moving," Abigail said. "Do you want me to drive?"

"What?" he asked, distracted. "No, I'm fine."

He started the car but didn't immediately drive anywhere. He just stared out the windshield, lost in his thoughts.

"You OK?" she asked.

He looked at her. "Yeah, sorry. It's just a lot to take in. That's why you brought me along, right? You recognized my father's name and you're keeping me safe for him?"

She nodded, deciding to withhold some information. Haatim didn't need to know that Frieda didn't trust her father or that she hadn't told him where Haatim was. Best to skew the details, at least for now.

"And I wasn't exactly sure what was going on when I first found you," she said. "So I brought you along to keep you safe."

"OK," he said.

"Your family knew you were in Arizona, right?" she asked.

"Yeah," he said. "It was where I went to college, so it's where I returned to after my sister died. I just couldn't stand being around my parents anymore. I told them I needed space."

Abigail nodded. "I can sympathize. I wouldn't talk to anyone for months after Arthur was taken."

"What happened?"

Abigail wasn't planning to tell him about this part of her life, considering it off-limits, but she started speaking before she could stop herself.

"I was possessed," Abigail told him. "Several months ago."

"Wait, what?"

"A demon lived inside me for several hours. I don't remember what happened during that time, I just remember waking up in a hospital bed almost a week later. Apparently when they found me I was half-dead and delirious."

"That…" Haatim said, trailing off. "That's crazy."

"Tell me about it," she said. "The demon who was inside me took Arthur back to hell with it. I've been trying to find him ever since. The little girl, Sara, was linked to Arthur."

"OK."

129

"When I…when I saw her, I found out that she couldn't help me find out who the demon was. But, it doesn't matter. I already know."

"You do?"

"Yes," Abigail said. "Or, at least, I knew *before* it possessed me. It hid the memories from me, but at one point I knew it's name. Now I need someone to help me retrieve that memory."

"People can do that?"

"I know a guy," Abigail said, "and that's where I'm headed next, as soon as we get to Raven's Peak and you head back home to be with your family."

"Why not just go there now?"

"I have to check this out for the Council," she said. "It's my job. How far are we from Raven's Peak?"

"An hour," Haatim said. "Maybe less. I picked up a map to help us find our way. I don't think GPS is going to work that far into the mountains."

"Probably not," Abigail said.

"What's in Raven's Peak?"

"I don't know," Abigail said. "Probably nothing, Maybe something. We'll find out when we get there."

"So you don't know what we're looking for?" he asked.

"No idea," she said.

"Like…" he said, "more demons?"

She was silent for a long minute. "It's possible," she said. "But more likely just strange activity and weird lights. It's usually just odd things and has nothing to do with the supernatural."

"Do you—"

"I think that's enough for now," she said. "I promised I would fill you in and I wouldn't lie, but I'm exhausted. The only thing you need to know for now is that I'm waiting for a call from a friend to find out when and where I'm dropping you off. You'll be back with your family in no time."

"OK," Haatim said.

She reached over and flicked the radio on, spinning through the static to find music. They managed to pick up an oldies station and a few country ones. She flicked it back out and let out a sigh, having no desire to listen to either.

They drove on, passing mile markers and exits only in a monotonous pattern. She felt like she was in the middle of nowhere, and it had with it a strange sense of déjà vu. It was as if she'd driven on this road before. Maybe she had, when she was younger and traveling with Arthur. They'd gone all across the country on various jobs through the years.

She thought back to the moment she'd touched Sara's forehead and the sheer intensity of the connection. Bits and pieces of memory had flooded back to her, intangible details only the fragments of which she could remember.

The demon had come here looking for something, she remembered. It was here for a reason, but she didn't know what…

"How did you get started doing this?" Haatim asked suddenly, interrupting her thoughts. It had started raining, she realized, the drops pattering against the window. It was soothing, a sound she'd always loved.

"Started doing what?"

"Fighting demons," he clarified. "You said Arthur trained you."

"Yeah," Abigail said. "He was my mentor."

"Were you like chosen or something?"

"It's a long story."

"Indulge me."

"It's what I've always done," Abigail answered after a moment. She was looking out the window, facing away from him. "The earliest things I remember. I was born into it."

"You don't remember anything from before."

"No," she lied. The cult she'd been kidnapped by, she decided, was off-limits. "I don't remember anything before it."

"It just seems so…" he said. "Crazy. I mean, most people don't think things like this are real, and you battle against them on a daily basis."

"It is what it is."

"Why don't you tell people about it?"

"Tell them what?" she asked. "That the monsters they hear about in stories are real?"

"Yeah."

"Because it couldn't possibly benefit me. For one thing, people wouldn't listen to me or believe me. For another, there are people out there who would actively try to stop me."

"What people?"

"Politicians, state officials, police. Not a lot of them, but enough to make my life miserable. If you can think of a group of authority figures, they are involved in hindering the work we do. And there aren't a lot of us left to do it anymore, anyway."

"Do what?"

Abigail glanced over at him, frowning. "Keep the world from falling apart."

✳✳✳

They reached Raven's Peak after only a little while longer. It was just before nightfall, the sun dipping below the horizon. The last bit of driving was down a two lane road weaving up the mountains on a switchback path

The map Haatim had purchased showed the little town being backed up into the side of the Smokies, and this road was the only way in or out without trekking across empty countryside for days. Secluded didn't even begin to describe it.

There was little traffic: a few cars or semis heading out of Raven's Peak but nothing else. There was the occasional house set off the road, some of which looked abandoned, but it wasn't until they were only a few miles outside the town that they started to regularly see gas stations, diners, and motels.

"Should we stop here for the night?" Haatim asked as they passed one such motel. It was just inside the city limits. "It's really late."

Abigail shook her head. "No," she said. "We need to keep moving. I was supposed to take care of this problem today, and I plan to be out of here by tomorrow. I just need to talk to a few people and find out if anything strange is happening in our around the city. And then I'll report back to the Council and move on."

"OK," Haatim said. He kept driving farther into the city.

They continued into Raven's Peak, passing municipal buildings and various small shops. The entire city could have fit into one district of Phoenix, less than a half mile in diameter.

It couldn't have had a larger population than a few thousand people, Haatim realized. This late at night the entire city appeared empty; there weren't even very many lights on and most of the buildings were closed for the night.

"It's so quiet," Haatim said.

"Places like this usually are," Abigail said.

"It feels disconnected," Haatim said. "Like we aren't in America anymore."

"I know," Abigail said. "Like you left the twenty-first century and traveled back to the fifties."

"Yeah," he said with a chuckle. "Like that."

"I was born in a town like this," Abigail said.

"Oh?" Haatim prompted. She ignored him, staring out the window and watching the city flow past. It had stopped raining, but there were still clouds overhead like it might start again at any moment.

He continued driving slowly, studying the buildings and shops. Most were short with barely a few standing above two stories. Quaint little structures with old fashioned signs: a post office, a pair of corner restaurants (Italian and Mexican), and several storefronts with dirty glass windows selling antiques. They were all built before prefab construction existed, each artistic and unique in its own design, but it made the town feel old.

"Not a lot of money in a place like this," he said.

"No, not much," she agreed. "Coal mining, probably. Places like this used to be everywhere. But the mines closed years ago, and the towns went with it. Everyone who could leave, did. The ones that are left just try to get by and survive."

"What's that over there?" he asked, pointing toward an enormous structure on the east side of town. It towered above the other buildings and looked to be at least the size of a football field, maybe bigger.

"A factory, I think," she said, squinting to see it. "They must manufacture something here. It's probably the only thing keeping the people in town employed."

"What do you think they make?"

"Hard to say," she said with a shrug. "Textiles, maybe. We can check it out tomorrow."

"Where are we heading?"

"Not sure," she said. "Everything looks closed."

"There's a store up ahead," Haatim said, pointing down the road. "Looks open."

"Couple of bars, too. Go ahead and park and let's check around this area."

He pulled into the parking lot and switched off the car, then climbed out and followed Abigail toward the entrance. There were puddles all around, filling potholes from a recent rain. It didn't look like the city fixed the roads very recently, and he doubted they would spare the expense. The air tasted cold and fresh, a lot cleaner than he was used to.

On the way across the lot he saw an SUV pull in from the other direction. The woman driving was wearing a brown overcoat and seemed exhausted. Her son—probably no older than ten—sat in the passenger seat.

Haatim started to look away when the boy suddenly turned to look at him. Haatim felt his stomach clench and the world shift as their eyes connected. The boy stared with a blank expression on his face, but his pupils were filled with an energy and intensity that made Haatim shiver.

It was only a momentary glance, but in that moment Haatim took a stutter step and suddenly felt very cold. Something about that child was terribly, horribly wrong.

"You all right?" Abigail asked. Her voice ripped him back to reality and he felt his hands quivering.

He turned to her. "What? Yeah, I'm OK."

"You sure?" she asked. "If you don't think you can do this…"

"I'm fine," he reiterated firmly. She nodded and disappeared into the building.

Haatim glanced back at the parked car one last time. The mother was climbing out, saying something to her son, and he was facing away from Haatim once more. Nothing out of the ordinary, just a boy and his mother stopping to get snacks on the road.

Pull yourself together, Haatim, he chided himself. *Just a kid. Stop seeing ghosts where there aren't any.* With a calming breath, he turned and followed Abigail into the building.

It was a corner store called Aunt Jane's. A bell tinkled overhead as they walked inside. The shelves were dusty and half filled with canned goods and boxes of cereal and pasta. The lettering was fading on half of the boxes, and he was afraid to look at the expiration dates.

There weren't any patrons inside, just an old, matronly woman manning the front counter while filing her nails. Her skin was leathery from long hours spent in the sun, and she wore a polka-dot dress.

"Can I help you?" she asked.

"I hope so," Abigail said. "We've been driving all day, and we were hoping to find somewhere to refuel."

"There's a gas station on up the road," the woman said, gesturing vaguely back outside. "Just on the outside of town. They only take cash."

"Oh," Abigail said. "I think I have some, so we should be all right."

"Are you campers?"

"Excuse me?"

"Are you heading to the campground," the woman clarified. "It's why most people come out here, and the gas station is on the way. The last place you'll pass until you reach the campground. It's is our only tourist destination."

"Yeah, that's why we're here," Abigail lied. "Spending a few nights."

"Hope you rented a cabin," the woman said. "After the rains today the ground is going to be muddy."

"We did."

"If there's anything you're running low on you'll want to pick it up here. Once you head down that road you won't have anywhere else to buy toothpaste or soap."

"I think we have almost everything we need," Abigail said. "It's just a little farther down the road?"

"About an hour," the woman said. "But, if you're hoping to get there tonight, you'll want to leave pretty quickly. The campground gets a little less inviting at night."

"Oh? How so?"

"Just odd stuff lately. Campers have said they saw strange things in the woods. Things going missing. If I had to guess, we've got some thieves trawling the grounds, but no one knows for sure."

Abigail nodded. "I see."

"It's pretty out there," the woman said. "Just watch your belongings."

Abigail nodded and gestured to Haatim. He followed her down the aisle, out of earshot of the woman.

"We passed a bar about a block back. I'm going to go check in there and see if there is anything interesting going on in town."

"Do you think there's something weird at the campground?"

"No idea," Abigail said.

"She said there were strange things in the woods."

"She said *campers* thought there were strange things in the woods," she said. "But, people who don't grow up in a town like this tend to think everything is strange, and the rustling of an animal can become terrifying."

Haatim shrugged. "True. It's probably nothing."

"Still," she said. "It's worth checking out if nothing else shows up. You stay here. Pick us up some dinner and breakfast, and I'll be back in a bit."

"All right," he said.

Abigail headed off, and he heard the tinkling of a bell as she disappeared outside. He looked around at the offered wares in dismay.

There were pastries in a display case that appeared like they'd been there since the forties and cans of soup from Campbell's that looked older than Andy Warhol's.

He also managed to find stale bread and soggy bologna and figured they could make some decent sandwiches. He continued walking down the aisles, looking for the most edible items to add to their dinner.

✳✳✳

The bar turned out to be a dimly lit dive joint called Fred's Blue Moon. It was dirty and dark, smelled like piss and ashtrays, and filled with clouds of smoke; the perfect kind of place to get a cheap drink and information.

There was a pool table in the corner with a faded and peeling finish and a couple of chairs throughout, but the floor was mostly empty. The floor was sticky, and the walls were covered in country music posters.

The entire place was empty except for the bar at the front and a pair of booths in the back. An old man looked to be sleeping in one of them, and a woman in her fifties sat at the other, nursing a martini. Four grizzled looking men sat on the barstools watching TV and sipping beers. If she had to guess, she'd put them in their late twenties to early thirties.

A burly old man stood behind the counter, leaning against a shelf of cheap whiskey and vodka and watching his patrons. News was on the tube above his head, but the sound was turned off and no one seemed to be paying attention to it.

They all glanced over as she came in, but each of them dismissed her in turn as she walked up to the bar. It was chipped and covered in stains but appeared modestly clean. She sat down on a stool a few seats others so she could listen in on their conversation.

One of them was wearing a police uniform, and the other three wore plain clothes but definitely worked in some profession requiring a lot of manual labor: they were muscular with thick necks and beards.

The bartender leaned against the counter as she came up. "Want something

135

to drink?"

"A whiskey," she said. "Jameson if you've got it with a splash of coke."

He poured out her drink into a smudge covered glass and slid it across the counter to her. She took a sip: it had decidedly less than a splash of coke in it, but she wasn't about to complain.

She sat with her drink for a few minutes, listening to the group of friends talk. They mostly just bitched about their wives or their jobs; a lot of talking, no substance. She sipped her drink and listened, pretending to read the captions on the television. Eavesdropping and being invisible was a skill Arthur had taught her early in her training.

The conversation shifted and they started talking about the group of campers that had come through a couple of days ago, a bunch of college kids. The cop told them about a blonde chick he was hoping to bust with something just so he could pat her down.

It was clear after only a few minutes, however, just how much they disliked the college group. That didn't surprise Abigail. She doubted any of these men had ever been to college, and they had a sort of tribal aversion to people who did.

One of the four men got up a few minutes later, finished off the last dregs of his beer, and headed for the door. He stood above two meters tall and had a scraggly black beard and flannel shirt. "See you fellas tomorrow."

"You leaving?" the cop asked.

"Yeah. Going to pop into Jane's and get something to eat and then head home. I work early in the morning."

"All right, Tim. See you tomorrow."

Tim headed out of the bar and disappeared down the road, walking toward the corner store. Abigail was about to follow him, but was interrupted when one of the other men spoke to her. He had a receding hairline and intense eyes.

"Where you from?"

"Arizona," Abigail answered.

"On your way to the campground?"

"Yep," she said. "Just staying the night with my husband."

"You should watch yourself when you're out there. Group of stuck up college guys rented out Owl Cabin."

"That a nice one?" she asked.

"It's the expensive one. The other one is Hawk, and it's a few hundred bucks cheaper."

"They've got money," the cop said. "Spoiled little rich kids, if you ask me."

"No one's asking you, Mike."

The cop shrugged and took a swig of his beer. "It's too bad then, because if it were up to me I'd shut down the campgrounds altogether. We don't need it, and it brings in too many outsiders who don't give a damn about us. They just want to see the old town."

"The old town?" Abigail asked.

"Out in the woods is the original location of Raven's Peak. This was back when they were still mining, but it was too hard to get to once the mines were closed. They moved it here about a hundred years ago, but the remains of the old town are still out there, just a ruins."

Something about the thought of ruins sparked Abigail's memory: secluded ruins in the middle of the nowhere sounded familiar, but she couldn't quite place it.

"Have strange things ever happened in those ruins?"

Mike chuckled. "All the time, if you ask tourists. It's a ghost town, spooky, so I can understand people getting scared. They hear strange things. Just the usual tourist bullshit."

"You don't sound convinced."

"It's just a bunch of old buildings. People come out here because they think it's something to see, but they don't care about us."

"Do they cause problems?"

"Vandalism, mostly," the cop answered.

"And littering," another guy spoke up. "We've been out there three times this year and taken in over ten bags of garbage."

The cop nodded. "People just toss their garbage and expect us to clean it up."

Abigail sipped her drink. "Still, it's tourism money?"

"We don't see any of it," the cop said. "The guy who owns the campgrounds doesn't even live here. He lives in Minnesota, I think. We don't see a dime."

"I see," Abigail said.

"We should just close the roads and put up a blockade. That would keep people out."

"Yeah," another guy added, chuckling. "Or use those police spikes. The ones they use to flatten tires."

"Yeah," the cop said. "Something like that. I'd kill for an opportunity to drop those."

Abigail listened to them talk for a couple of minutes longer, but they quickly lost interest in her and went back to their own conversations. She wasn't surprised that they were disgruntled about tourism, especially if they weren't seeing any money from it, but she was surprised at how openly hostile they were about it.

She felt almost like they were trying to threaten her. A petty machismo effort, because she knew they would never actually do anything to outsiders, but it did show how closed off this town was from the rest of the world. They were cut-off from outside influences and kept to themselves.

Which meant it would be hard getting any real information out of them. She stuck around for a few more minutes, though, and listened just in case they happened to mention something else that might be of use.

✱✱✱

Haatim finally settled on a few cans of fruit that weren't expired, some ravioli, baked beans, and a couple of cokes. He was worried about perishable items, but he did find a few wrapped cookies baked by a local pastry shop that looked rather tasty.

He passed the woman in the brown overcoat a few times as she shopped. She hadn't brought her son in with her and was picking up snacks. She offered him a smile, but it didn't quite reach her eyes.

He was hugging the items to his chest and wishing he had grabbed a basket when he heard the doorbell chime again. He assumed Abigail was back and started making his way toward the counter.

He realized almost immediately that it wasn't her, however. The footsteps sounded like heavy boots. He peered around one of the aisles and saw a tall and overweight man in a flannel shirt, jeans, and a cowboy hat walking up to the register.

"Where is she?"

The woman at the register stood up from her seat, a concerned look on her face. The other shopper, the one in the brown overcoat, slipped away into one of the aisles, out of sight.

"Tim, what's wrong?"

"Where is she?" Tim asked again, an edge of anger in his voice.

"Where is *who?*"

"Elizabeth," Tim said. "I know she's here."

"Tim…"

He turned and cupped his mouth over his hands, shouting toward the back room: "Elizabeth! I know you're here. Come on out and let's go home."

"Tim," the woman said, her voice sympathetic, "Elizabeth isn't *here.*"

"I know she is," Tim said. "Stop hiding her from me, Barbara."

"I'm not, Tim," she said. "You know I'm not."

Tim looked confused for a second, like he was trying to process what she was saying. Suddenly he noticed Haatim, standing in the aisle and watching. He stormed over, and Haatim almost dropped all of the items he was holding. The guy was tall, maybe five inches more than Haatim. Enough to make Haatim feel really small.

"Have you seen Elizabeth?" Tim asked. He had rough features and a scraggly black beard. He looked like he was in his late forties, but it was hard to tell.

"I'm sorry, I don't know anyone by that name," Haatim said. "I'm not from around here."

The man thought about this for a second and then nodded. "Well, if you see her, tell her to come home, all right?"

"All right," Haatim agreed, thoroughly outside his element.

Then Tim turned and disappeared back outside. The bell tinkled again, and then it was completely silent in the store. No one moved for a good thirty seconds.

Haatim finally walked up to the counter and set his pile of goods down. The woman at the register—Barbara—stood staring at the door, shaken up.

"Are you OK?" Haatim asked after a few seconds. She slowly glanced over at him, a vacant expression on her face.

"What?" she said, shaking her head. "Yes, I'm fine."

"Who was that?"

"Tim Melloncamp."

"Who was he looking for?"

"His wife, Elizabeth. She used to work here."

"Used to?" Haatim said.

"Yeah," Barbara said, grabbing the items and scanning them. "But she died."

"Oh," Haatim said. He glanced back at the door. "Is he...?"

"He's not taking it well," Mary said. "I was sure he'd gotten over it, because it happened a few months ago, but I guess something must have snapped. There's no telling how someone's grief will go."

The woman in the brown overcoat reappeared from up the aisle, carrying a bag of chips and some drinks. "That's terrible," she said.

"Elizabeth was a great person," Barbara agreed. "She had liver cancer. Is this all?"

"Yeah," Haatim said. "Just some snacks for tonight."

She finished scanning the items and bagged them for Haatim. He paid, thanked her, and headed for the door. The woman in the brown overcoat went to the register, setting her items on the counter.

"Do you know if there's a vacant motel in the area?" she asked.

"There's one a few blocks west. They never fill up all the way. Most people just continue down the road to the campground."

"Heaven's no," the woman said. "We stayed in one of the cabins the last two nights, but I'm not staying out there one night longer. My son was almost lost in the woods and it gets scary at night. We have the cabin rented for three more days, but I just can't be out there another second. We just need somewhere to sleep before heading back to Chicago."

"Then the motel is your best bet. I think it's a Super Eight."

"Thanks," the woman said.

"I would recommend sleeping on top of the sheets, though," the woman said. "If you know what I mean."

Haatim bit back a laugh and pushed the door open. He stepped out into the cool night air and glanced around. Abigail was still gone, and there were very few streetlamps lit up, so it wasn't very bright in the area.

After he loaded all of the supplies into the backseat, he sat on the hood of his car and waited for Abigail to return. It was chilly out, and the wind nipped at his skin, but he could see a myriad of stars in the sky, more than he'd ever imagined. He had to admit, living out in the country did have its perks.

✳✳✳

Abigail showed up at the car about ten minutes later. Haatim was lightly dozing on the hood of his car, not quite asleep but definitely not awake, either. He felt a tap on his shoulder and jumped, almost falling off the hood. When he saw it was Abigail, he sat up. She had a bemused expression on her face.

"Get everything?" she asked.

"Yeah," he said, "I might have found something interesting in the store, too."

"Me, too," she said. "You first: what did you hear?"

"A guy lost his wife," Haatim said.

"That's it?"

"He isn't taking it well, and he was acting strange."

"When did she die?"

"A few months ago," Haatim said. "But he was really freaked out, like he didn't even remember that she was dead."

"Too long ago to be what we're looking for," Abigail said. "And grief can do funny things to people."

"What did you find?"

"I overheard another tidbit about the campgrounds. A group of college kids went out there a few nights ago to stay in the expensive cabin. They have been stopping in every night at the bar to purchase drinks, but no one showed up today."

"Are they missing?"

"No one knows for sure. I spoke to a cop who said if they don't show by tomorrow night they'll go have to send someone to check on them."

"You think that's what we're looking for?"

"If there's anything here to find, it's probably out at the campgrounds," she said. She climbed into the passenger seat and started looking through the bags of stuff Haatim had purchased. "Let's head there and check it out."

Chapter 11

By the time they reached the campgrounds it was pitch black outside. Haatim was thoroughly exhausted from driving all day and ready to collapse. It was getting cold, too, and he wished he'd brought a jacket with him. Truth be told, he wished he'd brought dozens of things with him.

He wondered, and not for the first time that day, what the hell he was doing. He had dropped everything to drive halfway across the country with a woman who told him she battled demons. Even knowing it was true, he still felt she was at least a little crazy.

Maybe he should have taken her up on the offer to stay behind. If he hadn't told her who his father was, she would have just left him back in Arizona for the police to find. She had told him it would be safe and that the people who snatched him wouldn't be after him any longer, and he doubted she would lie.

He would have had to face the repercussions of what had taken place in his apartment, but he was confident they wouldn't find him guilty of anything. He hadn't been involved in any of shootings or deaths, and she'd already destroyed all evidence of his stalking. He was simply a victim in the situation.

But, if he was being completely honest with himself, then he found this entire situation to be exciting. It was messed up, he knew, but nevertheless he couldn't deny it. His life had taken a drastic turn the moment George Wertman had sat down across from him in the library. Growing up, things were always strict and rigid; he always played by the rules and did what he was told. Abigail was nothing if not a rule breaker.

"We're here," he said. Abigail didn't hear him, staring out the window at the woods. "I said: we're here."

This time he got her attention, and she blinked at him. "Sorry, I was lost in my thoughts."

"No worries. What are we looking for?"

She glanced around. It was dark, with only a few lights showing them the way. The campground was a giant roundabout. Gravel clearings jutted off the roundabout, and the central area was grass and picnic tables. No roads went farther into the forest; it simply made a giant circle and headed back to Raven's Peak

141

Two of the gravel clearings led to cabins that were a million times more advanced than the one Abigail had taken him to earlier in the day. They looked like expensive multi-level behemoths, though one was clearly better than the other.

He drove slowly down the roundabout, listening to gravel crunch under the tires. One of the cabins was dark and empty, but the other had lights on inside.

"I don't see any power lines," he said. "Do you think they ran them underground?"

"It's a possibility," she said, "but more likely they are using generators. See that shack? That's probably where they have to refill the tank."

Music could be heard playing in the interior of the first cabin they rolled up to. The doors and windows were closed, so all they could hear was the bass.

"Probably the college kids," Abigail said offhandedly. "This is Owl Cabin."

"Owl Cabin? That's…strange."

"I didn't come up with the name."

"I suppose it's better than 'Sturgeon Hangout,'" Haatim offered. "The other one was probably where the woman and her kid were staying."

"What woman?"

"A tourist I met back at the store. She couldn't stand being out here in the woods and bailed on the cabin three nights early. Seemed like a city kind of girl. I think they checked into a motel earlier and are leaving tomorrow."

"A motel? Seems like a downgrade if you ask me."

"I was thinking the same thing."

"Did she say anything strange happened?"

"No," he replied. "She just said her kid went wandering out in the woods, and she didn't want him to get lost or something."

"All right. We can stop by and talk to her on our way out of town tomorrow, if you think it'll do any good."

"What about the college kids? Should we check on them now or wait until the morning?"

"Let's talk to them now. We should at least make sure they are doing all right. Just knock on the door."

Haatim nodded in agreement. They sat in the car, staring at the cabin, and a long minute passed. He glanced over at Abigail and saw her staring at him.

"Well?" she asked. "Go on."

"Wait, you want *me* to do it?"

"Yep."

"Why don't you?"

"Because, like the townsfolk, I don't like spoiled college kids very much. They seem more like your kind of thing, and I'm sure you'll hit it right off. I'd rather just wait in the car."

"What if something *is* wrong with them, though? What if they're being

142

attacked or something?"

"Then I'll be right here to watch your back, ready to come rescue you at a moment's notice," she said. Then she smirked and added: "Again."

He stared at her and knew that if looks could kill he'd be doing some serious damage right about now. "Not funny."

"It's a little funny."

He sighed and opened the door. "Fine, I'll go."

He walked up onto the porch and to the front door. It was oak and quite beautiful with designs carved into it. He knocked lightly and listened. He waited for a moment without getting a response and then glanced back at the road. Abigail was still in the passenger seat, yawning.

She gestured her hand toward him with a knocking motion and mouthed the words *"knock louder."*

"Yeah, you rescued me. But, I wouldn't have needed rescuing if you weren't a crazy person with demons chasing you," he muttered, knocking again. He waited, and then knocked louder still, but there was still no response.

He headed back to the Chevy just as Abigail was climbing out. She said: "If they are drunk and passed out inside, so help me..."

"What do we do now?"

"Wait here."

She walked up onto the porch and wandered along the wooden walkway on the outside. A patio ran across the front, about three meters wide. Abigail glanced in the windows, and Haatim waited next to the car. After a few minutes she waved for him to come up.

"I don't see anyone," she said. Her entire demeanor had changed, and the joking side of her was gone. Now, she was all business.

"You think they are missing?"

"It's a possibility," she said. "I'm going to check it out."

"Want me to wait out here?"

"I want you to stick close to me," she said. "We don't know what we're dealing with, and until we know I don't want you out of my sight. I don't want to come back to find your dead body."

He felt his pulse quicken. She said so nonchalantly, like she was talking about inconvenient weather.

Abigail walked to the doorway, her revolver appearing in her hand and a frown on her face. She knocked a few times, and Haatim waited near the window. Nothing happened.

It was quiet. She tested the doorknob and found it to be locked. She knelt down, pulling small metal tools out of her pocket, and after a few seconds he heard the lock click.

"Count to thirty and then follow me," she said.

With one last glance at Haatim, she stepped into the living room. He watched through the window as she moved silently through the foyer, past the garbage on the floor, and into the dining room. Furniture was scattered, and a large oak table was covered with half-finished food and wrappers.

Abigail made it to the doorway of the living room and rounded the bend, disappearing from his sight. Haatim finished counting and then walked into the foyer behind her. The music was loud and spilling out of a pair of speakers along the right wall. They were cranked up to the max, and the music was cracking every few notes.

Haatim stepped gingerly across the dining room floor, dodging furniture and trash, and clicked the power button on the radio. The sound cut out, leaving him in a jarring silence.

A moment passed, but he couldn't hear anything from farther into the cabin. "Find anything?"

No response. He walked slowly toward the door leading to the living room, straining to hear. The place was eerily quiet, and he could feel the hairs standing up on the back of his neck. Something was wrong. As he got closer he could smell a sweet metallic scent wafting out of the living room, like copper. He peeked around the corner and—

"Haatim."

He screamed. The voice came from behind him. He scrambled forward and sideways, tripping and falling into the doorjamb. He saw behind him at the entrance of the cabin; Abigail was standing there, frowning at him.

"Where…where did you come from?"

"I went out the back and checked the perimeter," she said. "They are all dead."

"All of them?"

She shook her head. "Five bodies, but the cop back in town said six of them came out here together."

"What is that smell?"

He started to turn, trying to locate the strange scent. He felt a hand on his shoulder, pulling him back, but not before he caught a glimpse of what was in the living room.

Bodies, splayed out and with terrified looks on their faces. They were drenched in blood, though most of it looked dry and caked to their clothes and skin. One had his stomach cut open and his intestines were strewn across the floor, and another's arms had been removed and laid across his stomach.

The image burned into his memory, even with only a second's glance. He looked away in horror and saw Abigail standing next to him, a concerned expression on his face.

"Don't look in there," she said.

"Too late," he replied. He felt light-headed and sick and started to wobble. He'd thought the decomposing corpse at the warehouse was the worst thing he would ever see in his life; he'd been wrong.

He put his hands on his knees and took deep breaths, swallowing down bile.

"Need to vomit?"

He didn't reply, just kept breathing. The image...the blood...

The smell, he realized: that is the smell of their blood.

Haatim ran back outside, leaned over the railing, and threw up.

Abigail followed casually and leaned against the railing next to him. "Guess so," she said.

"Oh, God," he muttered. "I'll never be able to eat again."

"Is that so?"

He nodded. "Never."

They stood in silence for a minute, breathing in the cool night air.

"Happened a few hours ago," she said finally, after giving him some time to recover.

"You said one of them wasn't here."

"No, the sixth is missing."

"You think he left?"

"Maybe," she said. "But I don't know if he was heading to town or somewhere else. It's too late to track him down tonight, so we'll have to wait until morning."

"Do you think he killed them?"

She hesitated. "I don't know. It's pretty terrible in there, so I'm guessing something supernatural was involved."

"That's awful."

"I know," she said. "I'm sorry you had to see that."

"It isn't your fault."

She shrugged. "Let's hope your father sees it that way."

"What do we do now?" he asked. "Should we head back to town to get a motel room?"

"Too long of a drive," she said. "Plus, why bother heading back when we have perfectly good accommodations right here?"

Haatim looked back at the cabin he'd just fled out of, feeling a lump in his throat. Abigail chuckled.

"No, not that one. The other cabin. The one you said the woman had rented. Grab the stuff from the car, and I'll get the door open."

Haatim did as he was told, grabbing the bags of food out of the backseat and carrying them over to the other cabin. By the time he was there, Abigail had the door open and the fireplace turned on. It was a gas fire with fake logs, but the warmth felt amazing.

This cabin was considerably cleaner than the last, neat and tidy. They checked over the rooms to make sure everything was in order before finally

145

settling into the living room to relax. Haatim sat on the couch and watched the fire, trying to push the image of the blood and corpses out of his mind.

"You all right?" Abigail asked. She was sitting on the other couch, studying him.

"What? Yeah," he said. "I'm OK."

"You sure?"

He was silent for a long moment. "I don't know," he said.

She nodded. "Things like this, they take a long time to get used to. I'm surprised you're holding up as well as you are."

"Am I?" he said.

"The first time I saw a dead body, I cried for a week," she replied. "I was seven at the time, but I don't think that matters too much. Death is death. You've seen a lot of it today, and the fact that you aren't a heap of emotions on the floor means you're doing pretty well."

They sat in silence for a few minutes, and then Haatim started to feel hungry. His stomach growled, and he heard Abigail chuckle.

"Never going to eat again, huh?"

"Maybe that *was* a little dramatic," he agreed.

"Want me to fix something to eat?"

"No," he said. "I'll get it."

He went to the kitchen and started pulling supplies out of the plastic bags. He poured some canned beans into a bowl and tossed it into the microwave, then started making sandwiches.

"Shouldn't we tell the police?" he asked. "You know, about the dead college kids."

"We will," she replied. "But not until we are long gone and can call from a payphone. I'd rather be able to finish my work without having locals breathing down my neck."

"Makes sense," he said.

"Plus," she added. "How are we supposed to explain *this*? We stumbled across a cabin in the woods filled with dead twenty-something kids? Most of the time when people find something like this, they're usually the cause of it."

Haatim finished heating the food up and made them both a plate. "So, we just stay here tonight? And then what?"

"Tomorrow we find out what happened and whether or not their missing friend did this or if he's a victim, too."

"You think their friend could have done something like this?"

"The wounds were caused by a short serrated knife, and there were a lot of them. They were also imprecise and full of hesitation, so it wasn't a professional."

"Do you think he might have been possessed?"

"Demons don't usually hesitate when they are killing people."

"So you think he just snapped?"

"Maybe," she said. "But, it isn't likely that someone just *snapped* and did this, which means I'm thinking something provoked him. I'm just not quite ready to say it was a demon yet. There are several things that could trigger something like this."

"What if he comes back tonight?"

"Then we won't have to go out looking for him, will we?"

Haatim thought to object again and then changed his mind. He walked back over to the couches and handed a plate to Abigail, then started eating. He was starving, though he'd barely noticed until he actually had food in front of him. After all of the excitement from the last couple of days, he still felt entirely out of sorts, and his body was taking a while to catch back up.

It wasn't until he'd devoured half of his food that he noticed Abigail was watching him. He froze, mouth full, and then chewed slowly. She smiled and shook her head.

"Hungry?"

"I guess so," he said.

"And here I thought those dead bodies would steal your appetite."

The thought of the blood and corpses made his stomach twist. Haatim set his plate on the table. "Not hungry anymore."

"Good," she said. "Don't need you with a stomach ache."

"Funny," he said.

"I'm going to get some sleep. It looks like there are two rooms upstairs, so I'll take the one on the left."

"OK."

She finished eating, set her plate on the table, and then headed for the staircase leading up to the second floor. She paused at the landing and glanced back at Haatim.

"Get some sleep, because I expect you to be ready to go when I knock on your door in the morning. We're going to have a really long day."

Chapter 12

Despite what she'd said to Haatim, Abigail was barely able to sleep that night. She lay awake, thinking about her lapses in judgment over the last couple of days with Haatim, Delaphene, and the demon that was holding Arthur.

If the Council found out she'd gone to visit Sara without their permission they would be furious, and no doubt they would be able to find their way back to Delaphene who was still locked in her cabin in Colorado. She had to hope that if they did find Delaphene they would destroy her and send her back to hell before asking any unsavory questions.

But that didn't concern her nearly as much as her interactions with Haatim. She knew Frieda would be furious when she found out everything Abigail had told him regarding the Council and his father, but worse were the things she'd told him about herself.

She considered herself guarded and never talked about personal details, yet she'd told him about Arthur, her fears, and other details of her life she never told anyone before.

After her possession six months earlier, Frieda had slowly distanced herself from Abigail. It wasn't necessarily that Frieda didn't trust her, it was just that Abigail had become damaged goods. No one else on the Council had any faith in Abigail, and that put Frieda in an awkward position: backing Abigail meant losing credibility.

Which meant that she didn't talk to Frieda very often and never about the real things going on in her life. Even being friends, she knew Frieda would be beyond angry if she found out Abigail had spoken with Delaphene or used a forbidden ritual to create a connection to the demon holding Arthur. It was an unforgivable crime, maybe even enough to get her discharged from the Order.

When Haatim had shown up there was just something about him that made her trust him. She had been desirous to vent her problems to another human being, and he'd broken down her defenses. She had let her guard slip and told him things she should have kept to herself. A mistake which could turn costly if any of it made it back to the Council.

She awoke early the next morning, just after six, and went through her morning stretches and exercises. Arthur had taught her that staying limber was the most important part of her ability to fight. When she was young, he would have her stretch for three or four hours at a time, but now it usually took her a little over an hour to finish warming up her body.

She knocked on Haatim's door. She expected to find him sleeping, but he answered almost immediately. He was dressed and ready, but he had bags under his eyes and was still exhausted. *Guess he didn't sleep well, either.*

"Ready?" she asked.

"Not really," he said.

"Did you pick up any coffee last night?"

"Instant," he said. "It's all they had."

"It'll work. Make us a couple of cups. I have to grab some stuff from the car."

She headed outside and started rummaging through the trunk of Haatim's car for the large duffel bag she'd stuffed in there. It was loaded with two changes of clothes, various toiletries she liked to keep on hand, and lots of weapons: holy water, guns, knives, vials of miscellaneous poultices and poisons, and a variety of rare herbs and dried flowers gathered from all around the world.

Tucked at the bottom was her most prized possession: a small bible. It was the only one she'd ever owned and had been a gift from Arthur on her twelfth birthday. She had never fully accepted Christ into her heart, and Arthur had never been insistent that she should, but the book meant so much more to her than the words on the page.

She left most of it in the bag. For now, she grabbed an extra nine-millimeter pistol and a handful of sage. It wasn't as potent against demons as many other things she had, but it was common and easy to acquire and worked on many weaker supernatural threats.

By the time she got back into the cabin, Haatim was mixing her coffee.

"How do you like it?"

"With as much milk and sugar as possible," she said. "You didn't happen to pick up any caramel syrup, did you?"

He stared at her.

"Didn't think so."

She accepted the cup and took a sip. It was still bitter even with the sugar and milk, but she drank it anyway. It would help her stay alert. Haatim offered her a breakfast bar, but she shook her head.

"I don't like eating this early in the morning," she said. "I usually just wait and eat a big lunch."

"You should eat breakfast," Haatim said. "It's the most important meal of the day."

"Not for me," she replied.

"Suit yourself," he said with a shrug. He unwrapped the bar and took a bite. After a few seconds chewing, his eyes went wide. He rushed to the trashcan and spit it out, then looked at the wrapper.

Abigail couldn't help but laugh.

"Expired?"

"Two years ago," he said.

"Come on," she said, finishing her coffee. "We need to get moving."

Then she headed outside. Haatim gulped the last dregs of his own cup and rushed to follow. She paused on the porch and offered him the pistol.

"Here," she said. "Keep this with you."

"I don't know how to shoot a gun," he said.

"You point and pull the trigger," she said. "It isn't rocket science."

Tentatively, he accepted the weapon. He held it up, eyes wide as he stared at it. He looked vaguely like a terrified puppy.

"Which way do I point it?"

"On second thought," she said, taking the gun back. "I'll hang onto it for now."

She slipped it into her jeans at the back and headed off into the woods, looking for tracks around and behind the cabin. Haatim followed, looking at the scenery surrounding them.

"It's quite beautiful out here," he said. "I've never been to this part of the country."

"Just Arizona?"

"Yeah," Haatim said. "I never really got to travel because of my class loads."

"I hate Arizona," she said. "It's too dry and dusty. Not enough greenery for me."

Haatim shrugged. "I suppose."

"Found the tracks," she said, noticing a footprint in the mud. "Looks like someone headed away from here pretty fast yesterday."

"Think it's the missing student?"

"More than likely," she said. "Let's see where it leads."

She followed the trail, looking for broken branches and footprints to know they were heading in the right direction. It went basically due east and didn't deviate much, so it wasn't difficult to track. Haatim followed silently for a while, but after about fifteen minutes of talking he spoke up:

"How can you tell we are going the right way?"

"The footprints," she said, pointing at the ground.

"What footprints?" he asked. He looked where she was pointing. "That? That just looks like a scuff mark."

"What else would make a mark like that out here?"

"A deer?"

"Deer have hooves," she replied.

"A squirrel?"

"That's just ridiculous," she said. "This track is way too big."

151

"OK, then what about a bear?"

She looked solemnly at him. "It's a definite possibility."

The expression on his face was priceless as she turned and headed back into the woods. He hesitated for a couple of seconds and then rushed to catch up.

"You don't really think it could be a bear, do you?"

She ignored him, spotting something farther up ahead in the trees. It looked like the roof of a building, though it was resting at about ground level. She stopped walking, feeling an intense wave of déjà vu wash over her.

"I've been here before," she said.

"What?"

"Here," she said. Her hands were shaking. "I've been *here*."

"What do you mean?" he asked. "I thought this was your first time to Raven's Peak?"

She didn't answer and started walking quickly toward the buildings. She had a sudden flash in her mind, a memory of being attacked in these woods. A man in rotting flesh had killed her friends and taken her captive.

She crested the hill and gasped, looking down at the little town. There, in the center, was the Church.

The Church.

Frieda had told her the Church was in Europe, somewhere in Germany, and that it had been destroyed by the Council after her possession. But now she knew that had been a lie. Here it was before her, exactly how she remembered.

How she remembered…

She ran down into the town. Haatim was shouting behind her to wait, but she barely heard him. She didn't care and just kept going. She saw the spikes standing in front of the doors, though the heads had been removed, and ran quickly up the steps. She pushed into the room and was assaulted by more memories.

The demon had dragged her here, barely conscious. It was carrying the heads of her friends as well, laughing and singing the entire time. Their faces were plastered with terrified expressions, the last ones they wore before the demon ripped their heads off.

And then…I was taken…

"What's going on?" Haatim asked, stumbling into the Church behind her.

She spun and grabbed him, slamming him against the wall before she even realized what she was doing. His expression shifted from curiosity to fear and he put his hands up in submission.

"Hey, hey, I was just trying to help," he said, eyes wide.

She relaxed her grip and shook her head. "Sorry…I just…It was a reflex."

"It's OK," he said. "Do you mind letting me go?"

She pulled back, releasing her grip on his shirt. "Sorry."

"It's fine."

Haatim was staring over her shoulder, and she turned to look. Next to the rightmost wall of the Church sat a twenty-something guy wearing a black t-shirt and jeans. He was using his fingers to paint a word on the wall:

Belphegor.

He was currently writing the last letter.

"Who's that?"

"Belphegor?" Abigail said. "I think it's a demon."

"I know who Belphegor is," Haatim replied. "I meant the guy."

"Probably our missing college student."

"What's he doing?"

"I don't know," Abigail said. She walked across the Church. "Hey!"

No answer. The guy kept writing on the wall in his big scrawling letters. He reached up toward his face, seemingly to scratch his cheek, and then back to the wall and kept drawing.

"Hey, you!" Abigail said again, glancing back at Haatim. She had one hand resting on her revolver, ready to draw it at the slightest provocation.

Still, there was no response. She stepped forward, footsteps creaking on the floorboards, and reached a hand out. She grabbed the college kid on the shoulder and spun him to face her.

She heard Haatim gasp behind her and couldn't really blame him. The guy had dug his fingers into his own eye-sockets and ripped out his eyes. He was using the blood and ichor spilling out as the paint to write the demon's name.

The student hissed when she touched him and cowered back, curling into a ball next to the wall and flailing his arms at her. He looked disheveled and was covered in dry mud.

"What the hell?" she muttered.

"What...?" Haatim said, visibly shaken up. "What's he doing?"

"I don't know," Abigail said. This wasn't what she was expecting, and she certainly had never expected anything like *this* to be out here. "But something is *really* wrong."

"Is he possessed?"

"I don't know. I think so. I can't think of another reason he would do *this*."

She turned and headed back out of the Church, brushing past Haatim and to the town outside. He followed after her, a few steps behind.

"What do you mean?" he asked. "What's going on?"

"What did you mean?" she countered. "When you said you knew of Belphegor?"

"I read about him in one of my classes. It was on demonology."

"Where?"

"College?"

"Are you asking me?"

"No," he said firmly. "It was part of my graduate studies. We studied demons from all over the world."

"You didn't think that would be useful to tell me?"

"It was about theoretical demons that are supposed to be metaphorical. I didn't think any of it was *real.*"

She picked up the pace to a quick jog as she headed back toward the cabins. She heard Haatim breathing heavily behind her, trying to keep up. "Where are we going?"

"Back," she said. "I have a phone call to make."

"For what?"

She kept running and picked up the pace again, dodging around trees and underbrush, expecting Haatim to fall behind. She could come back and get him later.

He lasted a lot longer than she expected, making it almost all the way back to the cabin before finally slowing down and clutching his side.

"I'll uh...I'll catch up," he shouted after her.

She made it back to the clearing and went to the car. Her phone didn't have any reception out here, but she had something better. She popped open the trunk and pulled her satellite phone out of her duffel bag. She punched in a number and waited for Frieda to pick up on the other end.

As soon as it clicked, she said: "What the hell?"

"Abigail, this isn't a good—"

"You *knew* I'd been here before," Abigail interrupted.

"Abi—"

"Why didn't you tell me *this* was where the Church was located? Or that it was still standing at all? You lied to me, Frieda. You told me it had been torn down."

"The Council thought it might be good for you to experience this organically. When you were asked about it during the debriefings, you had no memory of the location or surrounding are, and the doctors thought coming upon it unexpectedly might trigger some memories."

"So I was a Guinea pig?"

"All in the pursuit of finding Arthur," Frieda said. "They thought sending you out there would spark your memories, and you might remember something vital about the demon that took him."

"And you didn't think any of this was worth telling me about beforehand?"

"It didn't seem relevant," Frieda said tersely. "The doctors insisted you not know and I needed an excuse to send you. I made up the reports about disturbances in Raven's Peak, so I knew you wouldn't be in any real danger. Look, Abi, I'm sorry if you feel like we've wasted your time, but clearly you remember *something*—"

"No disturbance?" Abigail echoed incredulously. "Tell that to the five dead

154

college kids."

Silence. "What?"

"I've got five college kids out here who've been hacked to pieces and another one who gouged out his own eyes to scrawl Belphegor's name on the wall of the Church. The Church you found me in but decided to keep secret from me."

Abigail spun, raising her revolver and aiming it at Haatim's face as he rounded the corner of the cabin. He stopped, raising his hands, and she slowly lowered the revolver. He walked toward her, keeping his hands up.

"Abi, there were no reported disturbances in your entire region."

"There sure as hell is one now," she said. "And I've got a possessed college kid out here who needs help."

"You said he was writing Belphegor on the wall? Definitely Belphegor?"

"Yeah, why? What's it matter?"

"I'm going to have to call you back," Frieda said.

"Wait—"

Abigail heard the line go dead and cursed, throwing the phone back into the duffel bag.

"You OK?" Haatim asked, still holding his hands up.

"Put your hands down," she said.

He did, resting them at his sides. He was still panting and drenched in sweat. "Are you OK?" he asked again.

"I don't like being screwed with," Abigail said angrily. "I'm *not* a piece on someone else's chessboard."

"I don't think he's possessed," Haatim said.

"What?"

"The guy in the Church. I don't think he's possessed."

"Then what?"

"I don't know," he said. "But Belphegor is bad news, if you believe the tales. He used to be called Baal-Peor, and he spreads insanity wherever he goes."

"What do you mean?"

"In Kabbalic mythology he spread paranoia and distrust. He would find a weakness already existing in a person and exploit it, pushing them over the edge. Usually he was after wealth or influence, but something he did it for the fun of it."

"So you're saying the demon found this guy's buttons and pressed them?"

"Yeah," Haatim answered. "Except nothing in Belphegor's history said he ever actually controlled people. He manipulated them, but left them to do their own business. I doubt he was ever inside this guy, because then he wouldn't be able to spread more insanity."

"What do you mean?"

"I mean," Haatim said, "Why turn your host crazy, when you can ride in one host and make everyone else go crazy? It seems counterintuitive and not Belphegor's style."

Abigail hesitated. "You mean he's still out there?"

Haatim's expression told her that was exactly what he meant.

Chapter 13

Abigail drove in silence back toward Raven's Peak, trying to work through the turmoil of emotions inside her. It was sprinkling, and the only sound in the car were raindrops on the windshield and the occasional scraping of the wiper blades.

She couldn't believe Frieda had manipulated her so completely, or even that Frieda would do such a thing. She'd thought she could trust Frieda. She knew they'd had a sort of falling out ever since Arthur was taken, but she'd never believed it could get this bad.

On the flipside, she could understand why Frieda did what she did, and was actually a little grateful that Frieda was looking into Arthur's disappearance.

Still, it hurt: it felt like a complete betrayal. She expected things like this from the other members of the Council, but she'd always thought Frieda was different.

"It's really foggy," Haatim said after a while.

"From yesterday's rain," she said. She couldn't see more than about twenty or thirty meters in front of the car, but to be honest she barely noticed. She was too wrapped up in her own thoughts and trying to figure out what was going on.

"Do you think it will start pouring again? I don't mind *this*, but I don't really like being stuck in a downpour."

"Let's hope not," Abigail said. "We need to figure out who Belphegor is riding inside of and stop them—"

"The kid," Haatim interrupted suddenly. "The kid I saw with his mom."

"You think it's him?"

"His mom said he went out wandering. It makes sense," he replied. "He might have stumbled onto something he shouldn't have. And when I saw him at the store, there was something about him that gave me the creeps."

"You should have told me."

"I thought I was just overreacting," he said. "I'm new to this, so I kind of thought I was just jumping at nothing. Can you blame me?"

She shrugged. "Not really."

"Actually, it explains Tim, too. That guy I told you about who came into the store and was acting weird. He would have had to walk past the kid in the car to get inside, so maybe the demon got to him in the parking lot."

"Makes sense," Abigail said. "You said they were staying at a motel, right?"

"Yeah," Haatim said. "And then they were planning to head back to Chicago today."

"Let's hope they haven't left yet."

They fell silent for a long while. "How do we stop this demon?" Haatim asked.

"The same way we stop all demons," Abigail said. "Kill it."

"What if it has infected other people?"

"I doubt it can infect too many people in this short of a time frame," Abigail said. "Or, at least I hope not."

"How long does it take?"

"I honestly don't know," she said. "I've never dealt with anything like this before."

"What if it has infected a lot of people?"

"Then, if we're lucky, killing the demon will put a stop to it. And, if we aren't, we'll need to come up with a plan B."

"Plan B, as in kill them?"

She didn't answer.

A long minute passed, then Haatim asked apprehensively, "Do you think it's infected us?"

"No idea," she replied. "But, if you start acting funny, I'm going to have to shoot you."

"Ha, ha," he said. "Very funny."

Abigail stared ahead, determined not to crack a smile.

"That was a joke, right?"

"We're almost back to the city. First we're going to stop in at the motel and see if we can find the—"

Suddenly there was a loud cracking sound as a gun was discharged behind them. It came from a quarter of a mile back from somewhere off in the woods. She saw the vague outline of the gas station maybe a hundred meters in front of them.

"What was that?" Haatim asked, tense.

"Something bad," she replied. "Hang on."

They were just on the outskirts of Raven's Peak. Another shot rang out; this second bullet thudded into the trunk of their car, ripping a huge hole in the aluminum frame. The gas station parking lot was empty except for a behemoth red pickup truck with monster tires.

"Someone is shooting at us!" Haatim shouted, clutching the door, tense in his seat.

"No kidding."

"What do we do?"

She ignored him and kept driving, picking up speed. She weaved back and forth so the shooter wouldn't have an easy target. With any luck she would slip right past the gas station and find some cover.

Then, she spotted another two guys hiding behind the red truck. They were also carrying rifles but hadn't fired yet and were hunkering down for an ambush. They were just now lining up their shots.

"Hang on!" she shouted, slamming on the gas pedal. She grabbed Haatim and yanked him down so his head was below the windshield. She aimed the vehicle straight down the center of the road and then ducked next to him.

Loud gunshots ripped into the engine block, and she heard a hissing sound as something hot started venting out. The windows exploded around them, showering them in glass, and Abigail pushed Haatim even lower into the seat.

They roared past the gas station and the firing men. The side and rear windows were little more than fragments now, and cold air whipped past her head, blowing her hair wildly.

She sat back up in the driver's seat and tried to get her bearings. The front windshield had a hole in it and a spider web of cracks, making it difficult to see out, but she was fairly certain they were heading the right direction.

"What the hell is happening?" Haatim asked, breathless.

"I don't know," she said. They raced on, seeing the other buildings of Raven's Peak looming in front of them in the fog. More gunshots behind them, but the gas station was barely visible through the sheet of fog.

"Do you think we lost them?"

Abigail didn't get the chance to reply before a cop car came speeding off a dirt road and slammed into the back left corner of their vehicle. It made a huge crashing sound and ripped control of the vehicle from her. They spun and skidded down the road.

Haatim started screaming, and Abigail closed her eyes, trying to keep her body oriented against the centripetal-force pressure. The wind whipped her hair and sucked her breath away.

They slammed into the side of a building just inside the city. She felt her body jarred from the sudden impact, and a spike of pain shot up her leg. She was dizzy and disoriented, but she couldn't allow herself time to recover.

In the street behind her she heard whooping and hollering and another gunshot thudded into the car. Her door was pressed against the wall, blocking her in. She slipped off the buckle, twisted her body, and kicked the windshield.

It took two kicks to break it off, and she slid out onto the hood. Haatim sat dazed in the passenger seat, blood streaming from his forehead and a concussed look on his face. She hoped he was OK.

But, right now, she had more important things to worry about.

She slipped her gun free, slipped down the front of the car, and then peeked around the edge.

Six men were running down the road toward her, shouting and whooping. Two were in police uniforms, and one looked like the guy she'd met at the bar the night before.

She picked one of them men near the front and fired off a shot. It was long ways off, but she hit him just above the knee, and he staggered to the ground. His gun slide away, and he clutched his leg, screaming. Abigail grimaced in satisfaction and ducked back out of sight.

They returned fire, and more bullets thudded into the wall and engine block. They were still fifty meters away, and she knew if they got much closer, their accuracy would increase dramatically.

She had to find cover, but first she had to get Haatim out of the car.

"Haatim!" she shouted.

He groaned but didn't answer.

"Haatim, get up!"

More gunshots barked around her, forcing her to duck lower behind the engine block. She was running out of time.

"Wha...what?" he heard Haatim say, followed by a series of curses.

"Climb toward me out the front of the car," she said. She slipped around the corner and fired off two more shots. She didn't have time to aim now that they knew where she was, but it was enough to keep them from advancing on her position easily.

She heard jostling inside the car.

"I can't. I'm stuck."

"Did you unbuckle your seat belt?" she called back.

A hesitation, and then: "Never mind."

A few seconds later Haatim crawled over the hood of the car and landed next to her on the pavement. He crouched, still dazed but at least able to partially focus. She slipped the pistol out from her pants, flicked the safety off, and handed it to Haatim.

"You want me to shoot them?"

"No," she said. "I want you to shoot *at* them. I'm going to run into the building while you fire; then I'm going to cover you and you're going to follow me. Got it?"

"Got it," he said.

"Only shoot a few—"

Haatim put his arm over the hood of the car and started firing back toward the advancing men. He closed his eyes and faced away from the gunshots. He furrowed his brow while he pulled the trigger.

Abigail scrambled, running to the doorway leading into the building. It was a FedEx office and was locked, but it was also a glass door. She busted it with the butt of her gun and ducked under the bar to slip inside.

She heard a clicking sound as Haatim ran out of rounds. She waited a few seconds, leaned back through the door frame, and started firing back toward the approaching group of men.

"Come on!" she shouted to Haatim. Bullets thudded into the wall and car, and Haatim scrambled across the ground to her position, moving on all fours. She allowed him to slide past her and then ducked back into the office behind him, taking a deep and steadying breath.

Haatim's entire body was shaking in terror. "They are shooting at us," he said again.

"I know."

"I shot at *them*."

"Don't worry," she said. "You were never in any danger of hurting anyone."

He looked at the gun. "Do you have more bullets?"

"In the car," she said. "I was trying to tell you to conserve ammo."

"Oh."

"They're in there!" a voice shouted from outside. Abigail grabbed Haatim and pulled him farther into the store. She spun open her revolver and spilled the spent rounds onto the floor. She had a handful in her pocket and started slipping them into the chambers.

"See those cardboard boxes," she said, pointing to a stack in the corner.

"Yeah," he replied.

"As soon as they step through the door, I want you to throw the heaviest things you can find at them. You don't have to hit anyone, just distract them."

"OK," he said.

"And stay behind the counter while you do it. Just throw them at the door."

She ducked around a corner leading farther into the FedEx building, leaning just far enough to have a clean view of the door. The first man came charging in after only a few seconds. She fired low, hitting him in the shin, and he screamed in pain. He collapsed and started thrashing on the ground.

A second later an empty box soared out from behind Haatim's desk, landing on the guy's chest. He barely noticed, shoving it out of the way, and just continued thrashing. Another guy came into sight a second later, trying to step over his comrade. This time Abigail shot him in the stomach. He went down, too, dropping his gun and writhing in pain.

They were just charging in blindly, barely caring about the fact that she had a safe position to shoot at them. No tactics, no planning, just blind anger. She knew there were at least two more men coming, but they hadn't quite caught up with their friends.

Or maybe they had just circled around to the back.

There was a gunshot from behind her at the rear door of the FedEx building. This one was also locked, and someone had just blown out the lock.

She spun, ducking, and saw another two men charging into the room behind her. She didn't have time to line up wounding shots. Both stopped

161

approaching and raised their guns when they spotted her a few meters into the room, but they were too slow.

She hit one in the shoulder and the other in the chest. The first dropped to the ground, screaming in pain and clutching the bullet hole.

The second fell to the ground, dead before he landed.

"Damn it," she said. She strode across the floor and kicked the wounded man's gun away, then kicked him in the face for good measure, silencing his screams.

She hadn't planned to kill him, but she hadn't really had time to react any differently. If Haatim was right, then these people weren't possessed or willing accomplices, and that meant she'd accidentally killed an innocent man. These were just normal people locked in the throes of some psychotic break.

She took a steadying breath and listened to the room around her. It was quiet; the only sounds were moans from the wounded men. She held her gun ready, waiting to see if there were any other attackers on their way, but there was nothing.

She headed back through the FedEx building to where Haatim was hiding. He was huddled low, clutching another box to his chest and staring at the entry with unbridled terror.

He jumped when she approached, letting out a little screech. "Come on," she said, heading toward the exit. Glass crunched under her steps. "We can't stick around."

She paused at the doorway and listened, but she couldn't hear anyone outside, either.

"You think it's over?" Haatim asked.

Abigail stepped outside. The city was still foggy, but the fog was lifting, and she could see more of the town laid out before her. All around them the streets were empty.

Down the road a few hundred meters she saw a building on fire. It looked like it had been burning for some time, but there wasn't a fire truck or anyone tending to it. More smoke rose in the distance. Two other buildings on her street had their windows smashed in and looked to have been looted sometime in the middle of the night.

She heard a police siren sounding in the distance. It was followed by a series of gunshots and a loud shriek.

"No," she said. "I think it's only just begun."

✳✳✳

She headed back to Haatim's Chevy. It was riddled with bullets and leaking various fluids. Smoke wafted out, and the engine was hissing; she knew it wouldn't work anymore, and probably never again. Haatim paused beside her, looking at his vehicle with an expression of utter despair on his face.

"My car," he muttered.

"Better it than you."

"Yeah, I know. But, still…"

"Don't worry, you can buy a new one," she said.

She walked toward the trunk. It was smashed where the other vehicle had crashed into it and popped open. She pulled her duffel bag out and checked it for bullet holes.

It looked to be intact, and she let out a breath she hadn't realized she'd been holding. Several of the items in it were incredibly rare and valuable and she didn't have the funds to replace them.

"What's that?" Haatim asked.

"What's what?" she asked.

"That high-pitched ringing sound?"

"It's the after effect of the gunshots," she said. "Don't worry, it'll go away."

He ignored her and glanced into the car, then leaned inside and started digging around. After a moment he came back out of the car holding her satellite phone. It was chiming softly.

"I meant this," he said. He handed it to her and she clicked it on.

"Hello?"

"You need to get out of Raven's Peak," Frieda said immediately.

"I can't. We've got a couple of civilians injured, and I need you to send some doctors. Multiple gunshot wounds. They attacked us, and at least one of them is dead. We need a clean-up crew as well to—"

"They've declared Raven's Peak a dead zone."

Abigail fell silent, utterly shocked. "They what?"

"It's happening in two hours. Napalm. They're going to make it look like a forest fire. Belphegor is too high risk to deal with any other way. This needs to be contained."

"Contained, yes, but what you're talking about…" she trailed off, shaking her head. "There are thousands of people living here."

"I know," Frieda said softly. "But if Belphegor gets out of Raven's Peak, it won't be long before the casualty count is in the tens of thousands. You've seen what he can do, Abi. You know we don't have the resources to handle something like this."

"Forest fire? That doesn't sound like an ideal alibi if you ask me."

"This isn't an ideal situation," Frieda replied.

Abigail rubbed her face. "What if I could stop Belphegor?"

"You can't."

"But what if I could?"

"Then we could call off the strike. But it doesn't matter, Abi. This threat is beyond any of us. The Council isn't taking any chances, and they're going to kill everyone. It's been over a thousand years since Belphegor has had access to a body, and the last time the death toll was catastrophic."

"How long do I have?"

"Not long. Your priority is getting yourself and Haatim safely out of the city."

"I never said I had Haatim with me," Abigail argued.

"Abigail this isn't a joke. I still haven't told the Council he's with you and they are launching a full scale investigation to locate him. If they find out he's been with you this entire time or, worse that *we* put him in danger, then things will go badly for both of us. You *need* to leave now."

"Then all of these people will die."

"They are already dead."

"I need time," Abigail pleaded. "I can do this. Please, Frieda, I'm begging you: have faith in me."

Frieda was silent for a long minute. "I'm sorry, Abigail. I have all the faith in the world for you, but my hands are tied. The Council has already made their decision."

Then she hung up. Haatim was staring at her, a look of worry on his face.

"Everything OK?"

"No," she said. "No, it sure as hell isn't."

Chapter 14

"We have to leave," Abigail said. "They are about to burn the city to the ground."

Haatim stared at her, wondering if maybe he'd heard wrong. He had hit his head during the car crash, so maybe he had a concussion. He shook his head.

"I'm sorry, I thought you just said they were going to burn the city down."

"That's what I said," Abigail replied. "We don't have much time, and I need to get you out of here."

"But, then everyone here is going to die."

"I know," Abigail said. "I wish I could help them, but if we stay we will die along with them."

"We can't just let them die."

The look of helpless resignation on Abigail's face floored Haatim. "I know," she said. "But there is no other way. They would never call off an airstrike because *I* asked them to. I'm a pariah."

"There has to be something—"

"What?" Abigail asked. "What could we do? We have *minutes* before they drop their bombs and kill everyone. Your father would kill me if I let something happen to you."

"Does he know I'm here?"

Abigail shook her head. "He doesn't know you're with me at all, and he's not exactly the forgiving type."

"Could you stop this? Could you save these people?"

"I don't know," Abigail admitted. "But, I don't know if I can live myself if I never even try."

There was a sudden bout of shouting from farther up the road. Voices were spilling out of an Italian Restaurant on the corner. The front door was open, and they could hear the sounds of breaking glass inside.

"What was that?"

"I don't know," she said. "I'm going to go check it out. You stay here."

She set the satellite radio on the hood of his busted up car and then moved quickly up the street, scanning the area and moving toward the restaurant. Haatim waited inside the FedEx building, trying to wrap his mind around what was happening.

165

It was insane to think that so many people would be killed because of something like this, and the idea that his father might have something to do with it was unthinkable. His father had always been stern and unwilling to compromise. But to think that he would willingly be a part of mass murder like this...

Haatim pulled his phone out of his pocket and turned it on. After it finished booting he clicked the button to call his father. Aram Malhotra answered immediately.

"Haatim! Thank God. Where are you?"

"I'm in Raven's Peak."

The other end of the phone was silent. Haatim could feel his father's anger and disapproval spilling through the speaker.

"What is going on? Who are you with—?"

"It doesn't matter, Dad," Haatim said. "I need you to call off the attack on the city."

"How do you know about—?"

"Call them off," Haatim said, "Or you'll be killing your own son."

A long silence. "There are things at work here that you cannot possibly understand, Haatim," his father said.

His voice was quivering, but the words were like a punch in Haatim's stomach, solidifying everything Abigail had told him: his father was involved in this in some way, and he'd kept it from Haatim for his entire life.

"I know," Haatim said, "but that doesn't change the reality of *this* situation. If you don't call off the airstrike, then I'll be dead."

"I cannot call it off."

"Then delay it," Haatim replied. "I don't care how, but I'm not letting you murder all of these innocent people. Not when there is a chance that Abigail can save them."

"You are with Abigail? I knew it. Frieda was lying. Son, trust me, Abigail cannot handle something like *this*."

"You are always the one telling me to have Faith, father."

"I have *no* faith in Abigail."

"Then have faith in me," Haatim said. "This is my decision, and it's already been made. Call the Council and delay the strike. I won't ask again."

"Haatim, you do not understand. Leave the city, now. I beg of you."

"No," Haatim said. "I'm sorry."

Then he hung up. The phone battery was almost dead, and with a sigh he dropped it on the floor. His hands were shivering and he couldn't think of any time he'd ever stood up to his father before. He'd always been terrified of his father while growing up.

But, now, everything had changed.

Abigail was back a minute later. She saw the expression on his face and cocked her head in confusion. "What is it? What's wrong?"

The satellite phone started to ring, bouncing on the torn up hood. Haatim picked it up. "It's for you," he said.

He clicked the speaker button on the phone. There was a moment of silence, and then Frieda said:

"You have one hour, Abigail. Don't mess this up. Haatim, when this is over with, you and I will exchange words."

Chapter 15

"Words?" Haatim echoed after Frieda closed the connection. "Should I be concerned?"

"Only if you enjoy living," Abigail answered. "I only get that tone from her when she's really pissed off. What did you do? How did you get them to give me more time?"

"You can stop this, right?" he asked.

Abigail stared at Haatim. "You called your father."

"We had a nice chat."

"That was stupid, Haatim," Abigail replied.

"Not if you can stop this," he said. "Then it'll be worth it. These people don't deserve to die."

Abigail picked up her duffel bag and started walking down the street. It was quiet and empty, which even for a town this small it felt unnatural. She walked toward a couple of cars that were parked in front of a coffee shop.

"What do we do now?"

"*You*," Abigail said, testing the door—it was locked. "Are getting out of town right now. There is going to be a roadblock somewhere outside the city, but it will be one of ours. Tell them who you are and who your father is, and they will let you through."

"No way, I'm not leaving you."

She hesitated and turned to face him.

"Thank you for trusting in me," she said. "But this is where our paths diverge. You need to get back to your family."

"I want to help."

"You already have," she said.

Abigail went to the rear window and hit it with her elbow, shattering the glass. Then, she reached in and unlocked the front door.

"What are you going to do?"

"I," she said, "am going to kill Belphegor."

***

"Will that stop what's happening?"

"Yes," Abigail said. "I think so."

"You think so?"

"I've never dealt with something this crazy before, but situations like this usually end when the source is destroyed. If I can find him and take him out, then at the very least I know he won't be able to spread this madness anywhere else. And, thanks to you, I now have an hour to do it."

"Is it enough time?"

"More than enough," Abigail said. "By the time this hour is up, either he will be dead or I will."

She leaned into the front seat of the car she'd just opened and started hot wiring it. After a quick splice of the wires the car sputtered to life. She dropped her duffel bag into the backseat and started rifling through it, finally pulling out a hand crossbow and a pouch of tiny darts.

"A crossbow?"

"Great for administering doses of sleeping medicine," she said. She loaded a dart and slipped the rest into her pocket. "I'm not a fan of blowguns."

"Doesn't prayer work?" he asked. "Banishing demons with litanies and the Lord's words?"

"It does," Abigail said. "But it was never really my thing. Arthur was an ordained Minister, and he taught me a handful of prayers, but I never really took it seriously. For me, guns are what I use to pray with."

As if to emphasize her point, she pulled out a short-barreled shotgun and a pack of twenty-gauge shells. She also slid the satellite phone into her pocket. It was bullet-proof and expensive but bulky and frustrating to carry with her.

"How many weapons do you keep with you?"

"Enough," she replied. She loaded the shotgun and then glanced at Haatim. "Time for you to go. The car has half a tank, which should be plenty to get you past the blockade. Don't stop until you're well clear of this entire area."

"OK," he replied. "What about your stuff?"

"If I make it out of here, I'll come get it."

Haatim hesitated. "If?"

She shrugged. "Optimism was never really my strong suit. Now go."

He started to climb into the car and then hesitated. He wrapped her up in a hug, catching her off-guard. "Thanks," he said. "For everything."

"No problem," she said, extricating herself from the hug.

"Be safe."

"I will," she replied. "Take care of yourself, Haatim."

He nodded and climbed into the car. She watched him drive off, heading out of town, and then she turned and looked back toward the center of town. The fog was almost completely gone, and the city was a scene of devastation: fires raged, people were shouting, and it was mass chaos.

If Belphegor was here, he'd be building up some kind of army to protect himself. If Abigail wanted to find him, all she would need to do was follow the people who are acting crazy.

✳✳✳

Haatim drove along the outskirts of town, heading for the road leading away from Raven's Peak and back toward civilization. Part of him was relieved to be getting away from all of the insanity, even though he was leaving Abigail behind. He hadn't known her for that long, but he had come to like and respect her.

It was hard to believe so much had happened in so little time. Only two days ago he would have laughed if someone told him things like demons were real, and now he had seen them with his own two eyes. It was actually quite terrifying when he admitted it to himself.

If it wasn't for Abigail, he would have died several times by now. She constantly risked her life protecting the world from horrible things, and her only concern while facing this impossible challenge was that she wouldn't have enough time to even die in the effort. He hated the idea that he was abandoning her.

But what help could he be? This wasn't his world.

Except...

Maybe it was.

His father was a deeply religious man and had raised Haatim to be educated and spiritual. He never would have imagined his father could be a part of something like this, but the more he thought about it the more it made sense.

It explained his father's many absences from his upbringing and his lofty sentimentality about bettering the world. It explained why he always taught Haatim to have Faith in and to trust in God.

But, just echoing the prayers and saying the right words didn't mean much of anything. Haatim had never considered himself a true believer. He'd thought of religious teachings as fanciful tales people told so children would behave.

He had lost his faith when his sister died. He'd given up all hope in a greater plan, and his father had been furious when he turned his back on religion. Now, however, Haatim felt that his faith was back. But, even after all of this, it hadn't been his father who had rekindled his faith.

It had been Abigail.

Not her belief in the supernatural, but rather her utter belief that she was doing the right thing by risking her life to save others. Her complete trust in the decisions she made and that there was good in the world. She might be arrogant and off-putting at times, but she was the bravest and most selfless human being he'd ever met.

✳✳✳

Abigail walked down the street, shotgun slung over her shoulder and hand crossbow at the ready. She fought the urge to glance at her watch, but she knew she'd already lost ten minutes of her hour before the attack came.

She knew how risky this was. No, risky wasn't the right word: *insane* was better. Maybe even suicidal. She was wholly unprepared and unready for something like this.

But she also didn't have any other options.

The Council had declared Raven's Peak a dead zone. They didn't do that unless they felt things were unsalvageable, and it had been almost two-hundred years since the last time they had employed scorched-earth tactics like this. If they felt there was any other way to deal with Belphegor, they would have used it instead.

Which meant they didn't think she was a viable alternative. Hell, she didn't even blame them for their lack of confidence in her. The last time she had come to Raven's Peak she was with two more experienced Hunters than herself and both of them were dead.

But she had to try. She might only have an hour, and this might be an insane plan, but she couldn't just stand by and let these people be burned alive. Arthur had taught her that when good people stood by and watched others die, then they died with them.

The day Arthur rescued her was the first time in her life she'd felt there was something good in the world. It was a feeling she embraced wholeheartedly, and he'd taught her the difference between just being alive and really living.

She heard a shout from up ahead and saw a man come charging out of the town's municipal building. He sprinted across the street toward a fast food restaurant that was on fire. He was also naked and screaming.

She saw someone else chase him out of the building and into the street. This second man was carrying a rifle and wearing a police uniform. Abigail started to raise her crossbow, but she was a split second too late.

The pursuer dropped to his knee, aimed, and fired at the naked man. The bark of the gunshot echoed past her, and the fleeing man fell face-first onto the road.

Abigail fired, putting a dart into the cop's chest. He froze, still on his knee, and slowly his grip loosened on the rifle as the sleeping medicine went into effect.

His hands were shaking as he tried to stay conscious, but by the time he hit the ground he was completely out of it.

Abigail ran to the man in the road but quickly realized that he was already dead. The cop had fired a high caliber round that passed through his body, shredding everything in its path.

"Damn it," she muttered. "Figures something like this happens in a town where everyone owns a gun."

She loaded another dart into her hand crossbow and moved on down the road. She heard more gunshots in the distance, but they sounded far enough away that she didn't worry about them.

The motel was about a block ahead, and that was the first place she planned to check for the boy. She doubted he would still be there, but she might find some clue as to where he had gone.

It was a one story "L" shaped structure with fading green paint and a white roof. It was quiet in the area and an old sign stood out front with the word "vacancy" lit up despite it being late in the morning.

A car had smashed into the front of the building and was parked in the lobby, but there was no driver inside. Abigail approached it cautiously. The door was open, and the keys were still in the ignition. Smooth jazz blared out of the speakers. Abigail reached in and flipped the car off, then closed the door.

She held her hand crossbow at the ready and slung the shotgun over her shoulder, moving slowly through the lobby. No one stood behind the desk, and most of the keys were hanging up and unused. Only two sets were missing: rooms four and six.

She walked along the front of the motel, working her way down the numbers from ten. By the time she reached unit six, she could hear laughter spilling from inside a room farther down the way. No doubt, it was coming from unit four.

A cursory glance inside the window showed that unit six was locked and empty. The bed wasn't made and clothing was scattered all over the floor, but it looked like whoever had been staying there had left some time ago. She kept moving.

The laughter intensified, and it sounded like a woman cackling hysterically. The door to unit four was cracked open. Abigail gently pushed it open and crept inside.

A woman in a brown overcoat was sitting in a gray chair, laughing and resting her head against a busted mirror. Blood ran down the side of face, and her hair was matted and unkempt. The television was on and playing a Spanish soap opera.

There was no one else in the room. Abigail hesitated in the doorway, trying to decide if she should address the woman or keep moving.

She didn't get to decide when the woman turned to face her. She grinned.

173

"Come in! Have a seat!"

Abigail considered her options for a second, and then strode into the room. She sat in another arm chair facing the woman and rested her crossbow on her knee.

"Hello."

"Hi!" the woman said, laughing. She rocked her head, gently tapping it against the glass, and smiled at Abigail. Her left eye was twitching. "You're very pretty."

"Thank you."

"Do you think I'm pretty?" the woman asked.

Abigail hesitated and then nodded. "Yes. Quite pretty."

"But I'm not," the woman said. "My husband thinks I'm a wretched, awful woman. He hates me, and that's why he beats me."

"He beats you?"

She nodded, perky. "Though he's rarely home, anymore. I hate him. I would divorce him, but I'm afraid he would kill me. So I'm going to kill him instead."

Then she burst out laughing like it was the funniest idea in the world. She clutched her stomach.

"He didn't come with you?"

"No," the woman said. "He's off sleeping with his secretary, and I don't even care. I just don't want my son to know he beats me. He shouldn't hate his father. He shouldn't."

"He should know what kind of man his father is."

"Oh, heaven's no!" the woman said. "A boy looks up to his father. He cannot possibly know the truth: all men are terrible."

"Where is your son?"

"He went with the others."

"The others?"

"The ones he called for. They came when he asked. And they swore to protect him. Do you think they can protect him?"

"I don't know," Abigail replied. "But I can help protect him. Do you know where he is?"

"They took him to the factory. They said they could keep him safe there."

"OK," Abigail said, standing up. "Thank you."

"Wait," the woman said, suddenly suspicious. "I don't trust you. You're Abigail. He told me not to trust you."

The woman launched herself from the chair, fingers outstretched and lips curled in a feral grin. She screeched, charging across the room. Abigail raised the crossbow and fired, but the woman was too close and her dart skimmed past her shoulder.

Abigail ducked as the woman reached for her face. She looked like a

174

ravenous animal trying to scratch and claw her eyes out.

Abigail slid past her to the center of the room and then kicked the woman in the shin. Off balanced, the woman clawed at the air and got ahold of Abigail's hair. She yanked on it, pulling Abigail to the side, and then scratched her face with her other hand.

Abigail rolled under the woman's arm, punching her twice hard in the kidney. The woman doubled over, releasing her hair, and Abigail punched her in the neck, dropping her to the ground.

For good measure, Abigail shot her with another crossbow dart. She growled in frustration and fixed her hair, tying it back into a ponytail.

"*That* is why I usually wear my hair short," she explained to the unconscious woman. "And how the *hell* did you know my name?"

Naturally, she didn't get a satisfactory answer. She blew out a breath of air and loaded more darts into her crossbow. It held three at a time, and she only had a couple left. She'd need to be careful not to waste them.

At least now she knew where she was heading. The factory.

She didn't have a lot of time left, but she also didn't want to rush out in front of some maniac with a gun. She moved through the streets cautiously, weaving down alleys and avoiding the main roads.

Gunshots sounded at random intervals, and people shouted and screamed all around her. Someone was singing, belting out the lyrics to a Jimmy Buffet song.

She heard dogs barking and people shouting and stayed out of sight. On one side street she spotted a brawl going on with a group of five men and women pummeling each other, but she was able to skirt around it and keep going.

Finally, she reached a group of buildings that stood outside the enormous factory. These were smaller strip-mall type structures, probably owned by the same company that owned and operated the factory. They were old and rundown but looked to still be in use.

The factory itself took up at least five acres of land and stood four floors high. She heard shouting coming from up ahead and moved quietly, staying out of sight.

Out front of the main entrance she saw a group of men gathered, yelling angrily at another man they were circled around. The guy in the center was small and cowering, pleading with them to let him go. Two of the men were carrying guns, and the rest had baseball bats and other weapons.

Abigail watched as one of the bat-wielding lunatics smashed the cowering man in the knee. They roared and laughed and another man followed that attack with a swing from a golf club. The guy in the center screamed in pain.

The rest jeered and cheered, and the pleading man collapsed to the ground, crying. Abigail counted seven of them in total, including the one they were encircling.

Abigail glanced up and down the front of the factory, looking for another way inside. It didn't look like there were a lot of entrances, at least on this side of the building. There was a factory entrance on the right wall eighty or so meters away, but all of the loading bay doors were pulled closed, and she doubted they would be easy to open.

Which meant her best entrance would be this main one here. She would need to go through these idiots, and the more of a surprise she could get on them, the better. At least only two of them were carrying guns.

She looked at her crossbow, making sure it was cocked and ready to go. She would get three shots, so she needed to make them count. The poison worked quickly and would knock a bear out for hours.

Abigail slipped out of hiding and strode confidently toward the group of men. She waited until she was about four meters away and then raised her crossbow. She fired the first two bolts in rapid succession, hitting the two gun-wielding men in the necks with darts.

The third dart she fired was at the biggest man in the group, a hulking brute towering over six and a half meters tall. He was big, but no match her the poison. The dart hit him in the shoulder, and he fell heavily to the ground with a grunt.

The rest of the group looked around in confusion as those three sunk to the ground. Abigail quick stepped forward and kicked the nearest man in the back of the leg. He shouted in anger, dropping to one knee, and Abigail followed with a roundhouse kick to the side of the head.

The other two men had spotted her by now and were ready to fight. One was short and built like a barrel with thick muscles and wearing an ugly flannel shirt. The other guy was tall and scrawny with bushy sideburns and a sharp nose. This one had his sleeves rolled up and tattoos covering her arms.

Scrawny was closer, and he stepped in with a growl and launched a clumsy punch at Abigail. She slipped past his arm and hit him forcibly in the side. He grunted and launched another attack, but she was already stepping back out of his reach.

The short one entered the fray, laughing like a lunatic as he tried to kick her. She could tell within seconds that he was better at fighting than his tall friend. She stayed out of reach, circling around to his side. He followed with a series of controlled punches, and the last one connected with her shoulder, knocking her back a painful step.

She rolled with the attack and scrambled back as he pursued her. She dodged one punch, deflected a second, and then launched a kick of her own back at him. She hit him in the stomach, but he barely seemed to notice.

Scrawny was using the opportunity to run to one of his downed friends who had been carrying a gun and was trying to extract it from the unconscious man's grip.

Abigail slipped back, realizing this fighter would be harder to bring down

176

than she had thought. She slipped her revolver loose and lined up a shot, first shooting the short guy in the knee. She followed with a kick to his face, knocking him unconscious as he staggered to the ground.

Scrawny had gotten the gun loose and was bringing it back up to line up a shot. His first bullet went wide as he pulled the trigger in panic, and then Abigail was on him. She rushed forward, swatted the gun out of his hand, and then punched him in the nose. It broke, blood pouring down his face, and she kicked him twice in the stomach.

He collapsed and rolled on the ground, groaning and clutching his broken cartilage. Abigail rubbed her shoulder and stretched it out from where the short guy had hit her. It hurt a lot.

She glanced around, making sure everyone was out of the fight. They were all either unconscious or had lost all interest in attacking her.

The doorway into the factory was clear in front of her. She readied her shotgun, took a few steadying breaths, and walked into the factory.

Chapter 16

Haatim pulled off to the side of the road about half a mile outside the city. He kept the car idling, divided by the raging emotions inside his heart and mind.

He hadn't seen any other people on the road, and it was quiet out here in the woods. Hard to believe that a mile behind him, an entire town was falling to anarchy and disrepair.

If he left Raven's Peak now, then he was abandoning Abigail to face this threat alone. He would be leaving her alone, and if she didn't make it out alive he would effectively be sentencing her to death. After everything she had done to rescue him and protect him up until now, he didn't think he could live with himself if she didn't survive.

Still, he wasn't sure what he could do to help. This wasn't his world, and he didn't know what she was facing. If he returned to Raven's Peak, he might be able to do nothing else except die along with her.

But, surviving and knowing that he might have been able to do something and chose not to would be worse.

He put the car back into gear and made a U-turn, driving back toward the city. He wasn't exactly sure where he would find Abigail, but he figured there was a decent way he could follow her.

Just follow the gunshots.

He drove back into town and turned east, heading down a road toward the central district. Abigail had been traveling in that direction when last he saw her, and he hoped he might come across her along the way.

He spotted something ahead and slowed the car to a crawl: as he got closer he realized two people were copulating in the center of the street. Their clothes were scattered all around them and they were laughing and moaning wildly.

Haatim hesitated in shock and then drove around them, running up on the curb to avoid their activities. He shook his head and let out a nervous chuckle. The pair barely seemed to notice his vehicle driving past them only a few meters away.

He kept going passing through the center of town and heading farther east. He was watching carefully for any sign that Abigail had been here. There was a body on the road, and he was fairly certain the guy was dead, but then he spotted a police officer farther up the way.

He climbed out of the car and checked the officer over, noticing a dart in the man's neck. He was heading the right way.

He kept going and drove past a man diving into an industrial trashcan in one of the side alleys. This guy was wearing a torn up business suit and rambling to himself as he tossed things out. The best word Haatim could think of to describe him was: ravenous.

Farther down the street a naked man ran across the road in front of his car, forcing him to slam on the brakes. This guy pounded his hands on the hood and made gyrating motions before squealing and running off. He disappeared into a house, shouting and laughing.

Haatim let out a sigh and kept moving. He hadn't seen any clues of where he might find Abigail yet, but he was coming up to the factory they had seen on the eastern side of the town. Then he would have to double back and check another street.

✳✳✳

Abigail crept slowly through sparsely furnished office space, careful not to make any noise. It was silent and dark, a long carpeted hallway that eventually emptied onto the factory floor. She'd tried the light switch, but the power was out. Only a handful of windows were letting in any outside sunlight.

It was around forty meters from the entrance to the factory itself, and she was walking past old and cramped offices. The furniture looked like it had been pulled from the last century. People—the group out front, she assumed—had been through here already and much of the equipment was broken. Papers and trash were scattered across the floor and computers were smashed by bats and clubs. She checked each room, determined not to pass by any threats.

Her footsteps were the only sound padding across the soft carpet. She listened, but there was no evidence that anyone else was in the office with her. She kept moving, breathing as softly as she could.

She held her shotgun at the ready; it was loaded with specialized shells packed with salt. It had a short-barrel and would spread the salt in a wide pattern. Demons moved quickly, but even a little bit of salt could slow them down.

She didn't want to use it on the kid if she didn't have to, but she doubted the demon was going to give up the body willingly. That, of course, required that the demon was still inside the kid. It might have moved on by now and found another host. If she underestimated Belphegor, she would get both herself and the host killed.

She wiped the sweat from her hands, breathing deeply and keeping herself calm. She was almost through the offices, only four meters from the cavernous factory floor beyond, when she heard a voice behind her.

"I wondered when I might meet you."

Abigail froze midstride. It was the voice of a young child. It came from one of the side rooms she had already cleared. She turned and saw a young boy, maybe ten or eleven, standing in the doorway of the office and studying her. He looked normal, if a little pale, with dark hair and bangs on his boyish face. His eyes, though, were dead and empty.

He hadn't been there a second ago, she was sure of it. Nor had she heard any footsteps on the carpet. With how quiet it was in the room she was certain she could have heard a pin drop on the carpet, let alone a boy's footsteps.

Yet, there he stood, watching her with an immutable expression. She forced herself to swallow and slowly swiveled around to face him. If he was at all concerned that she was carrying a shotgun, he didn't show it.

"Meet me?"

"Yes," the demon said. "I was hoping we might bump into each other. After all, I know Arthur so well now, even since he was brought to my master."

She felt a chill run across her spine. "What are you talking about?"

"I know your mentor *intimately*. I've been speaking with him rather often these last months, and suffice to say he has a great many things to say about you," the child said. "All good things, of course. He's quite fond of you. He'll be *so* thrilled to learn that we spoke."

"What are you doing to him?"

"You wouldn't even begin to imagine," the demon said. "After we broke him and turned him into our puppet."

"You aren't the demon that took him."

"No, I'm not, but *he* remembers you well. He speaks of the time he spent inside you in the Church and how delicious it was to dominate you. Perhaps you would like to feel that again? To have him slip inside of you like a soft glove."

"Shut up."

"He told me that you were a true fighter, but he broke you. That was before he took Arthur, of course. Now we have a new plaything."

Abigail felt her hands shake. "Don't speak of him…"

"Oh, are you sad to talk about Arthur? You should be. You're the one that sent him to hell."

Abigail didn't respond.

"You don't think so? I do. We had a nice long chat about it. Arthur didn't want to talk. Not at first. Funny how despair changes one's perspective, and by the end he couldn't stop himself from telling me everything. He told me you were the one who finally brought him in and locked him in that prison. He explained how you were the reason he butchered all of those people."

"He didn't…"

"Oh, he *certainly* butchered them," the demon argued. "Gloriously and without remorse. He thought he was doing the right thing."

"He thought they were infected."

"They *were* infected."

"But he didn't need to kill them. There was another way."

"Was there? Is that what the Council told you?"

Abigail didn't reply.

"A pity," the demon said. "And here, I thought you might be more than a simple lap dog."

Abigail started to raise her shotgun, but she felt a sudden compulsion to set it on the floor instead. She resisted, and her hands started shaking, but she couldn't regain complete control. The demon wasn't possessing her, it was just suggesting a course of action, but she could tell it was powerful

"Now, now, let's not get ahead of ourselves. This need not turn unpleasant. After my time with Arthur, I was hoping we might be able to end things amicably."

"Why are you here?" she asked.

"To finish the business my associate began so many months ago."

"And what business is that?"

"It isn't your concern," the demon said. "What *is* your concern is what I have to offer you."

"What you can offer me?"

The demon smiled.

"I can offer you your greatest desire," the demon said, "*if* you assist me."

"Assist you with what?" Abigail asked. "My greatest desire? How could you possibly know what I want?"

The demon ignored her. "This body is too weak to go into the tunnels where a certain knife was hidden long ago. However, older bodies would be too weak for me to use for an extended journey, so I'm at an impasse. I want you to retrieve the blade and bring it back to me."

"And why would I do that?"

"Because when you bring the knife here, I will return Arthur to you. Whole and alive."

✳✳✳

Haatim heard shouts from above and peered through the windshield, leaning forward in his seat. The sounds came from above on the roof of a nearby home.

He was almost through the residential street near the outskirts of the town. A man was standing on the roof of his two-story home. He was flapping his arms like they were wings and making bird sounds.

"Uh oh," Haatim said. He hit the brakes and put the car into park, and then jumped out. "Hey!"

"Hey!" the guy shouted down at him. "Watch this! I'm about to fly!"

"You can't fly," Haatim called up, cupping his hands over his mouth. "Humans can't fly!"

"I can," the guy said. "And I'll be rich and famous. The human birdman!"

"Trust me," Haatim said. "You are just going to hurt yourself."

"No, I'm not," the guy said. "Watch!"

Haatim watched the man jump off his roof, flailing and flapping his arms. He shouted and screamed in panic. He hit an awning about four meters down and then rolled off and thudded bodily into the bushes in front of his house.

Haatim sprinted over to check on the man. He was thrashing and groaning in the bushes, but he looked mostly unhurt. The bushes had cushioned his fall.

Haatim blew out a breath of air and rubbed a hand through his hair. "What the hell is going on?" he asked no one in particular. "This just keeps getting crazier and crazier."

He got back into the car and kept driving. Up ahead he saw a strip mall of shops and stores in front of the factory. They looked to have been broken into and looted like the other shops; one of them was on fire.

He pulled up in front of the factory, planning to double back on another street and make another pass through town. Along the way, he spotted a pile of bodies out front of the enormous factory and decided to check it out.

Several men were lying on the ground, some barely conscious and others completely out. A lone man knelt in the center of the group, praying with his hands folded in front of his chest. He was scrawny and it looked like his leg was broken.

Haatim walked over to the man, eyeing the men on the ground in case one of them decided to get up. There were weapons lying everywhere, and he doubted these people were passive or just hoping they could fly in their insanity.

He spotted a small dart in the neck of a few of the unconscious men. Abigail's hand crossbow lying on the ground nearby, empty.

"Guess I found her," he muttered.

The man on his knees was rocking back and forth, hands folded in front of himself, and chanting. He had blood running down the side of his head; he barely seemed to notice the pain. He just kept shifting his body and chanting, eyes open and staring up at the sky.

"Are you OK?" Haatim asked.

The guy turned to him, but his eyes didn't seem to focus on anything. "The end is coming! The end of days is here! Rejoice, brother, the end is here!"

He turned back to the sky and kept chanting before Haatim could reply. The door to the factory was open, and it was pitch black inside. If Abigail was here, he knew, she would be in there.

183

He eyed several weapons lying on the ground, bats and clubs and even a few guns, be he knew they wouldn't help him. He didn't know how to use any of them effectively, and they would do more harm than good.

He steadied himself and then walked into the darkness.

✳✳✳

I will return Arthur to you. Whole and alive.

The words hit Abigail like a ton of bricks. The demon was offering to bring her greatest friend back, the sole objective she had pursued during the last several months. It had consumed her ever since that fateful day in the Church when the demon had taken her. Everything she had done was dedicated to finding her mentor: her father.

And this demon could give that to her.

Deals were dangerous things for demons. They served as contracts for them and weren't entered into lightly. Which meant that if this demon was promising her Arthur in a deal, then it had faith it could deliver its side of the agreement.

Which made her wonder, what must the knife be worth to the demon if it was willing to pay such a price?

Abigail stood there for a long while, piecing through the possibilities. She was trying to come to terms with the emotions raging inside of her. This was everything she wanted, and the possibility of seeing Arthur again had never been this close. In fact, it was more than she had ever expected, because she'd never really thought she could bring him back alive.

Yet, there was another truth that she couldn't ignore: if she went through with what the demon was offering, then she would be sacrificing everything Arthur stood for while he was alive. She would be willfully disregarding everything he had taught her. She might be able bring him back like this, but the cost would be too great.

She would find another way.

"Arthur is gone," she muttered, more to herself than the demon. "And I *will* bring him back. But, if I do this for you, then it won't matter if I do, because his ideals truly will be gone forever."

The gun started to shake in her hand as she pushed the demon out of her mind. The demon smiled again, but this time it was filled with rage.

"Like father, like daughter."

Abigail felt the grip on her mind disappear, but by the time she'd raised the shotgun the demon child was already moving. The gun roared, and the stock kicked painfully into her stomach. Salt pounded into the wall behind the demon in a wide pattern, but none of them hit the moving boy.

184

The demon dropped low and scrambled to the side, hissing at her. She heard a loud banging sound from her left and ducked just in time to avoid being smashed by a flying cabinet. It soared through the air and blasted through the wall, sending up a cloud of dust.

She stepped forward, pumped the shotgun, and fired another round. This one hit the floor behind the demon as it disappeared around the corner. A table flew out at her, and she barely managed to side-step it.

She pursued the demon and saw it flee out of the offices and into the open space of the factory floor. She pumped another shell into the chamber and stepped into the enormous vaulted chamber behind it.

The vaulted chamber was filled with machinery, conveyer belts, and shipping crates. All of it was off and silent at the moment. Behemoth tables were covered in tools and safety equipment, much of it old and covered in rust.

She heard a scuffing sound from farther in and walked carefully through the open area. There was more ambient light in here than the previous offices, but not enough that she could see comfortably.

The sheer size and emptiness of the chamber had an eerie effect on her. It should have been filled with hundreds of people working and laughing and the sound of equipment humming and grinding, but it all looked dead in the darkness.

She felt her blood pumping and focused on breathing and listening. It was silent in the chamber. Suddenly she heard the rushing sound of air and turned just in time to spot an enormous welding table come flying toward her.

She dove and scrambled to the side, barely getting out of the way before it crashed next to her. It was heavy enough to shake the ground. She sat with her back to an old wooden shelf, panting and staring at the several ton slab of metal that had missed her by only inches.

"You should have agreed to help me," the child said from somewhere off to her left.

She turned but didn't see anything except a line of four-meter tall metal shelves. She climbed to her feet and crept in that direction, shotgun ready. She moved to the corner and peeked around.

Nothing. The area was empty.

The factory floor was like a maze, offering endless hiding places for the demon to stay out of her sight. Metal walkways ran overhead, eight meters off the ground and overlooking the entire floor space. She moved cautiously toward a grated staircase, hoping to find a better vantage where she could spot the demon.

"We could have become fast friends," the demon said, his voice behind her now. "The things I could do for you are incredible."

A huge shelving unit came flying through the air, but this time she was ready. She stepped out of the way, feeling the ground shake as it landed, and kept moving. The voice echoed in the chamber, so she couldn't tell exactly where the demon was hiding.

She reached the staircase and climbed up, moving carefully so as not to make much noise. She reached the landing and moved along the grating, trying to spot the boy. After about a minute, she did:

He was about fifteen meters away on the ground floor, walking calmly between the aisles with his hands folded behind his back. A cross-walkway ran over his head, and he didn't seem to be paying much attention.

Abigail crept along the landing, moving gingerly and careful not to scuff her shoes. Beads of sweat dotted her forehead, and she fought the urge to brush them away.

"But now I'm going to kill you, and it feels like such a waste," the boy said. "We could have achieved much together, Abigail."

She was about ten meters away now, still too far for an effective shot. She took another ginger step forward, and the metal grate made a soft echoing sound. Barely noticeable under normal circumstances, but with how quiet the factory was she might as well have banged her gun against the railing.

The demon turned and looked straight at her, a grin on its face.

"There you are!"

She heard a shuddering sound as a table flew across the chamber toward her walkway. She angled her gun and fired off a desperate shot, spraying pellets of salt down at the demon. Several landed on skin, sizzling where they touched, but the demon barely seemed to notice.

She dodged forward as the table closed in. It smashed heavily against the railing, and the walkway shuddered under the pressure. It didn't give in, but it did rock on its foundation. Abigail was thrown to her feet and almost fell as it swayed and stabilized.

The boy started laughing, and she heard more rustling noises as the demon called upon its inner nature to telekinetically grab more items to throw at her. Behind it she saw dozens of tables with old tools and machinery spread upon it: saw blades, nails as long as spikes, and countless hammers, wrenches, and miscellaneous tools. They were shaking and vibrating on the table.

"Crap," she muttered.

The demon raised its hand like a conductor standing in front of his orchestra.

"Now, Abigail, it is time for you to die."

Abigail dove forward just as the tools started flying off the tables. She ran along the railing, hunched low and trying to keep as much of the grated floor between her and the objects as she could.

She heard metal thudding into the railing and floor around her, bouncing in every direction and flying away.

She was too exposed on the railing and needed to get back to the ground. She ducked low, scrambled to the edge, and leaped off the walkway. She landed with a thud on top of a metal shelf and dove immediately the three meters to the ground, tucking into a roll.

The demon laughed as the hail of tools and small objects smashed into everything. It was a violent cacophony, hurting her ears. Occasionally something would ricochet off other objects and collide with her, knocking her off balance, but she was able to hide behind modest cover and avoid the brunt of the attack.

She kept moving, staying low behind the shelving and machinery. A sudden burst of heat on her left side right above her hip told her she'd been hit, but she forced herself to keep moving until she could find some better cover.

The assault continued, larger objects now as the demon ran out of small tools. An endless barrage, it seemed, and the demon kept laughing through it all. A table flew through the air, narrowly missing her, and then she was able to duck out of sight and catch her breath.

She checked her side and saw a screw sticking out if it. Maybe four inches long, it had pierced through her flesh and gone almost an inch into her abdomen.

The barrage died down, leaving the area in total silence. Everything was wrecked around her with broken equipment scatted haphazardly. The railing was hanging sideways above her, teetering and rocking, and part of it had broken off and collapsed to the ground.

Abigail folded the collar of her shirt into a bunch and stuck it between her teeth. She bit down then yanked the screw out. It hurt where the serrated edges caught her flesh, and she couldn't contain a groan. She dropped the screw onto the floor and checked the wound. It was seeping blood, but hadn't done much damage.

"Come out, come out, wherever you are!" she heard the boy call, voice high-pitched and squeaky. "You can't hide forever!"

The barrage came again, and Abigail gritted her teeth and prayed.

Haatim heard an enormous din as he reached the factory floor. Everything was wrecked, and things were flying through the air and crashing into tables and equipment. He couldn't see much in the cavernous chamber, but he could hear a young boy laughing.

He saw a hail of items flying through the air, bouncing and thudding as they went.

He gulped.

Heavy thing, any one of which could rip through his body and end his life in only seconds. And there were hundreds of them, everything from hammers to saws to a hailstorm of nails that might as well have been bullets. They were being aimed at something on the other side of the chamber from Haatim, and he

187

guessed that was where Abigail was hiding.

This is too much, he realized, standing in the doorway and watching the attack in awe. *This is insanity.*

Why did he think he could help in a situation like this? This was sheer brutality on a scale he'd never even dreamed of. What could he possibly do to help Abigail survive something like this?

He was terrified just watching it; terrified that the demon would notice him hiding near the entrance of the factory and decide to kill him next.

It isn't too late to leave, he thought. He still had time to slip out before the attack came. He could get out of the city, and he still had the car. There was no way Abigail would be able to deal with something like this, even with his help, and there was no sense in just staying here to die.

But there was another voice in Haatim's mind telling him that he shouldn't back down. He should have faith and press on.

Haatim hesitated in the doorway, struggling between the two conflicting ideas. How could he have faith after his sister had died so horribly? He had been so angry when his sister died, blaming God for her death.

He was angry because God hadn't done anything to save her. Yet, it was his father who refused to seek clinical trials and treatments for her, putting her life in God's hands.

Haatim blamed himself. He felt like it was his fault because he hadn't pushed back. He hadn't fought against his father's decision and searched out treatments that might have saved her life.

He hadn't been angry with God, he realized. He'd been angry with himself.

And he knew he couldn't live with himself if he allowed Abigail to die here as well. The demon might kill him, but inaction definitely would. Haatim didn't have a lot of faith in himself, but he did have faith that he was doing the right thing.

He forced his hands to stop shaking and then walked onto the factory floor. Somehow, he knew everything would be OK.

✳✳✳

Abigail crawled, staying low to the ground alongside the machinery. She still had her shotgun and had two shells left.

She was leaving a trail of blood behind her on the floor, but she didn't have time to really close the wound just yet.

"Where *are* you?" the demon said in a singsong voice, and then laughed. "I don't have all day!"

Abigail popped up behind a box and raised her shotgun. The boy was about three meters in front of her, facing the opposite direction.

188

She squeezed the trigger just as the demon turned to face her. It side-stepped avoiding the brunt of her shot, but couldn't avoid the spread.

It was a grazing hit, most of salt going wide of her target, but enough hit him in the shoulder to throw him back several steps. It seared where it touched and should have weakened the demon inside, but if it had any effect she didn't notice it.

"There you are!"

Abigail scrambled as the demon threw more tools and metal equipment at her. She ducked and dove forward, narrowly avoiding a shipping crate hurtling toward her head.

She pumped her last shell into the chamber, ducked around the corner, and prepared to fire.

The demon was gone.

She spun, realizing her mistake, but it was too late. The demon was already behind her, eyes glowing red. It extended a hand at her, grasping her in its telekinetic grip. She felt her body lifted into the air, the gun falling limp from her grasp. She fought back mentally, struggling to free herself from its hold, but it was like punching a brick wall.

"Arthur was a fool, and you are no better," the demon said. The squeaky tenor of the boy was still there, but there was the undercurrent of a guttural voice there as well. "I will bring my master back, and he will ravish this world."

"No…" Abigail muttered. "You…"

She could barely breathe; the pressure was so great. She felt like something was wrapped around her chest and tightening, trying to crush her like an empty can.

"Witness my victory," the boy proclaimed. She felt her body lowered to the ground, knees folded into a kneeling position. "All will bow before me."

"You are a coward," another voice interrupted from behind the demon. The boy froze, hand still hovering in the air, and spun slowly to see who had spoken:

Abigail saw Haatim step out from behind a pile of broken machinery thirty meters away.

"No…" Abigail groaned. She tried to tell Haatim to run away, but she couldn't draw in enough air.

"You would dare speak to me? You are nothing but an insignificant insect!"

"You hide within that body because you are pathetic and malformed," Haatim said. "You are unwilling to show your true form to us. Isn't that so, Belphegor?"

"I am neither weak nor afraid, mortal."

"And yet here you are, cowering within the body of a child. You warp the minds of your followers because you know that if they knew the truth of what you really were, a sad and pathetic monster, they would never believe anything

189

you say."

"Silence!" the demon roared.

"It is you who should be silent," Haatim said, striding confidently toward the demon. "This is not your world. You spread anger and strife and do not belong. It is time you went home."

Abigail heard a rattling as the demon telepathically threw a large metal crate through the air. Haatim didn't even flinch as it approached, and it missed him by only inches.

"You cannot harm me," Haatim said. "For you are nothing against the greater design."

The demon threw more objects at Haatim. He strode forward, unblinking as they narrowly missed him. He began singing in Hindi, his voice loud and strong. Abigail didn't recognize the words, but she did recognize the conviction in Haatim's eyes.

The demon roared in anger and began throwing things even faster. Shipping cartons and tables blasted across the room, smashing into the walls and floor in a din. Haatim walked through it all, stepping on broken equipment and moving ever closer to the demon.

He stopped singing and began chanting. Abigail recognized his words as prayers, having heard them spoken by Arthur countless times while growing up. He'd taught her rudimentary Latin, but it had never been something she focused on. More objects were flying through the air, but Haatim stepped past them unfazed.

Haatim switched to Hebrew and continued chanting. Abigail felt the demon's control wavering as it released its grip on her to intensify its attack on Haatim. She could feel its frustration. It was focusing completely on the new threat, disoriented and confused by its inability to hit him with anything.

It threw a table saw through the air. Haatim took a gentle step to the side and it flew past, and the demon screamed in rage and frustration.

"Die!"

"You cannot harm me," Haatim said. He was only four meters from Belphegor now, stopping calmly and staring at the boy. "You have no power here. You must leave."

Abigail felt the demon release its hold completely, focusing all of its energy on Haatim. She climbed shakily to her feet, holding her side to pinch back the blood that was flowing out, and moved as quietly as she could toward the demon.

It was surrounded by a cloud of objects flying in all directions as it launched them at Haatim. Items soared over his shoulders and around his body, brushing against his clothes yet none actually collided with his body.

Abigail picked up a wrench off the ground as she went, creeping up behind the demon.

"Why won't you die?" the demon screamed at Haatim.

190

Abigail swung the wrench down like a club hitting the demon in the shoulder and sending it staggering to the ground. The whirlwind of objects ceased and items collapsed to the ground, breaking and scattering across the floor.

Haatim stepped closer just as the demon was struggling to regain its feet. He placed a hand on the boy's forehead and starting chanting in Latin. It was a banishment ritual, and his words were strong and full of power as they poured out of his mouth.

The demon cursed and spit at him, but was unable to pull away.

"This child is mine!"

"It is not," Haatim said. "By the grace of God, I order you to vacate this child's body."

"No!"

"By the grace of Allah I order you to leave. By the love of Krishna, I order you to be gone from this realm! Return from whence you came!"

"Never!"

"I order you out, vile creature! Out!"

Haatim screamed the last word, and it hung in the air, echoing in the cavernous chamber back at them. The demon receded with a guttural screech, leaving behind only the sounds of their breathing and the moaning of the child on the floor. The room was filled with a vast emptiness, and Abigail knew that the demon was gone.

Haatim had banished it.

Abigail knelt and checked the child's wounds. He had a torn cheek and some minor burns from the salt pellets and busted shoulder but he was otherwise OK. As long as they got help here quickly he would make a full recovery. Given the circumstances, that was a blessing she hadn't really expected.

She looked at Haatim, standing there with his hand on the child's forehead and panting. He was exhausted and drained, barely able to keep his feet. He staggered to the side and sat down, pale and sickly.

"What the hell was that?" she asked.

Chapter 17

"I don't know," he answered. "I just…when I was walking toward the demon, something told me it wouldn't hurt me."

"A guess?"

"A feeling," he said, shaking his head. "I can't explain it."

"Are you all right?" she asked.

He nodded. "I just need a minute. I'm exhausted."

He looked around at the room as though for the first time. He had a look of shock on his face, and Abigail could relate: the entire chamber had been demolished with broken equipment, conveyer belts, tools, and other miscellaneous objects spread all around. It looked like a tornado had ripped through and disappeared.

Abigail's side was agony, but her body was still pumping adrenaline, so she barely felt the pain.

"I'm not surprised that you're so tired," she said. "Doing things like that really take a toll."

"Like what?" he asked.

She hesitated. "Channeling."

"Channeling what?"

"We can talk about it later. I need to get in touch with Frieda and let her know Belphegor has been dealt with. They need to call off the strike."

"All right," Haatim said, yawning. "I'll be right here."

Abigail headed outside and pulled out the satellite phone. She stepped out into the cool air and dialed Frieda's number. Frieda picked up almost immediately.

"Are you OK?"

"I'm fine," Abigail said. "It's done. The demon is gone."

"You're sure?"

"Positive."

"All right," Frieda said. Abigail heard her speak with another person, telling them to call off the strike, and then Frieda was back. "We will send a cleanup crew and create a story to explain what happened."

"That'll be an interesting one."

"Are you injured?"

"I'm fine," Abigail said. "Couple of scrapes and bumps but nothing major."

"What about Haatim? Did he get out of the city?"

"Something like that," she said. "I'll tell you all about it when you get here."

"Is he safe?"

"He's safe."

"Good," Frieda said. "His father is furious with both of us."

"I assumed he would be," Abigail said. "But there's nothing we can do about it now. There's something I need to tell you. Something I heard about Haatim's father, and you aren't going to like it."

"What is it?"

"Not here. In person."

"OK. Don't leave the city, Abigail. We'll be there in a few hours."

"I need to check on something, but it's in the area so we won't have to go far. It's out near the Church where Arthur was taken."

"Why?"

"Belphegor was here looking for something, just like the demon that took Arthur. I need to find out what it is and why they were looking for it. I don't know, Frieda, but this feels important."

"All right," Frieda said.

"There's something else," she said. "When I spoke to the demon, it told me that they had Arthur."

"Who?"

"I don't know. Belphegor was working with the demon that took Arthur to hell."

"It might have been bluffing."

"I don't think so," Abigail said. "It was…convincing. Belphegor knew who I was and knew things…"

Frieda was silent. "I'll be there soon, Abi. Be careful, and keep an eye on Haatim until we get there."

"Will do."

She hung up the phone. She grabbed some supplies and patched up her side, and then went to find Haatim. He had a little more color in his cheeks but still looked thoroughly exhausted.

"You look like hell," she said.

"Thanks," he replied, smiling wryly. They headed for the exit, walking back through the dark office space toward the town beyond.

"I should be thanking you," she said. "You saved my life."

"Just returning the favor," he replied with a shrug. "It's funny, actually; I learned all of those prayers in my years of studies. Words in many languages for different religions. But, until today, that's all they were to me: just words."

"Now they are something else," she said. "Something to battle against evil."

He nodded. "I thought I knew what evil was, but I was wrong."

"Then what is it?" she asked.

"Ambivalence. Standing by and watching people suffer and die when you know you can help them. I realized today that I don't want to be someone that just sits by and does nothing. I don't think I could have let those people die without trying."

Abigail smiled. "I think Arthur will like you."

A moment passed. Haatim looked at the unconscious bodies of the men on the street. "What happens to them now?"

"The Council will send a cleanup squad. Patch everyone up and concoct a story about what happened."

"Seems like a pretty big thing to cover up."

"We've dealt with worse," Abigail said. "Apart from the people who live here, no one will ever believe anything strange happened. Over time even the people who actually experienced these events in Raven's Peak will start to wonder if their memory isn't just playing tricks on them."

"OK," Haatim said. "So what do we do?"

"We?" she asked. "Your father was quite angry with me when he found out you were here at all. I have been summoned before the Council, so I'll be arrested and held as soon as they arrive."

"I'll talk to my father," Haatim said. "Make sure he understands it wasn't your fault."

"I don't think he will care."

"I'll make him care."

Abigail shrugged. "Thanks. Any help I can get would be much appreciated at this point."

"No problem. So, now we just wait for them to get here?"

"Actually, I have one other thing to look into before I'm arrested."

"Oh?"

"You're welcome to come with me, but you don't have to if you don't want to," she said.

He let out a sigh and smiled at her. "So where are we headed to now?"

"The old Raven's Peak. The one we found up in the woods."

"The mining town? Why? What are we going to do there?"

"I'll tell you as soon as I know."

Chapter 18

Abigail searched the area surrounding the old mining town, and it didn't take her long to find what she was looking for: a hidden entrance at the top of a waterfall leading underground. It was covered by a number of huge stones, and it took them a good thirty minutes to clear the area.

Once they did, it revealed an ancient trapdoor built into the ground, covered in runes.

"What's this?" Haatim asked.

"It's what the demon was looking for," Abigail said.

"It wasn't that hard to find," Haatim replied.

"No, but that isn't the point."

"Wonder what's inside," Haatim said, reaching for the stone trapdoor. "It feels like there's something..."

Abigail caught his hand and pulled him back. She felt a tingle as her hand got close to the door, almost like electricity.

"Don't touch," she said. "Do you see these runes? They are old, at least a few hundred years, and loaded with energy."

"What kind of energy?"

"The kind that kills you," she said. "And the kind that destroys demons and sends them back to hell. That's why the demon wanted my help because it can't get past here."

"You can get past this?"

"No," she said. "Not precisely. I don't actually know many people who can get past runes like this, but these sorts of places always have a backdoor. There is definitely another way inside, we just have to find it."

"Oh," he said. "So what do we do now?"

She gave him a long look. "Ever been spelunking?"

Spelunking, it turned out, was the most horrible experience of Haatim's life.

He'd never really thought of himself as claustrophobic, but he'd never really understood what claustrophobia was before, either. He thought it only applied to people who didn't enjoy confinement in small rooms: however, being trapped deep underground in tunnels and holes beneath the earth was terrifying.

There was no light except for his and Abigail's flashlights, and even that was only a pinprick he could shine forward. The only sounds came from them scratching their way through the tight tunnels and his heavy breathing from the exertion.

Abigail was in front of him, first walking while they traveled down the miner's tunnels and eventually crawling. After about an hour they reached a split where the passage forked to the left and right. One pass looked manmade and was larger and lined with tracks for the carts, and the other looked like a wall had crumbled and led into tighter tunnels that looked ancient and rough.

"This must be where it's hidden," she said. She examined the stones. "Looks like it was broken open sometime in the past. Hard to say when."

"Where does it go?"

"No clue," she said. "But if the artifact is down here, this is where we're going to find it."

"Artifact?"

Abigail ignored him and kept moving. She slipped into the tight hold and disappeared. Haatim let out a sigh and followed. It led into a steep decline and was moist with water and mud. He half slid and half crawled down after Abigail, struggling to slip through the small tunnel.

"Shouldn't we have hats on?"

"Only if you're concerned with falling rocks."

Haatim frowned. "We aren't?"

"The likelihood of a falling rock killing us is way less than a cave in. That would cut us off and starve us long before a rock would kill us."

Haatim hesitated. "That doesn't make me feel any better."

Abigail didn't reply. He kept sliding after her, grunting from the exertion and feeling his body muscles burning from the strain. There were thousands of pounds of rock resting casually above his head, and he tried really hard not to think about that.

They reached a slightly larger room after about twenty minutes of crawling and Haatim could hear the rushing sound of water. It was difficult to tell exactly where it was coming from.

"What's that?"

"Underground river," Abigail explained. She gestured her hand toward a hole off to the right side of the little chamber. "I think that will get us down to it."

"Down to it?" he said. "You mean *into* the water?"

"Yeah," she said. "It's our only way forward."

"Then maybe we should turn back," Haatim said. "There's no telling where that would take us."

"It will take us farther into the caves. If it's a dead end, we'll backtrack and find another way farther down." She crawled forward to the hole and slipped into the water. "Come on."

"Are you sure about this?" he said.

"You can swim, right?"

"Yeah," he said. "Not great or anything, but yeah I can swim."

She untied a length of rope she'd wrapped around her waist and handed Haatim one end of it. "Hold onto this and don't get too far behind."

"Wait," he said, slipping into the water behind her. It was freezing cold, and he let out a shuddering breath. "How far will we have to swim?"

"I don't know," she said.

"How do you know it isn't too far?"

"I don't," she replied.

"Then what am I supposed to do?"

She pursed her lips. "Take a *really* deep breath."

Then she sucked in air and dove under the water. Haatim watched her disappear and tried to decide if he should follow her. He watched the length of rope slipping under and considered just letting it go.

But, he wasn't sure he could make it back out of the caves if he didn't follow her. They had taken a number of forks and changed course a few times and he knew there was a decent chance he would get lost if he took off on his own.

No, his best option was to follow Abigail…and maybe drown in the process.

He took a deep breath as the rope dwindled and dove under the icy water. The underground river was small and cramped and his flashlight did nothing to show him the way ahead. The water was too muddy.

He felt along the wall with his left hand and held the rope in his other. He couldn't feel a bottom to the river as he swam, and he imagined it going down hundreds of meters below his feet.

After a few seconds he felt his lungs burning, but when he reached up above his head he felt only smooth rock. There were no pockets where he might suck in a quick breath of air. *Stay calm*, he told himself. *It can't be much farther.*

He kept swimming, kicking his legs and pushing himself along the rocks. He felt the rope tension increase as Abigail reached the end of the rope ahead of him. He held on tight, refusing to let go and loose the one thing connecting him to her.

Seconds dragged by and he started to grow weaker as the cold and lack of oxygen shut his body down. He'd never been much for swimming and didn't have the greatest lung capacity. His head started to pound, and he wanted nothing more than to open his mouth and gasp for air.

His entire body started to burn, and he knew he needed air. But the rock above him remained just as smooth. He couldn't swim much now and mostly let the rope pull him through the trench. His vision narrowed to slits, and he couldn't see anything in front of him, and all he could do was fight down the urge to panic.

I'm going to die alone down here, he realized. Down in a cave, and I'll be stuck here forever. No one will ever know what happened to me.

He scrambled on, feeling his cheeks puff out and flailing with his arms. He could tell he was panicking, and all he wanted was a breath of air. He didn't want to die in this cave, stuck hundreds of meters below the surface of the world.

Come on, come on, come on…

He felt a hand roughly grab his shirt and drag him forward. His head burst above the water, and on instinct he sucked in a huge breath of air. A long moment passed where he just laid there, clutching the rock and breathing.

"See? That wasn't so bad," Abigail said, sitting on the rock beside him. She looked relaxed and calm, just waiting for him to recover. 'Told you we could make it."

Haatim tried to think of something clever to say in response, but his mind wouldn't work. The headache faded but didn't dissipate completely, and his body still felt weak and cold.

"Yeah," he offered finally.

"You good?"

"I'm fine," he said, pulling himself up on the rock edge next to her. He was soaked and his clothes felt heavy. She gathered up the rope and tied it around her waist once more.

"All right," she said. "Let's keep moving."

She slipped down another passageway and Haatim followed. He had to crawl on his hands and knees again, but it was much more difficult now. He couldn't remember any other time in his life he'd been this exhausted. All he wanted to do was lie down and take a long nap.

They paused for a breather about fifteen minutes later. Abigail seemed to be perfectly fine as she crawled through the tunnels, so he knew the break was for him. He must look pathetic, exhausted, and weary. He decided if he ever had the chance to go spelunking commercially, he would decline.

"I can still hear water," he said.

"It's flowing underneath and around us," she replied. "But the air doesn't taste as stale anymore, so I think there's an exit somewhere up ahead. Unless I missed my guess, we aren't far away from the waterfall we found."

They kept moving. Haatim felt a black tarry mixture on his hands, and the rocks were slick and difficult to maintain balance on. Abigail's clothes were covered in the gunk as well, which was at least a little reassuring.

"Remind me to stay behind next time you suggest I go somewhere with you."

"I gave you the option. Plus, Frieda didn't want me to let you out of my sight."

"I don't think this is what she had in mind."

Abigail shrugged. "Probably not. But, hey, it's a new experience, right?"

Haatim only grunted in response.

The sound of rushing water intensified and seemed to envelop them as they crawled until it sounded like they were walking in the middle of a giant river. Haatim tried to shout a question up at Abigail, but she couldn't hear him.

Finally, they broke out of the passageway into a taller cavern. It was maybe eight meters in diameter with a four-foot-high ceiling. Haatim still had to slouch over, but it was infinitely better than crawling.

There was also some ambient light, and as they moved forward he saw that it was coming from the other side of a wall of water.

"What's that?" he asked.

"The waterfall," she said, reaching out and running her hand through it. "Told you we were close."

He looked underneath where her hand parted the water and saw trees and sky beyond. It was the most beautiful thing Haatim had ever seen and he thought he might cry.

"Here, hold me," she said, leaning forward toward the wall of water. Haatim wrapped his arms around her hips as he leaned out, sticking her head through the sheet.

She came back in a second later, soaked hair plastered to her face. She brushed the strands away.

"What did you see?"

"Check for yourself," she offered.

Haatim leaned forward toward the water. He felt Abigail's hands on his pants, keeping a grip on him, and he stuck his head through.

He found himself looking down a steep cliff and felt water flowing around his head. It was crashing into a deep pool about thirty meters down.

He pulled back in and shook the water off his face. "Long way down."

"Definitely," she said. She started walking to other direction, hunched over. "Too far to jump."

Haatim turned to look at her. "Jump?"

"Yeah," she said. "Would beat having crawling all the way back out, you know?"

"True, I suppose," he said. He hadn't really thought about crawling back out, and the idea made him even more exhausted. "Still, jumping sounds a little insane."

"Ill-advised," she agreed with a shrug. "Though 'insane' might be a bit exaggerated."

She started walking along the walls, scanning them over and feeling the rock with her fingers. She stuck her flashlight between her teeth.

"What are we looking for?"

"I don't know where else we can go," she said. The words sounded funny spoken around the flashlight. "And this cavern is huge. We need to find a passage."

"What if there isn't one."

"There has to be," Abigail said. "This is what the demon was after. If it isn't here, then we're going to have to backtrack and try one of the other passages we skipped."

"OK," Haatim said. He hoped it was here, having no desire to do any more backtracking.

He went to the other side of the room and began scanning those walls, searching for any holes or crevices that might be big enough to slide into.

He found something strange after a few minutes of searching, a hole, but it was only as big as his fist. However, when he touched it, he felt the wall crumbling beneath his fingertips.

"I think I found something," he shouted across the room.

"What is it?"

"I don't know,'" he said. He heard Abigail start moving across the room toward him. He kept pulling out chunks of the wall and tossing it aside. It felt like a disgusting sludge. "I don't know what this is."

"No idea," she said. "But it smells terrible."

"Do you think there is methane gas in here?"

"We wouldn't be able to smell methane," she said.

"True."

"And I don't have a chemical meter to measure the air, so I have no way of knowing."

"Methane is flammable, right?"

"And explosive. That's the only reason we're using flashlights instead of lighters," she said, grinning sarcastically at him.

"OK, OK," Haatim replied with a chuckle.

"Methane won't be a problem for us unless it gets to at least ten percent of the air around us. Then it becomes firedamp and can explode. As long as there's nothing to light it, though, we should be safe."

"All right," Haatim said. He kept scraping at the stuff on the wall, dragging it out of the way, and revealed a small passageway leading farther into the earth.

Abigail knelt down and shone her flashlight into the hole. "Looks like a tight fit."

"Want me to wait here?"

"Up to you but…" She trailed off, peering into the hole. She ducked down farther, trying to get a better view.

"What?" Haatim asked. "What is it?"

"What is *that?*" she asked, turning her head sideways and shifting the flashlight.

"What is what?" Haatim asked, kneeling down next to her. He squinted, trying to make out a shape that was about seven meters ahead of them. He felt a breeze from up ahead as air flowed past him. "Those look like shoes."

"And legs," Abigail added. "It looks like there's someone—"

Haatim heard a distinct scratching sound from farther down the tunnel. It was hard to figure out exactly what it was, but he knew one thing it reminded him of:

Lighting a match.

He saw a spark from up ahead as the match was dropped to the ground near the feet of the person. Air was flowing down the tunnel in their direction, he knew, which meant flames would be as well. Without thinking, he grabbed Abigail's shoulder and jerked her back toward the waterfall.

"Come on!" he shouted, tugging and scrambling across the wet stones. She slipped to her knees but he picked her up and kept moving.

He glanced over his shoulder and saw the roar of the fire as it exploded out of the tunnel. It filled the entire room behind them. In only a second it was already catching up, and he could feel the heat smoldering around his body.

And then he dragged Abigail through the waterfall and into the empty air beyond. He felt his stomach drop with the sensation and heard an explosion of steam as fire burst through the wall of water above them.

He felt as though he was suspended in air, watching water droplets scatter in the air around them. He heard the huge sound of the waterfall filling his ears and overwhelming his senses and closed his eyes. They fell sideways, and Haatim attempted to align his body for the best possible position to hit the water below.

And then he slammed into the water and everything went black.

Haatim awoke sharply, his entire body crying out in pain. He was coughing and sputtering and felt delirious with exhaustion and weakness. He was lying on a bed of rocks and sand along the edge of the water, maybe thirty meters downstream from the waterfall.

He had no idea how much time had passed, but it was late in the afternoon now so at least an hour or so. He looked around but couldn't see his companion anywhere nearby.

"Abigail?" he said, climbing to his feet. He wobbled and felt stabbing pain in his side where he'd smashed into the water.

No reply.

"Abigail, are you out here?"

He couldn't see her or hear anything moving nearby. Just silent trees and the waterfall nearby. He wondered if maybe she'd been washed farther downstream, and he hoped she was OK. He started moving that direction.

He heard something behind him and glanced back just in time to see a form come diving out of the waterfall near the top edge. Abigail flew down in a graceful dive, splitting the water smoothly. She swam up near him on the beach and dragged herself ashore.

Haatim could tell that she was exhausted. "I went back to the other entrance," she explained. "At the top with the runes."

"Did you find anything?"

"The runes were destroyed. Someone had smashed through them, but I have no idea how. I found where the knife that Belphegor was looking for was being kept, but it's gone. Whoever just tried to kill us took it with them."

"What is the knife for?"

"I don't know," Abigail said. "But a lot of people are after it, so it can't be good."

"What do we do now?"

"Now," she said. "We go talk to the Council."

Epilogue

The trip back to Raven's Peak didn't take very long. The walk back to their borrowed car was the worst of it, and Haatim wondered if his legs might give out during the hike. He actually fell asleep on the drive back to the city, and Abigail had to wake him up when they were there.

By the time they got back there were dozens of rescue helicopters and hundreds of people filling the streets. Most of them looked like they were from out of town and part of various relief efforts teams after a natural disaster.

"What's going on?"

"This is what the Council does," Abigail explained. "Containment, isolation, and eventually story-building and propaganda. They'll spend millions of dollars on false articles and police reports to back up their story of what happened."

"That's insane."

They reached a blockade just inside of town, and two men carrying Assault Rifles came to their windows. Abigail rolled down her window as they approached. "State your name and business."

"Abigail Dressler," she said. "My business is my own."

The man recognized her name. "We've been looking for you. You'll need to report to the tents."

"Is Frieda here?"

"She is," the man replied, gesturing his gun toward the center of town where a hastily constructed tent stood. "And I'd suggest you head there right now. She isn't very happy with you."

"She never is," Abigail said, rolling up her window and driving in toward the tents.

Haatim saw dozens of people inside and heard a general din of conversation. Some people were treating injuries and others directing the unloading and distribution of supplies. Abigail parked the car nearby and rubbed her temples. Haatim could tell that she was exhausted, and she still looked a little scared; though, of what, he couldn't guess.

"Is my father going to be here?" Haatim asked.

"It is possible, but not likely," Abigail replied. "Not for something like this. The Council has strict rules about the gathering of its members. They never put more than a few in one location."

Haatim climbed out of the car. "Which one is Frieda?"

Abigail smiled wryly at him. "Trust me, you'll know when you see her."

They walked into the tent. Haatim saw a well-dressed woman with a white skirt and blouse barking orders. She had high heels and a mole on her cheek, and despite it all she looked incredibly pristine amid the chaos.

"Ah," he said. "I see."

As soon as Frieda noticed Abigail she came striding over. "Where have you been?"

"Following another lead," Abigail said. "Took a little longer than I'd hoped. What's the story you're planning to roll out?"

"Militants," Frieda replied.

"Militants?"

"It was short notice," Frieda said. "There is a radicalized group of militants in the area, and we are utilizing them. As far as anyone will know, there was a chemical released into the air, and one of the side-effects that will be leaked is hallucinations. Four men are being charged with terrorist activities."

"It's going to generate a lot of press."

"Yes, it will," Frieda said. "We're intending to oversaturate the market."

Which meant they were planning on leaking so many false reports and accusations that there would be no way to verify any real stories. Everyone from aliens to government plots would be offered in explanation, so most people would dismiss any outrageous reports outright.

"Wow…" Haatim said, shaking his head.

Frieda wheeled on him, as if noticing him for the first time. She pointed a finger at him. "And *you*. You were ordered to leave the city."

"I couldn't just go and let these people die."

"When I tell you to *leave* a place, you leave it, got it?"

He started to object again, but her look silenced him. "Got it," Haatim answered. Frieda didn't seem like the kind of person he should argue with.

"What do we do now?" Abigail asked.

"You will both have to stand before the Council and explain everything that happened. Haatim's father is going to try and raise a few claims against you, Abigail."

"OK. He wants to reprimand me?"

"No," Frieda said, frowning. "It's serious, Abigail. He's planning to get you discharged from the Order."

Abigail had a stunned expression on her face, mixed with fear. "What?"

"He's already gaining allies and rallying support against you. He only needs to get half of them, and he's almost got that number already."

"He can't do that."

"Do what?" Haatim asked, but both women ignored him.

"He can," Frieda said. "And he is."

"That won't happen, though, right? He won't be able to rule against me? That hasn't happened in hundreds of years."

"After what you did here today," Frieda said. "It's doubtful. You saved a lot of lives. But, with Aram it is impossible to say. He has a lot of influence, and most members of the Council support him."

"You can't let that happen," Abigail said.

"I'll do everything in my power," Frieda said. "I promise."

"What are you talking about?" Haatim asked again.

"We need to go," Frieda said. "There is a helicopter waiting and we need to get moving."

"Can't we get cleaned up first?" Haatim asked.

"There isn't time. It's going to be wild, these next few days. I hope you're both ready."

Abigail had a sad and resigned look on her face. "Me, too."

Frieda smiled sadly at her. "Chin up. You'll get through this."

"Through what?" Haatim asked. Frieda ignored them and ushered them outside to where a helicopter was idling. There were helmets waiting, and after only a moment they were airborne, heading off toward the horizon.

Haatim thought it was one of the most beautiful sights he'd ever seen, watching the mountains stretch beneath him. He watched for a moment, just relaxing, before turning his attention back to Abigail and Frieda.

"So my father is going to try and get Abigail kicked out of the Order?" Haatim asked as they flew.

Both women were silent for a long minute. "Not exactly," Abigail answered finally.

"Then what?"

Frieda was the one who responded. "Hunters serve for life. There is no way to leave the Order while someone is still alive."

"What does that mean?"

"Your father is going to try and prove Abigail can't be trusted. If he succeeds, she will be executed."

End of Book 1
Lincoln Cole

ABOUT THE AUTHOR

Lincoln Cole is a Columbus-based author who enjoys traveling and has visited many different parts of the world, including Australia and Cambodia, but always returns home to his pugamonster, Luther, and wife. His love for writing was kindled at an early age through the works of Isaac Asimov and Stephen King, and he enjoys telling stories to anyone who will listen.

http://www.LincolnCole.net/signup

CPSIA information can be obtained at www.ICGtesting.com
Printed in the USA
LVOW08s1721080716

495639LV00002B/281/P

9 780997 225976